Dear Reader,

Like my heroine—Hannah Ross—I'm a city girl, but I grew up in a small town that was like Timber Bay, Michigan, the fictitious setting for *Finding Mr. Perfect*. As I've changed over the years, so has my hometown. For instance, the drugstore, with its funky lunch counter, is now a sub-sandwich shop, but the glittering white band shell still graces the park on the bay and the library, where I spent so many hours as a kid, still stands. As does the opera house, sadly with no irreverent local hottie like Danny Walker to restore it—yet. And the tunnel that runs beneath the streets really does exist. Was it ever known as the *Tunnel of Love*? Hmm, maybe not. But as modern, practical Hannah finds out, a girl has *got* to believe in something.

I hope you enjoy spending the Fourth of July in Timber Bay with Danny and Hannah, and please come back soon to find out what happens when another big-city girl invades Timber Bay—and the heart of Danny's best friend, Lukas McCoy.

Best wishes,

Nikki Rivers

"I do not hawk cereal," insisted Hannah

"I am a research sociologist, working as an independent consultant." It wasn't her style to sound so haughty, but Danny Walker brought it out in her.

"What's a consultant?" Uncle Tuffy asked.

Danny replied before Hannah could open her mouth. "That's what a person does when she can't find a real job."

Kate, Danny's mother, looked up from her lunch plate. "Oh, you poor dear. Have you been out of work long?"

Hannah gave Danny a look she hoped would freeze his mouth shut. "I am not out of work, Kate. I feel very privileged to be with a company modern enough to hire a sociologist for this project. Your family was chosen, Mr. Walker, because they embody standards and values that Granny's Grains wants to promote. This contest, I mean project, was conducted in the same manner a scientific study would be."

Danny gave a short laugh. "Well then that explains it, Professor. I always knew these studies weren't accurate because if you think you're going to find normal around here, you've definitely taken another wrong turn!"

Finding
Mr. Perfect

Nikki Rivers

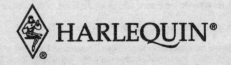

HARLEQUIN®

TORONTO • NEW YORK • LONDON
AMSTERDAM • PARIS • SYDNEY • HAMBURG
STOCKHOLM • ATHENS • TOKYO • MILAN • MADRID
PRAGUE • WARSAW • BUDAPEST • AUCKLAND

ISBN 0-373-44191-6

FINDING MR. PERFECT

This edition published by arrangement with Harlequin Books S.A.

® and TM are trademarks of the publisher. Trademarks indicated with ® are registered in the United States Patent and Trademark Office, the Canadian Trade Marks Office and in other countries.

www.eHarlequin.com

Printed in U.S.A.

ABOUT THE AUTHOR

Nikki Rivers loves writing romantic comedy because she believes that laughter is just as necessary to life as love is. She also gets a kick out of creating quirky characters, having come from a long line of them herself. Nikki lives in Milwaukee, Wisconsin, with her very own Mr. Right. She loves to hear from readers. E-mail her at RiversWrites@aol.com.

Books by Nikki Rivers

HARLEQUIN DUETS
66—A Snowball's Chance

HARLEQUIN AMERICAN ROMANCE
550—Seducing Spencer
592—Daddy's Little Matchmaker
664—Romancing Annie
723—Her Prince Charming
764—For Better, For Bachelor

Don't miss any of our special offers. Write to us at the following address for information on our newest releases.

Harlequin Reader Service
U.S.: 3010 Walden Ave., P.O. Box 1325, Buffalo, NY 14269
Canadian: P.O. Box 609, Fort Erie, Ont. L2A 5X3

To my editor, Kathryn Lye,
for the encouragement and the laughs—
and for always making me work harder.
Many thanks for helping give birth to my babies.

1

HANNAH ROSS HAD NEVER SEEN such a long table in all her life. At the head of its glassy expanse sat Randall Pollard, the jowly and robust CEO of Granny's Grains Cereal, Inc. On one side sat the CFO, a thin fierce-looking man, and on the other the impeccably dressed, bored-looking brand-new head of the marketing department. Hannah, in a tailored pantsuit that had cost more than she could afford even though it was on clearance, had the other end of the table all to herself. Plenty of room. But under her new suit jacket she was sweating as though she was in the middle of a crowded elevator stuck between floors.

Pollard had been on his cell phone ever since they'd sat down in the fifth-floor boardroom of the home office on Chicago's south side. The wait was making Hannah more nervous by the minute. She focused her attention on the banner behind Pollard's head. Printed in a font that mimicked cross-stitch, on paper that tried to look gingham, was Granny's Grains new slogan: *Granny is bringing America's families back to the breakfast table.*

A good slogan, but definitely problematic, thought Hannah. Chiefly because it was just as faux as the cross-stitch and gingham. The last three business quarters had been so dismal that Granny was in real danger of losing her ruffled apron.

It had been decided that the company's flagship product, Super Korny Krunchies, needed a new image. Unfortunately, the advertising firm that had been hired to provide it had determined that Granny's squeaky-clean image was at fault.

They were sure the numbers would improve considerably if the box was adorned with a girl barely into puberty wearing a push-up bra and a shrunken T-shirt. The ensuing ad campaign, pushed through when Pollard was in Europe tracking dead ancestors so he could join some posh country club in the suburbs, had gotten Krunchies kicked off the shelves of several Midwest grocery chains and had yielded bags of mail from scandalized customers. Nobody wanted to buy cereal that had to be wrapped in a plain brown wrapper before they could bring it home to the kids.

When Pollard returned from Europe, the old box quickly replaced the new one on store shelves across America. Along with a few department heads, the advertising firm had gotten the ax and Hannah, a research sociologist, had been brought on board to help marketing find a new direction. Trying to figure out what kind of image would put Super Korny Krunchies on top once again wasn't exactly what Hannah had planned to do with her master's degree.

Less than a year ago, she'd been perfectly happy analyzing whether the new single suburbanites impacted the economy in the entertainment sector of urban areas (yes, nobody wanted to drive all the way back downtown once they were home). Although she'd been working on a very interesting theory that the findings could be an early sign that an entire generation would eventually lack all spontaneity, the funding for the project became a fatality of the new economy.

Jobs in sociological research weren't exactly clogging the want ads. But consultants were in vogue for everything from jury selection to shopping for birthday presents. So when a friend from college contacted her about a consortium of consultants he was putting together, Hannah decided she'd been unemployed long enough. Granny's Grains was her first client as a sociological consultant.

Pollard ended his call. His chair creaked ominously as he leaned back in it and folded his hands over his protruding belly. "Well, Miss Ross," he said, "I hope you have something for us."

"Something we can actually use," the new head of marketing added cynically. It was no secret that he'd been against bringing in a scientist.

"I think you'll be pleased with my results," Hannah said as she opened her briefcase, took out a small stack of spiral-bound reports, and stood to hand them out. "The good news," she said as the men opened their reports, "is that the new slogan is right on the money. If you'll turn to page three you'll see that my research numbers show that Americans really do want to come back to the breakfast table. The cocooning that started in the nineties has spilled into the new century. On page five, you'll see that polls show a conservative shift in the nation and—"

Hannah spouted statistics and quoted studies until she noticed the CFO checking his watch. She decided it was time to lighten things up a bit. "So, in many ways, your new slogan is right in the ballpark." She smiled brightly. "Or maybe I should say *backyard*."

Nobody laughed at her little joke. Not even a tiny smile out of any of them. Which was a shame because it was the only joke in her entire presentation. Instead, Pollard threw his copy of the report on the table in front of him. Hannah winced as it slithered off the glossy surface and onto the floor. "These numbers mean nothing to me," he said. "What I want to know, Miss Ross, is why aren't the boxes moving off the shelves?"

This was the part that Hannah dreaded most. She was a good researcher and she was confident in her findings. But she didn't feel at all confident in how the client would react to her findings—or in her ability to deal with the reaction.

Hannah had never pictured herself in the corporate world. In the movie of her life that had played in her head, she'd never been a number gatherer for middle-aged corporate types who were going to use her findings for advertising. In the rarefied theater of her mind, her work not only had purer motives but she'd also been wearing yoga pants and cross-trainers, not confining tailoring and pumps that pinched. But it was more than just her yoga pants she missed. Face it, analyzing the cereal-buying habits of Middle America hadn't been anywhere at all on the preview reel.

But this was real life and the corporate types weren't expecting an intermission. She took a deep breath and gave them what they paid for. "I'm afraid it's partly because of the box itself." Hannah nervously gestured toward the oversized rotating cereal box hanging from the ceiling, hoping that no one would ask her what the other part was. She'd hate to have to totally alienate her first consulting client by telling him that his product tasted more like the cob than the corn. "The current box," she went on, "depicts an ear of corn wearing a superhero cape."

"We know that, Miss Ross," Marketing assured her with a long-suffering air. "Except for a brief period, it's been on the box since the early sixties."

"A classic, true," she said, quite pleased with the diplomacy of her ad lib. "But in today's world, your flying ear of corn isn't the image the consumer wants in a product."

"If you're talking about modernizing it," said the CFO, "that's been tried. To disastrous results."

"That's because the consumer group you need to target wants to buy a product that speaks of stability. They want a product that makes them think that if they use it their family will become what they wish them to be."

Mr. Pollard frowned, sending his jowls to a new low. "And what do they wish their families to be, Miss Ross?"

"Normal, Mr. Pollard."

"Normal?" The head of marketing spat out the word as if it tasted bad.

"Yes," Hannah said emphatically. "Normal. Simply, perfectly normal."

The three men at the table looked confused. Fortunately, Hannah was not confused. She knew all about what normal was *supposed* to be.

"Today's parents are older, more educated, more sophisticated than ever before. But society is coming full circle, gentlemen." This was more like it, thought Hannah. She was beginning to sound as though she knew what she was talking about. "What they want is really very simple. It used to be referred to as the American Dream. Picture, if you will," she said, pacing the length of the conference table, "front porch swings and backyards full of toys and rosebushes. Pies cooling on the windowsill in summer and jack-o'-lanterns glowing from front porches in the autumn. Snowmen in front yards in the winter and Christmas trees winking in frosted windows." As she paced, Hannah rhapsodized about tree forts and vegetable gardens, neighborly neighbors and Sunday picnics, painting the kind of picture that might be found in a 1950s magazine ad. And painting it well because, although she usually talked in statistics and averages, this was a subject close to Hannah's heart.

As a girl, Hannah had wished for normal on stars like some girls wished for boyfriends. She'd pined for pastel painted houses with ruffled curtains in the windows. Craved cozy family meals and story time before lights-out.

"Women today—and my statistics show that women still do the majority of the family grocery shopping—want a safe, happy home and family. And if they thought there was a cereal on the shelves that could inch them any closer to that image, you wouldn't be able to restock the shelves fast enough."

Hannah took her seat again while Marketing rolled his eyes and the CFO checked his watch again. Reluctantly, Hannah looked down the table at Mr. Pollard, expecting to see his jowls hanging an inch or two lower in disappointment. Instead, he was rubbing his pudgy hands together with relish.

"Yes, yes," he said. "I see what you mean. Splendid idea. Really splendid. My grandmother made this company a success on just such family values. She always said that the family was the backbone of America. So why not put the great American family on our box of cereal? We'll base a whole ad campaign on it. We could even do seasonal boxes. All featuring the same family." He turned to the head of marketing. "Call the modeling agency. We need to start searching for the perfect models immediately."

"No!" Hannah said with perhaps a little too much urgency.

"No?" Pollard said with the kind of tone that made her think the simple word was seldom said to him.

"What I meant to say was, models would be a mistake. Today's consumer is too savvy to fall for a cardboard retread of Norman Rockwell. They want the real thing. This is, after all, the age of reality television. I think the only way this idea will hit home with consumers is if you put a real family on the box."

Randall Pollard slammed his doughy hand on the table. "By George! That's it!" he yelled, his jowls quivering in excitement. "We'll put a real American family on the box. From a real American town. The most perfectly normal family from the most perfectly normal town," Pollard gushed like an old-time politician. "We'll make it a contest. Yes, a contest! And you, Miss Ross, will run it."

"Me? But—" Hannah's mind reeled. She'd never run a contest before. She'd never even entered one. She didn't have a clue. "Surely there is someone else who—"

"Nonsense," Mr. Pollard cut in. "Who better to choose our perfect family than a sociologist? We'll continue to pay your consulting fee, of course," he added, "plus, there would be a hefty bonus for you after the project was completed successfully. Shall we say—"

The figure made Hannah gulp. It would be enough to support her while she looked for another job in research. Maybe she'd never have to enter a boardroom again!

She could figure out how to run a contest, couldn't she? It couldn't be that different from doing a research study, could it? She'd merely gather data, analyze it, and—

"Miss Ross? We're waiting. Are you with us or not?"

"Of course, Mr. Pollard," Hannah said enthusiastically. "I'd love to run your contest."

"IT'S LIKE YOU'VE FALLEN into the absolute perfect job. Practically custom-made just for you," Lissa Hamilton enthused before she took a huge bite of her feta burger.

"Running a contest for a cereal company is the perfect job for me? You're going to have to elaborate on that, Lissa. And make it good," Hannah warned, "because otherwise I think I've just been insulted."

They were sitting in a booth at their usual Greek restaurant in the Lincoln Park section of Chicago, where Lissa, a freelance photographer, had a small loft. Outside the dirty plate-glass windows, the March wind was crisp and the trees were still bare as the Midwest experienced the usual slice of unpredictable weather that kept winter from becoming spring.

Across the booth, Lissa waved her manicured fingers around in the air, trying to express something as she chewed. Lissa was never very still for long, but she never talked with her mouth full, either. After she'd swallowed, she said, "Hey, don't get me wrong. I know it's not the research you want to be doing, but I'm the right-brained one in this twosome, remember? Believe me, you'll feel better about this whole thing if you look at this consulting job as the perfect opportunity to develop your creative side—not to mention that it will be an awesome playground for your inner child."

Lissa leaned forward, waving a French fry, thick with catsup, as she talked. "Think about it. You get to find the kind of family you always wanted—and you get to live with them for—oh, maybe a month?" she asked before she popped the fry in her mouth.

"Right. I'll have a month to do some advance work before Pollard and the marketing and advertising people arrive for the photo shoot."

"What kind of advance work?" Lissa asked.

"Gathering data for press releases, conducting in-field interviews, recording observations. Basically, I'll be compiling as much information as possible and evaluating it so I can assist the marketing department in building the family's image in the media."

Lissa smiled. "In other words, you have to get to know them."

"Yes. I guess you could say that. Certainly, anecdotal information would be beneficial to the—"

Lissa waved her fingers again. "No, no, no. That's the scientist talking. You'll be good at all that stuff—goes without saying. But this is what is exciting about this whole thing— you get to find your ideal family and give them to yourself for a present. And you get *paid* to do it."

Hannah stopped playing with her Greek salad. "Wow. I never thought of it that way."

"That's why we've been friends all these years, girl. We never think of anything the same way."

It was true. They were nothing alike. Lissa was an artist. A little wild. With clothes to match. While Hannah was a scientist. A little conservative. With clothes to match. One of the things they differed on was how they perceived Lissa's family.

"If I could pick the perfect family, I'd pick yours," Hannah said.

"Spoken like someone who never had to actually live with them."

"How is Aunt Alice, by the way?" Hannah asked.

"Still boring."

"Oh, she is not. You don't know how lucky you were to have so much family living together in that big old house. I would give anything if—"

Lissa laughed and shook her head. "That's my point. Here's your chance, girlfriend. Go find that family you've always wanted."

BY THE MIDDLE OF June, Hannah found herself driving a company station wagon loaded down with cartons of Super Korny Krunchies along a two-lane highway in Michigan's Upper Peninsula, squinting at directions taped to the dash and hoping fervently that she wasn't lost. But, no. There it was. As promised.

"Welcome to Timber Bay," Hannah read out loud as she drove past the sign made of rough-hewn logs. She glanced at the directions again and turned right at Ludington Avenue. The heart of the town lay before her, pretty as a picture from an old calendar.

She drove past a red brick courthouse with green benches scattering its lawns and sweet william lining the long walk that led to its doors. In the next block there was a barbershop, with an old-fashioned striped barber pole out front, alongside a grocery store that looked like the only thing that had changed about it in the last fifty years were the prices posted in the window. She turned right at Sheridan Road where a corner drugstore that advertised a lunch counter and a stately bank with a four-faced clock anchored the town square. Farther down Sheridan she passed a library with wide granite steps and a movie theater with an old-fashioned marquee jutting across the sidewalk.

"Perfect," Hannah murmured reverentially. It all looked so perfect. It all looked so normal. Which, according to the data Hannah had gathered, is exactly what Timber Bay, Michigan, was supposed to be. Okay, maybe not normal by today's standards. The town didn't appear to run on the same clock as the rest of the country. Timber Bay, no matter what the calendars in the town's kitchens read, was marching to the beat of a drum from 1952. From its unemployment rate to its crime rate, from its abundance of stay-at-home moms to its low number of high-school dropouts, Timber Bay was a town that could have stepped out of time. Exactly the image Super Korny Krunchies was looking for.

If the Henry Walker family, the family Hannah had chosen as Granny's Grains Great American Family, looked as good as the town they lived in, Hannah was going to be adding that bonus Mr. Pollard promised to her bank account in no time.

The sound of children drifted through the open car windows as Hannah drove past a park. Mothers sat on benches watching children play on swings and teeter-totters. An old-fashioned wooden band shell, painted white, graced the edge of a boardwalk. Beyond it, the body of water that bore the same name as the town spread out toward the horizon, glittering bright blue in the sunshine.

She pulled up to a Stop sign across the street from an old hotel. It had probably been the pride of the town back in the days of logging and lumberjacks, but now it was abandoned, its windows boarded up, its front steps crumbling. A shame since the little coffee shop on the other side of the hotel looked as if it had been refurbished. Cute café curtains in the windows, a wreath on the door, and—

"Oh, my," Hannah murmured when she noticed the man in front of the coffee shop.

He was sitting on a plain wood chair, tilted back far enough to raise the front legs off the sidewalk. His arms were up, elbows out, hands linked behind his head, eyes closed, his face tilted skyward, soaking up the afternoon sun. Above him was a sign that said Sweet Buns. And quite a delicacy he was, too. True, she couldn't see his backside so she had no idea if his buns were sweet, but what she could see was pretty yummy. His muscles did a nice job of filling out his simple white T-shirt and battered, faded jeans. His brown hair, brushed back from his face, was a little long and attractively tousled. He had a square chin, a strong jaw, and a wide, full mouth.

Beefcake. Right out there on the main street of town. But sweetly meaty specimen that he was, what made him even more compelling was the look of pure, obvious pleasure on his face. Hannah was still staring when he lowered his head, opened his eyes, and looked straight at her.

She'd never seen eyes that blue before. She wasn't sure how long she'd been staring but when she caught his mouth lifting into a wry little grin, Hannah decided she'd been looking too long already.

She jerked her gaze back to the road and started to ease her foot off the brake just as an elderly man with a cane stepped off the curb. She hesitated seconds too long and ended up having no choice but to wait for him to cross the street. Hannah concentrated on his shuffling feet, steadfastly ignoring the urge to look over at the coffee shop. She ran her hands through her windblown chin-length brown hair, trying to comb out the knots with her fingers, then took her time picking a piece of lint off her black suit jacket. But the pull from those blue eyes was stronger than the will to not embarrass herself again.

She gave in and turned her head—and found herself nose to nose with the beefcake in denim.

Oh, those eyes. They were enough to make a girl shiver.

"Lost?" he asked.

"Of course not," she said, using haughtiness to keep the shivers away.

The beefcake leaned his head farther into the car to look at the slip of paper taped to her dash. "That the address you're looking for?" he asked.

"Not that it's any of your business, but, yes, it is."

"Then you might not be lost yet, but you're on your way."

"Excuse me?"

"You made a wrong turn."

The last thing Hannah wanted to do was ask him for help, but she was already running late. She looked at her watch. The Walkers expected her for lunch and it was after one. She sighed. "Would you mind giving me directions, please?"

"That might be kind of hard to do, considering your bad sense of direction. Tell you what, I'll show you the way."

She thought he was going around to get into the passenger seat and she totally panicked. "I—I don't think that will be necessary," she yelled out the window. "I'd really rather you didn't get into—" she broke off when he plopped himself down on the hood of the Granny's Grains station wagon. Apparently, he had no intention of getting into the car.

"Make a U-turn," he yelled.

She stuck her head out the window. "Are you insane? Get off my car."

He rapped his knuckles on the logo emblazoned on the hood. "Doesn't look like it's really your car. Looks like it belongs to Granny's Grains. So unless you're Granny—"

"Save it. I've heard that same joke several times in several different ways all the way up from Chicago. I'm late. So if you would please—"

Behind her a car honked. And then another. She closed her eyes and groaned. Nice entrance. Holding up traffic in a town with such a low crime rate might be transgression enough to make the front page of the local paper. Mr. Pollard would not be pleased. Behind her, the honking started again so she set her jaw, stepped on the gas and made the U-turn, all the while hoping that the beefcake would fall off in the process.

He didn't.

Instead he'd turned into a talking hood ornament. "Full speed ahead," he commanded loud enough for her, and probably the whole town, to hear.

Hannah slunk down in the seat and started to drive, hoping to remain as inconspicuous as possible. Fat chance with the local hero waving and yelling at just about everybody they passed. Bad enough she'd had to drive all the way from Chicago in a bright red station wagon with the company logo displayed prominently in several places, now she had to arrive to meet the Walkers with the local beefcake perched on the front of the car like it was a float in the homecoming parade. She felt like she was hanging onto the last of her professional dignity by her very short, ratty fingernails.

Luckily, they'd only gone a few blocks when he yelled for her to pull over. She checked the address taped to her dash. Yes. This was it.

The house was large, its narrow clapboard siding painted lemon-yellow. The shutters on the windows that reached nearly to the ground were painted white, as was the trim. And there was a huge porch stretched low across the front with a swing swaying gently in the early June breeze.

"Perfect," she murmured again. Just the kind of house Hannah had always dreamed about. It was even better than the one Lissa had grown up in.

"Want me to carry your cereal for you, sweetheart?"

While she'd gaped at the house, Hannah had nearly forgotten all about him. He was leaning in the passenger window this time.

"No, thank you," she said stiffly as she got out of the car. She was glad she'd worn the black tailored pantsuit and the gorgeously tailored white shirt she'd borrowed from Lissa. It made her feel professional enough to put the beefcake in his place. He was draped attractively against the car, showing no sign of leaving. "I don't think I'll get lost between the front sidewalk and the front door," she told him. "You can go now."

She didn't wait to see if he did. This was too exciting a moment to let him spoil it. Okay, so maybe this wasn't a real scientific research study, but Lissa had been so right. It was going to be quite an adventure—getting to know the family that was going to represent not only Super Korny Krunchies but also her fondest fantasy.

It wasn't until she was standing at the Walkers' front door, ready to ring the bell, that she realized that she wasn't alone.

He was lounging there next to the door, his wide mouth quirked into a grin, his blue eyes glittering.

"Look, do you mind?"

"I don't know, sweetheart," he said while his gaze wandered suggestively down to her mouth. "That depends on what you're asking me to consider."

"I'm asking you to consider leaving."

"I already considered it. I decided not to."

Hannah groaned. This was ridiculous. The Walkers were her ideal family. She couldn't show up at their front door with this lunatic—albeit very attractive lunatic—at her side.

"Aren't you going to ring the bell?" he asked. Before she could stop him he reached past her and rang it himself.

Hannah was trying to decide if she could manage to disappear before anyone came to the door, when it opened.

"Hi, Ma," the beefcake said. "What's for lunch? I'm starved."

2

By the time Hannah had met Kate Walker, her husband Henry, and Henry's older brother, Tuffy, who lived with the Walkers, she was starting to recover from the shock of finding out that her beefcake hood ornament, aka Danny Walker, was a member of Granny's Grains Great American Family. It helped that he'd disappeared right after introductions. She knew it was probably very un-Great American Family of her, but Hannah fervently hoped Danny was having lunch elsewhere.

Mrs. Walker led her through a bright, charming living room and a dining room with crystal candlesticks and real flowers on the table to the kitchen at the back of the house.

It couldn't have been better if Hannah had dreamed it up herself. The cupboards were painted white and the walls were papered in tiny blue flowers. There were blue gingham curtains at the windows and needlepoint on the walls of a spacious alcove that held a big oak table already set for lunch. Something was bubbling merrily in a pot on the stove and the aroma was enticing enough to make her mouth water.

"This place is for you, Miss Ross," Uncle Tuffy said as he pulled out a chair for her then bowed in a courtly fashion.

"Thank you, Mr. Walker," she said as she took it.

Tuffy chuckled delightedly. "I'm not Mr. Walker," he said. "Henry there—he's Mr. Walker. I'm Uncle Tuffy."

"Then, thank you, Uncle Tuffy," she said.

He grinned and Hannah tried not to think of lawn ornaments. He was short, slightly built and wiry, except for a rather large potbelly that strained the buttons of his red plaid shirt. With round cheeks above a whiskered chin and white hair that stood out in wispy tufts from his pink scalp, he looked like a gnome. All he needed was a stocking cap.

From her seat Hannah could see out the windows to the backyard where a lilac bush was in full bloom and a swing hung from an old oak tree.

"I see you have a greenhouse."

"Kate raises her babies out there," Uncle Tuffy said.

"Her babies?"

"That's what I call my plants, dear," Kate Walker answered from the stove where she was dishing out plates of food.

How sweet, Hannah thought. Calling her plants her babies. Kate came over and put a plate of food down in front of Hannah. Creamed chicken on popovers. How classic was that? Served on china that was edged with blue forget-me-nots, it looked like a picture from the pages of a woman's magazine. Hannah raised a forkful to her mouth. Heaven.

"Mrs. Walker, this is delicious. But I hope you didn't go to all this trouble because of me. We do want you to just be yourselves, you know. I mean, that's the point, isn't it?"

"Why, I didn't go through any trouble at all, dear. Just creamed Sunday's leftover chicken, as usual," she said as she sat down to join them. "And please call me Kate."

Leftovers. The word brought back memories. Until she'd started hanging around at Lissa's house, the only leftovers Hannah had been familiar with were cold pizza or congealed Chinese. But at Lissa's the leftovers morphed into what Mr. Hamilton called surprise pie. He loved to joke that you never knew what would be under the crust. Hannah had made it a point to eat at Lissa's house whenever they had leftovers.

She took another forkful of food. It was so yummy that she wondered why the Walker family would want to eat the bland, oversugared cereal they would soon be representing.

But eat it they did, and, according to Hannah's data, they ate it in very large quantities.

"How long has your family been eating Super Korny Krunchies, Kate?"

"Well—um—let me see." Kate seemed a little flustered suddenly.

Uncle Tuffy beamed. "I been eatin' it since they been makin' it," he said proudly.

"And how long have you been hawking it?" Danny Walker asked as he came into the room and started to fill his plate at the stove.

"I do not *hawk* cereal," she answered. "I am a research sociologist, working as an independent consultant." It wasn't Hannah's style to sound so haughty, but Danny Walker seemed to bring it out in her.

"What's a consultant?" Uncle Tuffy asked.

"That's what some people do, Uncle Tuffy," Danny said as he slid into a chair right across from her, "when they can't find a real job."

Kate looked up from her plate. "Oh, you poor dear. Have you been out of work long?"

Hannah gave Danny a look she hoped would freeze his mouth shut. "I am not out of work, Kate. I feel very privileged to be working with a company modern enough to hire a sociologist for this project."

"Contest, you mean," Danny said as he poured himself iced tea from the glass pitcher on the table.

Hannah preferred to think of it as a project. "As I was saying—this *project*—"

"But, Miss Ross, it *was* a contest, wasn't it?" Tuffy asked, worry puckering his forehead. "We won, didn't we? We get the year's supply of cereal, don't we? I'm gonna be on the box, aren't I?"

"Yes, of course, you won—"

"Then it was a contest," Danny said, his blue eyes mocking

her like the devil. "So what did we have to do to win? Send in the most box tops?" he asked as he raised a glass of iced tea to his mouth.

"No, Danny," Tuffy answered enthusiastically. "We won for being normal."

Danny nearly spit out his iced tea. "Normal? Sweetheart, do you have any idea what normal is?"

Why couldn't the man have an addiction to fast food, thought Hannah with a sigh. Why couldn't he be out somewhere supersizing instead of sitting across from her, being super-irritating? "Your family was chosen, Mr. Walker, because they embody standards and values that Granny's Grains wants to project."

"So basically, sweetheart, this is just an advertising gimmick."

"No. Of course not. And I would thank you not to call me sweetheart. I have a master's degree in sociology. This contest—I mean project—was conducted in the same manner a scientific study would be."

He gave a short laugh. "Well, that explains it then, *professor*. I always knew those studies weren't worth the price of a two-penny nail."

Hannah wished she'd taken her suit jacket off. It was feeling a little tight what with all the bristling she was doing. "Exactly what does that mean?"

"It means, professor, that if you think you're going to find normal around here you've definitely taken another wrong turn."

Forget mocking *like* the devil. Danny Walker *was* the devil. Her own personal devil. Just what she needed. How on earth had he slipped through the cracks of the carefully prepared questionnaires the finalists had had to complete? He'd taunted and ridiculed her from the moment his blue eyes had first locked on hers. He was cocky and obviously irresponsible. Jumping on her car like he was some kind of teenager, Hannah scoffed inwardly.

According to her data, Danny Walker was thirty years old. He owned his own building company but still lived at home with his parents, which was one of the reasons she'd chosen the Walker family. Multiple generations of a family living together was a trait that Hannah's research determined a large number of Americans approved of today and looked to as an ideal worth upholding—and one of the reasons Hannah had always envied Lissa's hodgepodge of a family. So Danny had definitely been a deciding factor when she chose the Walkers as Granny's Grains Great American Family. But Hannah was beginning to wonder if she should have looked more closely at the family in Boise, Idaho, that had four children under the age of five. The fact that only one of the children could talk was definitely beginning to look like a plus.

Hannah decided to ignore Danny's last remark and turned pointedly to his father.

"Mr. Walker, I believe you always come home for lunch. Is that right?"

"Yup. Always do. Nothin' better than the wife's cookin'," said Henry before shoving another forkful of food into his mouth.

Henry Walker was a man of few words, apparently. Still, compared to her own father, he was almost glib. He didn't exactly look like what she'd envisioned a steel company owner would, but his flannel shirt might play well to their target group. They'd have to get rid of the coveralls, though. They were a little greasy and just a tad more blue collar than the image they were going for. Though Hannah could see that he had once been a handsome man. It was clear that Danny got his eyes from his mother because Mr. Walker's were brown, but the interesting angles of Danny's face he owed to his father.

A slurping noise from the other end of the table brought

her attention to Uncle Tuffy, who was noisily enjoying his iced tea. Although Uncle Tuffy also figured in Hannah's choice, he was somewhat problematic, as well. But maybe his childlike demeanor would be endearing to middle America. The old, simple bachelor uncle. And they could always do something with his hair before the photo shoot.

But Kate Walker was the real find. She was perfect just as she was. In a pale yellow cotton dress and a flowered apron tied around her waist, her champagne blond hair worn softly around her kind face, Hannah could easily see her picture making a box of cereal more attractive to a harried working mother. Betty Crocker come to life.

She couldn't wait to meet Sissy, the married daughter who lived close enough to take a walk over for a cup of coffee in the afternoon, and her husband and two children. Sissy was a stay-at-home mom. A rarity these days. And the Walkers were very much "hands-on" grandparents.

Hannah loved the whole Walker family setup. Sort of like a buffet of all-you-can-eat relatives. So there was one questionable dish on the buffet table? At least he was a gorgeous dish, she thought as she looked at him through her lashes while she dabbed her mouth with her napkin. His skin was tanned a warm, golden brown and there were streaks of pale blond in his hair. The sun that had browned his skin and bleached his hair had etched lines at the corners of his eyes—those striking blue eyes—that deepened when he smiled or when he laughed. Of course, he was mostly laughing at her. But still, Danny Walker, irritating as he was, was going to sell a lot of cereal.

The thought made her remember that she had business to discuss.

"I'll need to set up interviews for all of you and for Sissy and her family, as well. I also intend to meet with the mayor, the chief of police, and the high-school principal."

Henry grunted and Kate looked a little baffled. "Such a lot of work, dear. Is it really necessary?"

"I'm afraid so. One of my jobs is to supply the company with information they can use to create press releases. We expect there to be plenty of media interest in our Great American Family."

"That's us, isn't it?" Tuffy asked anxiously. "We get the year's supply of cereal, right?"

"Yes, of course. But, even better, in a month, Mr. Pollard, CEO of Granny's Grains, will be arriving with an advertising crew for a photo shoot. The entire family will be featured on a whole series of cereal boxes to coincide with our Bringing America Back to the Breakfast Table campaign."

"Sounds like advertising to me," muttered Danny.

"Mr. Walker," she said reasonably but firmly, "the results of my work will be used in an advertising campaign but that doesn't take away from the fact that the process used to select your family as Granny's Grains Great American Family was a scientific one. Now," she said, turning back to Kate, "these interviews will be informal so there is nothing to worry about. It's important that you just go about your regular daily lives so that I can get the flavor for how you live."

"Ma, you should take the professor out to the greenhouse for feeding hour," Danny suggested.

Well, thought Hannah with satisfaction, her tone had obviously worked. Danny had decided to be helpful. Still, he did have that twinkle in his eye—

"Are you interested in tropical plants, Hannah?" Kate asked.

"I'm interested in anything you do, Kate. I'd love to watch you feed your plants. In fact, the greenhouse should probably go on the list of possible sites I'm compiling to give the photographer when he gets here."

"You mean he might want to take a picture of my babies?"

"Oh, absolutely. The company has gotten whisperings of

interest from a few women's magazines. The fact that you're a gardener will, I'm sure, add to their interest."

"You mean a picture of me and my babies in *Gardening Today*?"

"Possibly, Kate. If we get the press we want with this, you might even make the afternoon talk shows."

"You could take your babies with you, Ma," Danny put in. "Let 'em perform on the air."

Hannah frowned. "Perform?"

Kate laughed and flapped her hand. "Oh, Danny is just being silly, Hannah. My babies can't perform. Although it can be very entertaining to watch them eat."

Hannah opened her mouth to ask another question, but decided it was just Kate Walker's rather singular way of speaking. Watching her plants eat, of course, merely meant watching liquid fertilizer sink into the soil.

"Come along, my dear. I'll introduce you to all my little darlings. You can even help me feed them!"

Hannah forgot all about the mocking devil sitting at the table watching her. She felt positively glowy inside. She barely remembered her own mother. She'd certainly never gardened with her. It seemed like such a mother/daughter thing to be doing. So sweet. So wholesome. So—well, so Great American Family.

She'd better take notes. It wouldn't do to forget what she was really there for.

"I'll just run and get my notebook and tape recorder out of the car."

"Don't be silly, dear, they don't chew loud enough to record," Kate said sweetly before she sailed out the back door.

Chew? "What did she mean *chew*?" Hannah asked Danny.

"You're the intrepid researcher, professor. Shouldn't you find out for yourself?"

Hannah opened her mouth to take the bait then thought better of it. Ignoring him, she left the kitchen and headed out to the station wagon for her things. When she came back through the kitchen with her notebook and recorder, Danny was, thankfully, gone.

Out in the backyard Hannah could hear Kate humming in the greenhouse as she made her way down the little brick walk lined with shrub roses that were just starting to bud. The song of birds and the scent of lilacs filled the air. This, thought Hannah with satisfaction, was just as it was supposed to be. Perfectly normal. Even better, it was perfectly perfect.

The greenhouse had a peaked roof and one of those doors that were cut in half like in the pictures you see of old country cottages. The upper half was open. Kate, wearing a wide-brimmed straw hat, was inside talking sweetly to her plants, holding one up in a hand that was covered by a cotton gardening glove sprinkled with tiny pink roses. In her other hand, she held a jar of—Hannah squinted and leaned in over the bottom half of the door for a better look. It couldn't be—

But it was. Kate, looking like something on a Mother's Day greeting card, was holding a glass jar of dead flies.

"There you are, dear," she trilled when she saw Hannah. "Come in and meet my babies."

Hannah sincerely hoped she wasn't talking about the flies. She pushed open the half door and went inside.

Long wooden tables on either side of the room were filled with the strangest-looking plants Hannah had ever seen. She reached out to touch the fringed leaf of one and Kate said, "Oh, no, dear. Mustn't touch. It makes them think you're giving them something to eat and they could never digest anything as big as your finger."

Hannah quickly pulled her finger back. "Excuse me?"

"Why, that's a Dionaea, dear. My favorite one, in fact. I call her Dee Dee Dionaea. She's highly carnivorous, you know."

Hannah gulped. "Carnivorous?"

"Why, yes. All my little babies are meat eaters. You probably know Dionaea as Venus flytrap. Those colorful ones over there are Byblis and those," she pointed with pride at a squat plant that looked like a specimen from outer space, "those are Australian Pitcher Plants. They drown their prey before digesting them."

Hannah looked from the weird flora to the jar of dead bugs in Kate Walker's dainty, rosebud-covered hand. For a second she thought she was going to lose her popovers. "And you feed them—"

"Flies, my dear. The neighbors have one of those bug zappers so I just go over there every few days and sweep them up from the patio." Kate looked around as if to make sure no one was listening, then she leaned closer to Hannah and lowered her voice. "They have a dog over there—one of those silly standard poodles—so there's always a lot of flies available. If you know what I mean."

Hannah knew exactly what she meant. Suddenly the greenhouse seemed awfully warm, the scent of damp rich earth nearly overpowering.

"Of course, they also eat live insects," Kate was saying. "In fact, they prefer them. Perhaps you'd like to take one up to your room while you're here, dear? Just to make sure you're not bothered by flies."

The idea of trying to sleep with Dee Dee on the bedside table slowly munching moths or whatever other creatures flew by night was enough to bring on nightmares.

"Um—no, I'm sure that won't be necessary." Hannah started backing toward the door. "Um, I think perhaps I'll take a walk around town and sort of get my bearings."

Kate looked concerned. "Are you all right, dear?"

"I'm—uh—fine." Hannah pressed a hand to her stomach. "Just ate too much at lunch, I expect."

"Oh, then perhaps a walk—"

Hannah didn't wait to hear the rest.

Outside again the air was cooler. She closed her eyes, took a few deep breaths, and her popovers settled back down.

Terrific, she thought as she crossed the back porch and went into the house. Just terrific. Meat-eating plants. Not exactly normal. Okay, so maybe it was her fault for expecting nothing more exotic than an orchid or two. Obviously, there should have been a follow-up question on the entry forms. *Do you garden*—followed by *just what the heck grows in your garden?* Or even better yet, *does your plant's lunch have wings?*

"Pollard isn't going to like this," she muttered to herself as she went through the kitchen. Maybe she could just cross the greenhouse off the list of possible sites for photo shoots. In fact, it might be better to keep the subject of gardening out of the picture entirely. "Calm down," she told herself as she went through the lovely dining room and the inviting living room. So there was one little thing that didn't quite fit the perfect picture. She'd just have to find a way around it, she thought as she opened the front door. Danny Walker was standing on the other side of it.

"Feeding time over already?" he asked.

Okay, thought Hannah with a groan, make that two little things that didn't fit.

"Would you please remove yourself from the doorway so I can pass?"

"What's the matter, professor? Did your data promise you a rose garden?"

"Very clever, Mr. Walker. Now, if you'll excuse me, I'm going for a walk."

"I'll go with you."

"No, you won't," she said curtly and started to step around him.

He put out his arm and braced it on the doorframe next to her, blocking her way. "But, professor, aren't you afraid you'll get lost again?"

This close to him, getting lost wasn't what she was afraid of at all. More like afraid her heart was going to jump right out of her chest. She thrust her chin up defiantly. "I think I can manage."

He lifted a hand and reached out to tuck a strand of her hair behind her ear, then he leaned in close, so close she could feel the heat coming off his skin. So close she could smell him. Sawdust and sunshine. Her pulse shot up at least another half dozen beats when he whispered, "But I know secret places in this town that no one else knows about."

She didn't doubt it for a moment. Already he'd found a highly erogenous zone in her ear that she hadn't even known existed. *Enough,* she told herself. You're a scientist, not a pushover for a cocky slice of beefcake. She stepped back from him and folded her arms across her chest.

"You might want to save all this charm for the local girls, Mr. Walker. It's totally wasted on me."

"Liar," he said.

"Unbelievable. You really think you're irresistible, don't you?"

He grinned and her stomach took a dive. "Well, aren't I?" he asked.

"Watch, Mr. Walker," she said. "This is me resisting." She ducked under his arm, crossed the porch, walked down the stairs, and started up the street. She could hear his laughter all the way to the corner.

3

LAUGHING, DANNY WATCHED Hannah walk away. She had a determined stride on her—no surprise—and long legs. Too bad she dressed like a man. For a moment he wondered what might be underneath that severe black pantsuit but shook off the thought in a hurry. Hannah Ross had so much starch in her a man could get hurt if he got too close.

He sauntered down the steps and out to his pickup parked in the driveway. Windows down and the radio blasting something about broken hearts, Danny drove across town to Lukas McCoy's freshly painted Victorian. He turned into the driveway and coasted around to the back where the old carriage house and stable was now home to Timber Bay Building and Restoration. He parked in front of the cumbersome double doors that his partner Lukas refused to replace. Never mind that the place housed a computer, a fax machine, and just about every power tool known to man. Lukas insisted on keeping the old doors for authenticity.

Danny got out of the truck and walked around to the side door that led to the office. Inside, Lukas sat at an old oak desk he'd restored, his fingers plunking away on the computer keys as he filled out an invoice.

"I thought you were going over to take some measurements at the church."

"Just want to get these couple of invoices in the mail, Danny. We can use the cash."

"Huh—no kidding." Danny picked up a stack of mail from

the desk and started to flick through it. Mostly bills. Bills needing that cash Lukas mentioned. "Any messages?"

"Not the one you want," Lukas said.

Danny threw the mail back on the desk. "Damn, I hate this waiting. And if I know the dragon lady, she's making us wait on purpose."

"Take it easy, Danny. It's only been two weeks since we sent the proposal to her lawyer. For all we know, the rumor that Agnes Sheridan wants to restore the old hotel isn't even true."

"That job would make all the difference to this company, Lukas. And if we don't get it because of me—"

"Ancient history. Agnes Sheridan is a smart woman. We're the best for the job and if she looks into it she's going to know it."

"*If* she looks into it."

"Will you chill? Tell me about lunch. Did the cereal rep show?"

Danny grinned. "With a little help from me."

Danny told Lukas about jumping on the hood of her station wagon and Lukas shook his head slowly. "Now that kind of behavior, Danny, is exactly the kind of stuff that always got you in trouble," he said, but Danny could see the laughter in his partner's eyes.

That's how it had always been. Danny had been the one forever in a scrape and Lukas had always been the good guy, admonishing Danny's antics but secretly admiring his guts. They'd been best friends since third grade when Lukas, who'd towered above Danny, rescued Danny's jacket from the basketball hoop where some older bullies he'd messed with had tossed it. Lukas, at six foot four, still towered over Danny's five foot ten. And he was still the good guy as far as Danny was concerned.

"I got a feeling that I'm going to be in a lot of trouble during the professor's visit."

"The professor?"

Danny shrugged a shoulder. "It suits her. She's got ice in her veins and she likes to throw her master's degree around. I don't know how smart she could be, though, if she chose us to be on that box of cereal. Perfectly normal, we ain't." He looked at his watch. "I'm going to head on over to the high school to have a look at those warped floors. Catch ya later."

"Yeah, later," Lukas said absently.

Danny left him to his hunting and pecking and headed back out to his pickup. He spent about an hour at the high school, taking measurements to replace warped floorboards in a few of the classrooms, then took a slow ride down Sheridan Road and pulled up in front of the old hotel that Agnes Sheridan still owned.

Man, he wanted that job so bad he could feel it in his skin. And not just for the money. He was tired of building kitchen cabinets and replacing floorboards. He wanted a challenge. Plus, a job like restoring the Sheridan Hotel would involve hiring sub-contractors and that would raise Timber Bay Building and Restoration to a whole new level. They were ready for it. They could do it. And if old lady Sheridan would meet with them, they could get that job. Danny just knew it.

If she'd meet with them.

An old restlessness started to stir and haunt. The kind of restlessness that always got him into trouble. He made a U-turn and started back down Sheridan Road with a vague idea of heading for the highway out of town. Sometimes, if he drove fast enough, he could outrun the restlessness. Then he saw her.

There was no mistaking that brisk, long stride or that ramrod-straight back. You'd think she was trying to balance that master's degree on the top of her head. He grinned when he thought of the look on her face after her visit to the greenhouse. Something told him Hannah Ross wasn't used to surprises. He chuckled. Wasn't it his duty as a human being to help change that?

"Danny boy, I think it's time to give back to your fellow man," he murmured as he pulled over to the curb just ahead of her and waited until she was walking past the truck. Then he leaned over to the passenger window and gave a long, low whistle. The surprise on her face when she turned her head made her look like the teenager he was feeling like inside.

"Hey, baby," he drawled in his best teenage male predator drawl, "want a ride?"

Hannah groaned. Danny Walker. She should have known.

She'd been walking around town all afternoon and had come to the conclusion that Timber Bay was just as she'd expected. Perfect. She'd found plenty of picturesque sites for possible photo shoots that more than made up for a few dozen meat-eating plants. Until she'd turned to see those blue eyes mocking her, she'd almost forgotten that there was another fly buzzing around the ointment—and, unfortunately, this one was too big to feed to Dee Dee Dionaea.

She decided it was better if she didn't break stride. "I'll thank you not to call me baby," she said, looking straight ahead. "And, no, I don't want a ride."

She expected him to laugh at her and speed away. She should have known she wasn't going to get what she expected from Danny Walker. He started riding the curb, slowly enough to keep pace with her. Why was there never an illegally parked car around when you needed one?

"Bet you were one of those kind of girls that never said yes."

That slowed her down a little. "Excuse me?" she asked, refusing to look at him.

"Bet you never let the boys pick you up."

"Of course not."

"Then let's make up for lost time. Come on, baby. Get in. You won't regret it. Promise."

Oh, he was impossible. "Will you stop it," she hissed out of the side of her mouth.

"Sorry, babe, didn't hear you," he yelled with the kind of gusto usually reserved for requesting encores at rock concerts.

This was getting embarrassing. People were starting to stare. She halted, turned, and stalked up to the truck. "Will you please stop it?"

"Stop what, baby?" His lopsided grin was insufferable. Sexy, but insufferable.

"Stop making you want to jump in my truck and let me take you for a ride?"

Oh, she had no doubt that's exactly what she'd be taken for if she got in that truck with him. "That's not likely to happen in this lifetime," she said as she turned away and started walking again.

He followed, still hugging the curb and begging her noisily to get in.

People on both sides of the street were slowing down and staring. A carload of teenagers went past, hooting and honking. Was she forever going to make a spectacle of herself in this town with this man? If word of these little scenes got back to Pollard, she had a feeling she wasn't going to see dollar one of that bonus—even if she could get rid of those meat-eating plants before his visit.

"Would you please get lost?" she said.

"Can't. If you don't say yes it'll ruin my perfect record."

Despite herself, that got her attention. She looked at him. "Your perfect record?"

"Nobody ever turned me down before."

Oh, she could believe it. There he was, his hair looking like someone just ran their fingers through it, his blue eyes glittering with mischief and one corner of his incredible mouth quirking naughtily. What girl wouldn't be tempted to take that ride?

But Hannah was no girl, she reminded herself. She was a grown woman, in Timber Bay in a professional capacity.

"Hey," Danny suddenly yelled, "there's the mayor. Didn't you say that you wanted to meet him?"

Hannah furiously looked around until she spotted an official-looking car coming their way.

"I'll call him over," Danny said then started to do just that.

Hannah gave in and got into the truck.

"That was dirty," she said as she slammed the door. "You knew I wouldn't want to meet the mayor this way."

Danny shrugged. "Hey, good guys finish last."

"And I bet Danny Walker is always first in line."

He laughed while he fiddled with the radio and she was slightly astonished at how much she liked the sound of it. It gave her a little jolt to know that she was the one who had caused it. When he stopped at a station that was playing a song she loved, a slow, sexy rock ballad, she started to think it was a good thing the Walker house was only a few blocks away. But instead of going straight down Sheridan Road, Danny made a right turn at Ludington Avenue.

"This isn't the way to your parents' house."

"Nope. It's not."

"Well, then, turn this truck around."

"Why?"

Why, indeed, wondered Hannah. There was sexy music spilling from the radio and fresh wind pouring through the open windows and the hottest-looking man Hannah had ever seen in the flesh was in the driver's seat. There had to be a reason this wasn't good. "Well—your mother is expecting us for dinner," she said, pleased that she'd remembered.

"We've got a little time."

"Where are you taking me?"

He looked at her briefly. But not so briefly that she didn't notice a spark of what looked like real interest in his eyes. "You really do hate surprises, don't you?" For once, his voice was soft, his smile softer. "Shame 'cause it looked good on you when I surprised you back there."

Why was he looking at her like that? When had the mocking look turned into something else? And why did it seem as if the truck had looked a lot bigger from the outside? It's like the thing had shrunk into one of those tiny imports.

"Mr. Walker, I've changed my mind. Please stop this truck and let me out."

He shot her a look. "Does that master's degree of yours tell you how you're gonna make me?"

Hannah bit her lip. Why had she brought up her degree, for heaven's sake? It wasn't her style. But he'd been so infuriating. He was supposed to be the all-American big brother, for heaven's sake. He wasn't supposed to act like a sixteen-year-old brat that you'd never in a million years want your girlfriends to meet. And now, here she was, in danger of succumbing to all that bad-boy charm. She'd do well to remember why she was even in the same town as Danny Walker in the first place.

"All right," she said as she opened her shoulder bag, "since you refuse to stop I might as well make good use of the time."

"I didn't think you were interested, but come right over here, baby," he said as he patted the seat next to him, "and we'll make excellent use of our time."

She refused to think about what it would be like to slide over next to him and ride off into the sunset. Absolutely refused to think about it. Instead, she got out her tape recorder and notebook. She flipped open to a page full of questions and turned the recorder on. "Interview with Danny Walker," she said into it. "Now, for the first question—"

"Hey, professor," Danny said as he reached over and turned the recorder off, "it's summer. No school."

"I have a job to do, Mr. Walker," she said as she turned it on again. "Now—how would you describe your childhood?"

Danny pulled to a stop at a red light and looked at the microphone and then at Hannah. That no-nonsense name sure fit. She sat there with her recorder, looking at him with that straight little nose of hers slightly in the air, all ready to put him under a microscope. Well, if she thought he was going to cooperate with this crazy contest, she was in for yet another surprise. "Come on, professor, have a heart. If I have to go to summer school, at least make the test multiple choice."

"It's not a hard question, Mr. Walker. How would you describe your childhood? Happy? Fulfilling?"

"How about wild and adventurous?"

She gave him a look. "I meant your home life."

"So did I," he said as he eased his foot off the brake when the light turned green. "Living in the Walker homestead can be a harrowing experience."

Danny could tell by the way she set her lips that she didn't like that answer at all. She scribbled something in her notebook and said, "Perhaps we can come back to that question later. Now, then, were you and your sister close?"

He shrugged. "We played it like we couldn't stand the sight of each other but when trouble came we were always right there for each other. Still are. But I wouldn't say we're all that close."

She started scribbling again and he leaned sideways a little trying to get a look at the notebook but she caught him at it and shifted it.

"What about your father? How would you describe your relationship with him?"

"Indescribable."

"That's no answer. It's too vague."

He gave her a grin. "So is my relationship with my father." She jotted something down.

"And your mother? How do you feel about her?"

"Hey, a guy loves his mother," he told her. And he did. He loved his ma to death.

"Yes, of course," she said impatiently. "But you must have other feelings, too."

What did he feel? His emotions concerning his mother had always been pretty mixed. There were times he wanted to hug her and other times she drove him up the wall.

"My feelings for my mother are complicated," he found himself saying. "I mean, she was always the first one there to feed the gang, always the first one there with the bandages, always the first one there with the pat on the back. She was great. But—" Danny let the word trail off and wondered when he'd started cooperating.

"But?" she prompted.

He shrugged. "Sometimes a guy wants a mother he can actually talk to."

"You feel you can't talk to her?"

Jesus, why was he saying this stuff to her? And what the hell was she writing down in that notebook?

"Look, Ma's great. Don't get me wrong. She's just a little dizzy."

The professor grimaced as she turned off the tape recorder. "Do you think we could pick another adjective?"

"Why? You think cereal eaters don't know what dizzy means?"

She arched her brow and stuck her nose in the air. "One wonders, Mr. Walker, since you seem to think so little of your parents, why do you still live with them?"

He looked at her. "Is that one of the questions you've got written down there?"

"No—I'd just like to know."

"Fair enough. I love my parents. But this is the real world, not a commercial. And as for why I live with them—you're the sociologist. I'm sure you have a theory."

"Money?"

"Not bad, professor."

"But I thought your business was successful."

"Successful enough," he said. "Let's just say I have a very expensive obsession."

Her mouth dropped open. "You mean you live off your parents so you can spend all your money on a woman?"

"Hey—get something straight. I don't live *off* my parents. I pay my own way. And who said anything about a woman?"

"What then? A gambling problem?"

Christ. Could her opinion of him get any lower? "You know, professor, you're starting to put a real damper on this car trip."

Danny didn't like this a bit. Hell, he was supposed to be the one riling her up, not the other way around. But damned if she wasn't starting to really bug him with her preconceived ideas and her useless studies. Well, he'd show her something that wasn't in her statistics.

"Hang on, professor, you're about to meet my obsession."

The truck tires squealed as he made a U-turn and headed back down Ludington, then took a right at Sheridan and a left just past the hotel onto Miller Street. Neither of them spoke until he pulled up to the curb in front of the boarded-up building that had consumed him for years.

"There she is, professor. The lady who takes my money— not to mention my blood, sweat and tears."

He wished he could relish the look of surprise that flooded her face, but he was too pissed off that she'd goaded him into bringing her here. This part of his life was not for publication to sell cereal.

"An opera house?"

"That's what it says above the door," he said, aware that he sounded surly as hell.

She looked at him. "You're obsessed with an *opera* house?"

"What's the matter, professor? Do your studies show that guys like me don't own opera houses?"

"You own it?"

He nodded. "The town wanted to tear it down. I went to

the council and got them to sell it to me. I've applied for historical status so I can get some funding, but in the meantime—" Danny broke off. He didn't appreciate the look on Hannah Ross's face. "Better close your mouth, professor, before your eyes pop out and drop into it."

"Sorry, it's just that—"

"It's just that your statistics show that men who work with their hands spend their free time watching wrestling on TV and listening to country on the radio. Proving once again the idiocy of statistics."

"You're insufferable, you know that?"

"And you're in way over your head."

She thrust her chin up stubbornly. "And just what does that mean?"

"It means that Granny picked the wrong person to run her contest."

HANNAH WAS BARELY ABLE to enjoy her meat loaf. The family dinner she'd been so looking forward to wasn't exactly cozy. Henry, still in his grimy coveralls, was hiding behind the sports section. Every once in awhile his fork would sneak out the bottom, load up some food, and disappear under the baseball scores again. Kate was fretting over a list that had something to do with her church group and Uncle Tuffy had taken his plate into the living room to watch cartoons. None of this was, in her opinion, Great American Family behavior. But what was even worse was the fact that Hannah had to, once again, sit across the table from Danny.

Danny Walker was shaping up to be the worst problem in the family. His demeanor was definitely not Great American Family caliber. She could clean up Henry and Uncle Tuffy. She could find a way to get Kate to keep her thoughts—and her greenhouse—to herself for the duration of Pollard's visit. But how on earth was she going to get Danny to stop acting like something out of a Tennessee Williams play?

She sure hadn't done much of a job controlling him that afternoon. She was still angry at herself for getting into his truck. But what else could she have done when he'd started waving and yelling madly at the mayor? What on earth would the Honorable Ed Miller have thought of her for standing out on the street of his low-crime-rate town having a shouting match? It just wasn't like her.

Big surprise. Danny Walker had the power to make a woman forget herself.

But even worse, she couldn't get what he'd said out of her head. *Granny picked the wrong person to run her contest.* It rankled big time—mostly because she'd wondered the very same thing once or twice that day herself.

Was Danny Walker right? Was she in over her head?

She raised her eyes from her untouched mashed potatoes to sneak a look at him. He caught her at it. Maddeningly, he winked at her and it filled her with the ridiculously childish urge to stick out her tongue at him. Instead, she filled her mouth with mashed potatoes, and filled her mind with new resolve. Danny Walker was *not* going to be right. Granny's Grains *did not* pick the wrong person to run their contest.

After dinner, Hannah insisted on helping Kate with the dishes.

"Besides," she said after everyone else left the kitchen, "this will give me a chance to ask you a few questions."

"What sort of questions, dear?" Kate asked as she poured pink dish soap into the running water.

"Oh, just family things. For instance, did your children eat breakfast before school when they were young?"

"Well, yes. Of course, dear. Breakfast is, after all, the most important meal of the day."

Yes! thought Hannah with relief. Kate was a normal mother, even if her taste in gardening was a bit bizarre.

"I'm sure your mother felt that way, too, didn't she?" Kate asked.

"I wish I remembered," Hannah murmured.

Kate looked at her, her eyes wide. "You don't suffer from amnesia, do you, dear? The people in my soaps are always coming down with it, but I've never known anyone in person who had it."

Hannah grimaced slightly. You never knew what was going to come out of Kate's mouth. She was never malicious, of course. She couldn't be sweeter. She was just a little—um—dizzy. The fact that Danny's word was a perfect fit didn't help Hannah's mood.

Hannah sighed. "No, Kate. I don't have amnesia."

"Oh," Kate said with a disappointed little frown on her face.

"My mother died when I was very young. My father raised me."

"Then who fixed your breakfast, dear? Your father?" Kate asked.

The image of Orson Ross trying to flip a pancake with that perpetually distracted air almost made her laugh. He'd have the pancake turner in one hand and an open book in the other and the pancake would end up on the floor, totally unnoticed, while he read. "I doubt if my father ever even thought about breakfast," she said. "Or any other meal, for that matter."

And it was true. Her father was a dear, but when he wasn't in a classroom or lecture hall, he was in his study with his papers and books. "I learned to order takeout when I was five and to make simple meals when I was six," she told Kate. "I used to bring him a plate in his study at night."

"You mean you didn't even eat together?"

Kate's face was all soft and concerned and Hannah realized she'd crossed a line. She was supposed to be asking the questions, not revealing personal information about herself. "Oh, I wanted to ask you about that," she said, segueing into the next question quite nicely. "Did your family always eat breakfast together?"

Luckily, Kate was easily distracted.

"Oh, yes! Always."

"Did you ever have a problem getting everyone to the breakfast table?"

"Why, no, I never did." Kate thought for a moment. "I think it was my meal system that did it."

"Your meal system?"

Kate nodded. "Pancakes on Monday, over easy on Tuesday, waffles on Wednesday, scrambled on Thursday and French toast on Friday."

Hannah frowned. Kate hadn't mentioned cereal. "But, didn't you—?"

"Oh, no, dear. I never varied it. That was the whole point, don't you see?"

Hannah forgot about cereal for the moment. "No, I'm afraid I don't see."

"Well, if you knew that you had to wait a whole week for another waffle Wednesday, wouldn't you eat them when they were put in front of you?"

It made a wacky kind of sense, Hannah had to admit. But where did cereal, particularly Super Korny Krunchies, fit in?

"Kate, when did you serve cereal?"

"Oh, I never served cereal when my kids were growing up. I always insisted they eat a cooked breakfast because everyone knows that—" Kate broke off, her hand flying out of the water to her mouth, sending little puffs of soap suds into the air around her head like a housewife's halo. Only the halo was a little crooked. "Oh, dear," Kate said.

Oh crap, thought Hannah. Another glitch. A huge one this time. Big. Very big.

"Got a problem, professor?"

She didn't have to look to know that Danny Walker would be leaning in the doorway, hip cocked, mouth quirked, wry twinkle in his eyes. With all the twists and turns this day had taken, one thing she could be sure of. If she had a problem,

Danny would be sexily draped somewhere nearby, ready to give her a hard time.

"You don't look so good. Meat loaf upset your tummy—or is it the taste of failure? Didn't I tell you that studies and surveys were bogus?"

Hannah glared at him. "As I said earlier, there is a margin for error in every research study. But if a subject is going to lie—"

"Watch it," Danny warned as he came away from the doorway. "Lie is a strong word."

"But it's the right word," she retorted. "I could go upstairs right now and produce the original entry form that states that your entire family eats Super Korny Krunchies. And that's not the only problem with that entry form, either. Several answers are definitely misleading."

"Or maybe you just asked the wrong questions," Danny said.

Hannah threw her hands into the air. "What difference does it make what the question is if the entrant is going to lie?"

"Uh—excuse me, professor, but I think that's an argument for my side. How can you possibly know what is and what isn't a lie when you read those forms of yours?"

"Oh—" Kate cut in "—I'm sure Uncle Tuffy didn't think he was lying."

Hannah forgot the insult she'd been about to hurl at Danny. She swung around to face Kate. "Are you saying that Uncle Tuffy filled out the original entry form?"

Kate nodded. "Tuffy is Henry's brother—not the—um—brightest in the family. So he might have gotten some things wrong. He's always needed someone around to take care of him. But he's got a kind heart and he really does love your cereal and he eats it every day," Kate assured her eagerly. "And he wanted so badly to win. It's just that the rest of us don't eat it. But when Tuffy figured out that he ate enough for a family of four, why he thought—"

Hannah held up her hand. "Wait—let me get this straight. No one else in the family eats Super Korny Krunchies?"

"Have you tasted it?" Danny asked.

"Of course, I've tasted it," Hannah answered impatiently. "Then don't ask stupid questions."

Hannah thrust her hands into the pockets of her pants. "You know I've about had it with you getting a laugh at my expense, Walker. This isn't very funny to me. First I find out that no one is really quite like they're supposed to be. You're like a family picture taken out of focus. And now I find out that nobody but Uncle Tuffy even eats the cereal you've been chosen to represent. And you stand there, with that mocking look in your eyes and—"

"Wait!" Kate cried. "Susie and Andy eat it!"

Hannah jerked her focus away from those mocking eyes and back to Kate. "Sissy's children?" she asked.

Kate nodded. "Whenever they're here they always eat it with Uncle Tuffy. Every morning and then again before bed. I try to get them to put fruit on it, but—"

"That's wonderful!" Hannah interrupted. She was desperate and could care less if the kids put crushed candy bars on it, just as long as they could eat a bowl of it in front of Mr. Pollard without gagging.

Whew. Close call with disaster, thought Hannah as she slumped against the counter. But just to be on the safe side, she had better ask a few follow-up questions.

"Is there anything else I should know? Any other information that might not be entirely correct?" she asked. "Sissy *is* a stay-at-home mother, right?"

"Yup," said Danny, his eyes twinkling. "In fact she never stops talking about it."

Hannah ignored the twinkling and asked, "And she has a traditional husband?"

Danny seemed to find this even more amusing. "Traditional is the perfect word for Sissy's husband Chuck."

So far, so good, thought Hannah. "When am I going to meet them?" she asked.

Danny nodded toward the windows. "Any second now."

Hannah looked out the window. Two children, a boy and a girl, were dashing across the yard, while a young woman carrying a huge tote bag was just coming down the alley behind the Walker house. She was followed by a young man who looked enough like Elvis to be the ghost of the King of Rock and Roll. He was talking urgently and gesturing a little wildly with his hands as he walked but the woman didn't bother to turn around. When she came through the gate to the backyard, she locked it behind her, leaving the Elvis look-alike on the other side, still pleading his case.

The children clattered up the steps and across the back porch. The screen door slammed against the wall as they tumbled into the kitchen. They were both towheaded and as golden-brown as their uncle.

"Children!" Kate exclaimed. "What are you doing here?"

"Mommy left Daddy again," the little girl said as if she'd announced nothing more important than what she'd just watched on television. Then, barely missing a beat, she asked, "Can we have some cereal?"

4

"MA DON'T YOU DARE give them any of that sugary junk. They've already had dinner," said the young woman who'd slammed in the back door with just as much force as her children.

"Sissy," Kate said, her hands on her hips, "what are you thinking?"

Sissy looked taken aback. "What? All of a sudden I'm not welcome in my own parents' house?"

"Sissy, this is *Hannah Ross*," Kate said pointedly. "From Granny's Grains."

It took a few moments for it to register on Sissy's face. When she finally got it, her hand went to her mouth much the same as Kate's had earlier. "Oh my gosh! I forgot all about Uncle Tuffy's contest. I guess I picked a lousy time to leave Chuck again, huh?"

Again? The word leapt out at Hannah and said *boo!* How could this be happening? Sissy and Chuck had looked perfect on paper. They'd been so absolutely—*right*. Now it looked like they were just another thing that was absolutely wrong.

"I think you better sit down, professor," Danny said.

Hannah automatically sat down on the chair Danny had pulled out for her. She was too dazed to even bother being irritated when Danny sat right down next to her.

"Does this happen often?" she asked him.

"So often the kids keep a second wardrobe upstairs in Sissy's old room. 'Course *old room* isn't really the correct term. The bed hardly ever has a chance to get cold before Sissy shows up at the back gate again in yet another skirmish in the employment wars."

"Employment wars?"

"Remember you asked if Sissy's husband was traditional?" Hannah nodded.

"Chuck is so traditional that he won't hear of Sissy working. While Sissy, who can cook up a storm, is on a constant crusade to transform the kitchen of the Belway family tavern. Make it like some bistro in Paris she read about. So every time Sissy sneaks something onto the menu, Chuck sneaks it back off again. And Sissy comes home."

Hannah leaned her elbows on the table and shoved her hands into her hair. "How long does she stay?"

Danny shrugged. "Varies. Anywhere from two days to two months."

Her head jerked up. "Two months!" The situation had gone from bad to worse with just those two words. If Sissy and Chuck weren't back together before Pollard and the rest of the crew showed up, Hannah was going to have a lot more to worry about than a taunting blue-eyed devil and a bunch of plants you could take out for a burger.

"We're not exactly what you planned on, are we, professor?" Danny asked softly.

Oh, fine. Danny Walker had picked a great time to talk nicely to her. And wasn't his smile just a little sweet, as well? The back of her throat started to ache, just like it always had when she was a little girl, forcing back tears. She'd be damned if she was going to cry in front of Danny Walker. She sat up straighter. "A few minor glitches," she said with a shrug. "Nothing I can't handle," she added nonchalantly, then turned to look out the window just in time to see Chuck finish climbing the fence.

"Time to play the helpful uncle," Danny said as he stood up. "Hey kids, I've got to run something over to the shop. Want to ride in the truck?"

The kids immediately lost interest in cereal. "Can we, Mom?" Susie asked.

"Go ahead," Sissy answered, then mouthed a thank you to her brother over the children's heads.

Danny shepherded the two children out of the kitchen just as Chuck appeared at the screen door and started rattling the knob.

"Come on, honeybunch, unlock the door," Chuck cooed, his face pressed against the screen.

"Don't you *honeybunch* me, Chuckie Belway."

"You can't call it quits over a couple of artichokes. Come on, sugar, admit it was a dumb idea, anyway."

"Dumb idea!" Sissy put her hands on her hips and stalked over to the door where her husband was clinging to the screen like a moth seeking a lightbulb. "Restaurants everywhere are putting gourmet pizzas on their menus. And if you hadn't been so all fired stubborn about tasting it you would have seen why."

"Well, this isn't everywhere. Most of Timber Bay has probably never even tasted an artichoke. They sure as hell don't want one on their pizza."

"You're impossible, Chuckie Belway," Sissy yelled before she slammed the kitchen door in her husband's face. Her bottom lip quivered as she turned to Kate. "Ma, I—I'm sorry if I'm messing things up for Uncle Tuffy, but I—I just can't stay married to a man who doesn't appreciate and nur—nurture my—my creativity." She sniffed and dashed at a tear slipping down her cheek. "H—How can you build a life with a man who won't even consider artichokes? I deserve artichokes, Ma."

"Of course you do, dear," Kate said as she took Sissy into her arms to console her.

Hannah was having a hard time picturing this tender scene on a cereal box. A *Moving Back in With Mother* edition? She was pretty sure Norman Rockwell never put that one on a magazine cover. She groaned and stood up.

"I can see you could use some time alone and I've got some paperwork to do so I think I'll just go on up to my room."

Nobody paid any attention so Hannah slipped out and went upstairs to the back bedroom Kate had shown her to earlier.

The room was sweet, with a flowered quilt on the bed and ruffled curtains at the window. The furniture was light oak and there was an old wooden rocker painted white. Soft and simple and feminine. Like a daughter's room. Hannah should be lying on the bed, staring at the ceiling and dreaming or sitting in the rocker at the window and watching as the soft, summer evening unfolded in the yard below. Instead, she sat down at the little oak desk, opened her notebook computer, and tried to compose her first daily e-mail report to Mr. Pollard. The task seemed to require the kind of fictional skills she couldn't quite summon at the moment.

She considered calling Lissa. But Lissa had been so upbeat about the whole thing Hannah hated to have to tell her that her inner child was on the verge of having a panic attack.

She closed the mail screen and opened a new document in the computer file on the Walkers. Okay, she thought as she thrust her hands into her hair and stared at the empty screen, no need to panic. Think it through. What exactly are the problems re: The Great American Family?

A fly buzzed around her head and she swished it away while typing *meat eaters in the greenhouse.* She stared at the line on the screen for a couple of seconds, tempted to delete it. The Venus flytraps seemed almost like a nonissue considering that the second generation Great American Family had been torn asunder over an artichoke pizza. On the other hand, she was pretty sure that Pollard didn't like weird—in any form. The flytraps stayed on the list of the day's debacles.

Next, she typed *Danny the Devil.* He could prove to be

worse than the flytraps, since there was no way at all, Hannah was sure, to contain that bad boy persona he was so fond of displaying. She wasn't going to fool herself that the few glimmers of kindness he'd shown were going to grow into the image Pollard was expecting in the Great American son. She'd just have to try to stay out of his way and hope that he'd lose interest in tormenting her soon. There had to be a girlfriend somewhere—or possibly several—that would eventually occupy his time.

Debacle number three, Sissy and Chuck. She typed and their names appeared on the screen. She stared at the letters, wondering if she could possibly find the money to send them all to Disney World for the duration. Unfortunately, until she got that bonus, she could barely afford to send them all out for an ice-cream cone.

Danny had said that sometimes the split only lasted a few days. So the Sissy/Chuckie problem might very well fix itself in time. But there would be consequences—from this split and from the earlier ones. She'd have to make it a point to spend some time with Susie and Andy so that she could see what kind of negative effects the parents' problems had on them. There were loads of statistics that showed that there would be some. When she found out what she was up against, she could then develop a strategy to work around any behavior that was less than perfect. They seemed like bright children. Maybe if she coached them a little and—

Great, she thought with disgust, now she was planning to finesse the situation for monetary gain. She'd better be careful or she was going to turn this into a game of *how low can the sociologist go?*

But what was she supposed to do? Pollard had insisted on meeting the winners and she knew he intended to make good use of photo ops. He'd be in the family's presence almost constantly. But could she stoop to using children to help pull her out of this mess?

Maybe she wouldn't have to. Susie and Andy seemed to be full of energy. They probably didn't stay in one place too long. With any luck, they'd sit still just long enough for the photographer to snap a few and then they'd be off. Who really expected perfect behavior out of children, anyway?

Well, okay. Maybe her father had expected perfect behavior and Hannah had wanted to please him enough to behave. But even Lissa and her brother acted out once in a while.

She looked at the old alarm clock on the bedside table. It was getting late. She'd wasted too much time obsessing. That report to Pollard still had to be written.

Typing furiously, using as much fiction as fact, Hannah filled the e-mail with lavish descriptions of the town and the house and just a very general, but glowing, description of the family. She sent it to Pollard and copied it to Marketing, and was filling in her daily log when there was a soft knock on the bedroom door.

"Come in," Hannah called over her shoulder.

She heard the door open, but no other sound. She turned around. Six-year-old Susie Belway was peering around the door.

"Hi," she said.

"Hi," Hannah answered.

"Can I come in?" the little girl asked.

"You certainly may." Perfect. Time alone with Susie Belway was exactly what Hannah needed.

Susie scampered in, leaving the door open, and flopped, tummy down, onto the bed.

"This is the best bed at Grandma's house to jump on," she said.

"Is it? I haven't tried it yet."

Susie giggled at this. "You're too old to jump on beds!" she exclaimed. "You should have come for a ride with us. Uncle Danny bought us ice cream."

"I've already been taken for a ride by Uncle Danny," Hannah said dryly.

"Isn't his truck cool?" Susie asked. Fortunately, the little girl didn't expect an answer. She held up a deck of cards while she sprang up and down on the quilt. "Want to play Old Maid?"

"I don't know how to play Old Maid," Hannah said as she got up from the desk chair and went to sit on the bed opposite Susie. "Can you teach me?"

Susie nodded enthusiastically. "Sure!"

Susie gave Hannah a quick lesson then started to deal.

"I can't stay and play too long. It's almost time for Grandpa to read me my bedtime story."

"That sounds nice," Hannah said as she took her turn discarding and drawing. "Do you like sleeping at your grandparents' house?"

Susie shrugged. "Sure. It's fun."

"Does it ever worry you a little?"

"Worry?" Susie's little face scrunched up. "I don't think so," she finally said as if she wasn't even sure what the word meant.

The little girl rearranged her cards with a minimum of fuss, then laid down three pairs. "I won!" she squealed. "Can I deal again?"

"Sure—go ahead," Hannah said. While Susie shuffled, Hannah asked, "By worry, I mean are you ever afraid because you don't know what to expect?"

"Wouldn't that be like being afraid of surprises?" Susie asked.

Hannah raised her brows at the question. Afraid of surprises? That wasn't what she'd meant. Was it? She decided to try another approach. "Do you ever feel out of control?" she asked.

"Oh, sure!"

Okay, thought Hannah. Now we're getting somewhere. "When do you feel out of control?"

"Well, like at school. When I have to go to the bathroom real bad. That's pretty hard to control."

Not what Hannah had expected. "But do you ever get angry?"

Susie screwed up her face. "At my teacher?"

"No—at your family."

"Lots!" Susie said it with enough enthusiasm to make the mattress bob up and down. "Especially at Andy when he won't play with me. He's the one who taught me Old Maid but he won't ever play it."

Well, that sounded pretty normal, thought Hannah.

Susie lay down another winning hand. "Wow, you're really bad at this. How come you never learned how to play Old Maid?"

Hannah shrugged. "Well, for one, I never had a brother to teach me. In fact, I really didn't have many other kids to play with when I was growing up."

Susie's mouth dropped open. "Wow! How come?"

"I was raised by my father. He was a professor at a college and we lived on the campus. Most of the other teachers there didn't have children."

"Didn't your daddy play with you?"

Hannah laughed at the idea of Orson Ross, with his leonine mane of gray hair and his tweed blazers with a deck of Old Maid in his hands. "I'm afraid he wasn't the kind of daddy that plays with you."

"That sucks," Susie said.

Out of the mouths of babes, Hannah thought as she drew the Old Maid.

DANNY HEARD THEIR VOICES as he came down the hall. When he got to the doorway, neither of them saw him, so he stayed, quietly watching.

With those silly cards in Hannah's hand and the way she was curled up on that patchwork quilt she looked like a teenager playing with her little sister. She was wearing a pair of men's cotton pajamas, blue-and-white striped, the sleeves so long they drooped over her hands. Her hair was tousled and the soft light from the bedside lamp turned it the color of the honey Lukas's sister served with her scones down at Sweet Buns. He would have known without overhearing what she'd just said that she wasn't used to much playfulness. Shame, because laughing with Susie like she was now you could see that there was potential.

Who knew? There might even be potential under those baggy striped pajamas.

Susie looked up from her cards and saw him. "Uncle Danny!" she cried.

"Hey, Susie-Q. You're not winning all the professor's money, are you?"

Susie beckoned him over with her finger. He moved close to the bed and bent down.

"Grandma says she doesn't have a real job so she prob'ly doesn't have any money," Susie whispered into his ear. Danny could tell by the way Hannah shot off the bed that she'd heard what Susie said.

He straightened and held out his hands, palm forward. "Hey, I didn't say it."

"Maybe not this time, but you started it," Hannah shot back.

"Are you two gonna fight?" Susie asked, looking from one to the other of them.

"You know what, sweetums? I think Grandpa is probably looking for you." Danny tapped his watch. "Time for your bedtime story."

Susie looked disgusted. "Oh, I never get to stick around when any grown-ups fight." Her bottom lip sticking out, she gathered her cards and stomped out of the room.

Danny knew he should follow her but instead he wandered over to the desk and tried to get a look at that notebook Hannah was always writing in. "So—you ready to throw in the towel yet?"

She reached around him and closed the notebook. "What do you mean?"

"Ready to admit that Granny picked the wrong person to run her contest?"

"Granny's contest was run exactly as it should have been."

"Then how come we won?"

She stuck that straight little nose defiantly into the air. "What do you mean? You won because your family fit—"

"Yeah, yeah. I know. We fit the criteria."

"Well, you do. This house couldn't be more perfect. Your mother is exactly like I expected her to be and your father does own his own business, right? A steel company?"

"He owns his own place, yeah. And steel is involved. Steel and scrap. But maybe not the kind of steel you think."

"It's true I don't know anything about steel, but it's all hard and cold, isn't it?"

His father's activities—with both steel and steal—were something Danny probably should warn Hannah about. But he wasn't feeling charitable. Besides, it would suit him just fine if she never really knew the whole story as far as his father was concerned. So instead he just asked, "What about Sissy and Chuck's ongoing pizza war?"

"Haven't you ever heard, Mr. Walker, that it's how a family handles problems that really matters?"

"Sure I have. And I agree. But I thought you were looking for normal."

"You don't seem to have a very high opinion of your family, Mr. Walker."

"My family, professor, is perfect just as it is. But normal? I'm all for fantasy, but that one is a real stretch." He walked to the door, then turned. "And, by the way, maybe you should start calling me Danny, considering we're going to be neighbors."

"Neighbors?" she sputtered.

"Yeah. My room is right next door. Sleep tight—Hannah," he said, and then he closed the door behind him.

SLEEP TIGHT INDEED. A half hour later Hannah was still tossing and turning. If she was going to lie awake all night the least she could do was to start preparing for future interviews. Instead all she could think about was the fact that Danny Walker was one much-too-thin wall away.

She closed her eyes tightly but they flew open again almost immediately. Did he sleep in the nude? Surely with his sister and niece and nephew back in the house he'd at least have underwear on.

That thought led to a mental debate with herself on whether he wore boxers or briefs. Statistics showed that most men in his age group—

The numbers flew out of her head when she heard the loud creak of a bedspring from the room next door. Something in her tummy tightened. Her nipples started to harden so she rolled over onto her stomach, as if burying her breasts in the bedclothes would help matters any. All the pressure did was make her wonder what a pair of roughened hands would feel like pressing where the mattress pressed now.

Another creak of the springs and Hannah groaned and pulled the pillow over her head.

How on earth could this be happening to her? This—this new earthiness? This lust for a man she'd first laid eyes on just that afternoon? She was not the kind of woman who got hot at the sound of a bedspring. She was the kind of woman who would rather curl up with a good article in a research journal than a man.

Of course, none of the men she'd ever had the chance to curl up to looked like Danny Walker. Harold, her first boyfriend when she was seventeen, had been thinner. And much taller. And his hands hadn't been rough so much as damp. And Richard, the boy she'd seen off and on for most of her college years, well, it'd been hard to tell just how tall Richard was what with his stoop and his unfortunate habit of looking over the top of his glasses. She'd had a brief fling with a professor in grad school. He'd been moderately good-looking in an elbow-patch sort of way, but he'd been as preoccupied as her father had always been. They'd spent a couple of months wrestling around his office but when it was over, Hannah wasn't sure if she'd ever heard him say her name.

The point was, she was pretty sure that she'd never even wondered what any of the men from her past were wearing under their baggy corduroys. None of them had been even remotely—well—hot. But that was all right. Hannah was the kind of woman who would choose brains over brawn anytime.

Wasn't she?

There was another creak from the mattress next door. All that brawn, tossing and turning.

And possibly naked.

She tried to force herself to start running data on the latest study on the sociology of the divorced family unit through her mind, hoping for some insight in how to handle the Sissy/Chuck situation, but it was no use. Danny Walker kept tossing around on the world's noisiest mattress—a mattress that was just on the other side of the wall. Six inches of plaster and wood between them.

It was going to be a long night.

5

THE NEXT MORNING, Hannah poked her head over the banister and listened. She'd purposely emerged from her room late, hoping Danny would be off doing something manly with wood. Facing him first thing in the morning when he was the reason she'd tossed and turned half the night was more than Hannah could handle. She was thoroughly disgusted with herself. Here she was, trying to hold onto the shreds of her professional dignity and all she'd been able to think about was whether or not Danny Walker was sleeping naked in the room next to hers. Every time she'd try to get her mind back on work, the bed next door would creak and her mind would clear of everything but the thought of what those thighs and that chest must look like naked. If this kind of preoccupation kept up she was going to be reduced to judging a male stripper competition and reminiscing about her more cerebral past when she ran a contest for a cereal company.

The house was quiet, so Hannah descended the staircase and tiptoed her way to the kitchen, greatly relieved to find Kate alone at the stove.

"Good morning, dear," Kate said. "How did you sleep?"

"Very well," Hannah lied. It was only a small lie, though. And the smell of bacon frying was already starting to revive her.

"Oh, good. Have a seat, dear, and I'll get your juice."

Hannah wasn't used to being waited on but she'd already decided that she liked it when Kate waited on her. Silly, she supposed, but it made her feel special. Maybe it had something to do with the way Kate seemed to enjoy it so much.

Kate smiled cheerfully as she put a glass of orange juice in front of Hannah, then filled the four-slice toaster. "Your eggs will be ready in a jiff."

"If this is Tuesday, it must be over easy," came a voice from the back door.

"Ina!" Kate exclaimed. "Come on in. I'm just about to break some eggs for Hannah. I'd be glad to add a few more."

"And I'd be glad to eat them," the woman said as she opened the screen door and let herself in. "This must be the cereal gal, huh?"

"Hannah Ross," Hannah said, holding out her hand.

The woman's handshake was firm, her hand slightly rough. She was tall, raw boned, with a graying pageboy haircut and a face that looked like it had never met a bottle of sunscreen. "Ina Belway," she said.

"Chuck's mother?"

"Yup," Ina pulled out a chair, "sad to say that lug head is my boy."

"Oh, don't be so rough on him, Ina," Kate said. "He's a good boy. Just a little set in his ways."

"His old man was the same way. Never wanted me to work next to him at the bar. Then he died on me and I had to learn it all in a hurry."

Ina said it without an ounce of self-pity. It made Hannah like her right away.

"It sounds like you're on Sissy's side."

"Hey, I got nothin' against artichokes."

Melted butter sizzled as Kate broke eggs into the hot pan. The toast popped up and Ina got up, grabbed it, and brought it to the table to butter. She placed two slices on Hannah's plate.

"Well," Kate said as she came over and started to dish out eggs, "it's true that those two fight like a couple of kids, but I know Sissy can be very high-handed. I keep telling her she has to choose her moments."

"So is she still in a snit?" Ina asked.

"She took the kids down to Whittaker's Department Store. They're having a sale on sandals. I expect that'll cheer her up."

"The two of you don't seem very worried," Hannah said.

"About what, dear?" Kate asked.

"That Chuck and Sissy's marriage is on the rocks."

"On the rocks? Why, whatever gave you that idea?" Kate asked with what looked like genuine innocence in her wide blue eyes.

"Huh," Ina grunted. "What's a few rocks? Those two are made for each other."

Hannah was about to ask how that could be when the phone on the kitchen wall rang. Kate excused herself and got up to answer it.

"Why Clem Hatchett, you just calm down. Are you sure it was Henry who took your fence?"

The back door banged open and Henry Walker burst in, took one look at Kate on the phone, and started to leave the way he came.

"You just wait one darn minute, Henry Walker!" Kate exclaimed.

To Hannah's surprise, Henry stopped in his tracks.

"I'll call you back, Clem," Kate said into the receiver then hung up. She walked up to her husband and poked him in the chest with her finger. "Henry, you know good and well that Clem wasn't ready to get rid of that fence yet!"

There was a mighty scowl on Henry Walker's face. "Well, he *should* be ready to get rid of it," he insisted grumpily. "Durn thing was half layin' in the alley. A public nuisance. I should get a key to the city for clearing it out of there."

"All the same, Henry, you know the trouble it caused when you took Mrs. Ludington's riding lawn mower."

"Well," Henry mumbled defensively, "it wasn't like anyone was riding it—"

Hannah rubbed her forehead with her fingers. She was getting dizzy trying to make sense of the conversation.

Ina chuckled. "You look confused, Hannah."

That was putting it mildly. "Care to help me out?"

"Happy to. One hot August day last year Ken Ludington took a break from mowing his lawn to go into the house to fetch a drink of water," Ina told her. "Henry had that mower on the back of his truck before Ken swallowed his first mouthful."

Mouth open in astonishment, Hannah looked at the Walkers who were still arguing about the fence. "Henry is a thief?" she whispered in disbelief.

Ina shook her head. "Nah. Those of us who love the old rascal prefer to call it wishful salvaging."

"Wishful salvaging?" Hannah asked, knowing she'd probably be better off if she hadn't.

"Yeah. Henry sometimes runs into trouble on a slow day of junk collecting. Gets impatient. He's been known to collect something before its owner is entirely ready to give it up."

Hannah frowned. "Junk collecting? But I thought Henry was in iron and steel? Steel with a double e," she added for clarification.

Ina laughed. "Oh, he's in steel and iron, all right. And plastic, wood, tin and paper. Salvage. He collects other people's junk. Sometimes prematurely," she added with a twisted smile. "But, if anyone complains, Henry always takes it back."

Hannah pushed her plate away. It looked like Henry Walker was going to need more than a wardrobe change to fit the Great American Family image. "Tell me this is one of those reality television shows and I'm the only one not in on the joke. Tell me anything—just don't tell me that the Great American Father has a police record."

"Is that all you're worried about? Henry doesn't have a record. Not yet, anyway."

"No?"

"Nah. Most people don't press charges and if they want to, Kate generally takes one of her mincemeat pies over to whoever the latest victim is and they usually change their minds."

"That must be some pie," murmured Hannah.

"It's the bourbon," Ina said out of the side of her mouth.

Hannah wondered if Pollard was a fan of mincemeat. After a couple of bourbon-laced pieces, the Walker family might start looking like they were supposed to.

"Henry!" Kate yelled, snapping Hannah's attention back to the latest debacle. "You get your hand out of that jar of sugar cookies."

"Oh, for pity's sake, I'll take the durn fence back if that's how you're going to be," Henry said grudgingly.

"That's how I'm going to be," Kate told him firmly while she held a cookie jar just out of her husband's reach.

"Aw, tell Clem I'm on my way," Henry said before he slammed back out the screen door.

Kate put the cookie jar down and turned to Hannah. "Are you going to finish that, dear?" she asked in her usual sweet voice.

"What?" Hannah was having a little trouble keeping up. She looked down at her plate. "Um—"

"Because if you're not, my babies just love bacon."

"Then by all means," Hannah said, losing her appetite completely.

"Perhaps you'd like to feed them yourself, dear?"

"I'd pass if I were you," Ina said out of the side of her mouth. "Kate is the sweetest woman I know but those plants of hers give me the creeps."

"Actually, Kate," she said as she pushed back her chair and stood up, "I have an appointment with the high-school principal in about fifteen minutes. So I better run."

"Mr. Swartz. Such a nice man," Kate said.

Hannah kept Kate's simple statement in her mind as she drove to the high school. She badly needed some success. But Simon Swartz had to be more than a nice man. He had to be at least a semigreat man. Which didn't seem like so much to ask. After all, he ran a school that had one of the lowest dropout rates in the Midwest. To accomplish that, he'd have to be a natural-born leader, looked up to by students and parents alike.

She parked in the school parking lot and got out of the station wagon, telling herself that it was silly to have such doubts about her own judgement. After all, she had been the one to evaluate Simon Swartz in the first place. She was a professional. She knew what she was doing. Didn't she?

Okay, she admitted to herself as she walked to the entrance of the building. Maybe she should have asked a couple of follow-up questions about Henry's occupation. But, to be fair, Hannah didn't even know there were places that actually salvaged junk—the Westbridge Campus certainly didn't have one—so how could she have known what to ask? And what kind of question could she possibly have put on the preliminary questionnaire that would have yielded the information that Henry sometimes collected junk before it had officially been thrown out by its owner? And didn't the Walkers have to take some of the blame for this mess? What were they thinking of even entering a contest when they were harboring things like wishful salvagers and revolving door marriages?

It was some comfort, at least, that, thanks to the camaraderie of a small town, Henry didn't have a police record. But she'd have to remember to keep her eye on him once Pollard came to town. Any more debacles and she was going to have to take up juggling.

The high school's heavy steel entrance door clanged when she opened it. The smell of chalk and floor polish welcomed her as her footsteps echoed in the cool, empty hallway. Growing up in academia had its downside, but the scents and sounds still made her feel a little safer.

She found the principal's office halfway down the first floor hallway. As she knocked on the door, she reminded herself to ask a lot of follow-up questions. Tons. That way, there wouldn't be any surprises as far as Simon Swartz was concerned.

Mr. Swartz himself opened the door.

Hannah's first impression was that he didn't look anything like a leader of men.

Luckily, she was starting to lose faith in first impressions.

For starters, Hannah had to literally look down at him. He couldn't have been more than five feet four inches tall. He was small and thin, boyish in his plaid cotton suit and dated bow tie. His sandy-colored hair was thinning but so far he hadn't succumbed to the comb over.

"You must be Hannah Ross," he said. "I can't wait to hear what you think of our little town." His voice was slightly squeaky, but when he warmly took her hand in both of his to draw her into his office, she could see how maybe his students might take to him despite his *über*-geek visage.

Hannah assured him that she thought Timber Bay was lovely and agreed that yes, indeed, everyone was very friendly. She quickly steered the conversation back to him.

"Mr. Swartz, I'd love to hear your philosophy on education and your views on the sociological impact the school family has on the home family—and vice versa, of course," she said as she took her tape recorder out of her bag.

For the next fifteen minutes she listened to him talk about the importance of hands-on parents and teacher/parent involvement. He described his open-door policy toward both students and faculty and the importance of pep rallies and hot-dog day.

"I'm sure hot-dog day is—um—delicious. But Timber Bay High School has the lowest dropout rate of any school in its class in the country. How do you account for such excellent numbers?"

"Oh, that's easy. I simply don't let anyone drop out."

Hannah blinked. "Excuse me?"

"Let me show you," he said.

Hannah followed him over to a file cabinet. He opened it and took out a metal box with a padlock.

"When a student expresses interest in quitting school, I have them fill out the proper paperwork and then I file it here." He put the box on top of the cabinet, unlocked it and showed her the thick manila folder inside. "And that's the end of it."

Hannah frowned. "The end of it? How can that be the end of it?"

"Because I never pass the paperwork on. That's the secret, you see."

"No, I don't see."

"Well, if the paperwork never goes through the proper channels, then it can't possibly be completed, can it? Thus, the student never drops out."

"But if the student is old enough to quit, wouldn't that be denying them their rights?"

Mr. Swartz looked genuinely puzzled. "Never had a complaint of that. No, what usually happens is I find some kind of project to distract them until they forget all about it. Before they know it, they're graduating."

"And that works for you?"

"It worked for me," Danny Walker said from the doorway.

Perfect, Hannah thought. Now that the usual witness to her degradation was present, the moment felt complete. "Don't you have anything better to do, Walker, than lurk in corners waiting to witness disaster so you can give me that cute little grin?"

"You think I have a cute little grin?" he asked with exaggerated innocence.

"Guilelessness doesn't work for you, Walker. Your ego pokes too easily through the thin facade."

Mr. Swartz laughed merrily. "Danny always was one to tease the girls, Miss Ross," he said. "But I assure you he's here legitimately. He has some warps to fix."

"More like he has some waves to make," Hannah said as she turned off her tape recorder and stuffed it back into her shoulder bag. "Thank you for your time, Mr. Swartz," she said.

Terrific, Hannah thought as she marched down the hall. Timber Bay High's low dropout rate had been skewed. And Hannah had been screwed—once again. Swartz had looked so damn good on paper, too. Now he was just one more disappointment. One more thing she had to figure out what to do about.

Outside, the day had gone as gray as her mood. She fought the wind as she walked to the station wagon. What the hell was she going to do about Mr. Swartz's interview?

She opened the door, threw her shoulder bag into the passenger seat, and got into the car. Her tape recorder had spilled out of the bag onto the seat. She picked it up, ejected the cassette, and stared at it. Maybe nobody would ever have to hear what was on it. If she never transcribed it, she could erase the tape and just act like the interview hadn't happened. She could leave Mr. Swartz, and the high school, out of her report to Mr. Pollard. Maybe concentrate on the grade school that Andy and Susie Belway attended instead.

She put the cassette back into the recorder and put her finger on the erase button.

"I think that would be a very big mistake."

Hannah turned her head, and once again found herself nose to nose with Danny Walker.

"Don't let me keep you from your warps," Hannah said, finger still poised on the button.

Danny reached over and took the recorder out of her hand.

"Have you any idea what you've got here, professor?" he asked.

"Not anything I can use, that's for sure."

"What Swartz told you in there is one hell of a story—and you know it."

"What he told me in there is quite possibly illegal."

"Illegal?"

Well, maybe she was reaching a little. "At the very least," she said, "he's imposing his own will on unsuspecting students not to mention falsifying school records. That doesn't exactly set him up for man of the year."

"Boy, for a chick who is running a contest for a cereal company, you sure have a way of sticking that straight little nose of yours up at other people."

Ohhh, he was maddening. It was as if those blue eyes could see right through her. She wasn't about to get into that conversation with him. "Forgive me if I'm a bit cranky, but on top of everything else I've found out since I got here, I didn't expect to find a principal who lies to make himself look good."

"You just don't get it, do you? That man in there saved a lot of asses—including mine."

"Is that what you meant when you said that it had worked for you?"

"Yeah," Danny answered. "As soon as I was old enough, I dropped out. But Swartz got me back."

Hannah's curiosity got the better of her. "How?"

"A couple of weeks after I stopped going to school, just around the time I was getting bored with hanging out, Swartz had it put in the paper that the auto shop was going to completely restore a '57 Chevy. At the end of the year, they were going to hold a drawing. Winner got the car."

"Let me guess. You wanted that car enough to go back to school."

"Not bad, professor. You're catching on. The '57 was my dream car—and just about everyone in town knew it."

"You're saying that Swartz—"

"That's what I'm saying. It took the class the rest of the semester to restore it. I never was so happy to go to school in my life."

Danny started to talk about the car and what it'd been like to work on it—and to dream about it maybe one day being his. As she listened to him, an image came into her mind of what he must have looked like, racing down Ludington Avenue, making every girl he passed wish she was in that car beside him—sitting up tight next to him, her hand on his hard thigh, his arm around her shoulders, the radio playing songs that would make them want to be alone.

Down girl, Hannah thought with disgust. She got busy rooting in her shoulder bag for the car keys. "Look, just because Swartz got you your dream car, doesn't mean that—"

Her fingers had found the keys when he said, "But I didn't win."

She looked at him. "You didn't win?"

"Nope. But it kept me in school the rest of the semester. To fill up my schedule, I took wood shop. That summer I worked for a builder and made enough to buy my own car. But even more important than the car, it led to my life's work and a partnership with my best friend."

But all Hannah could think of was that it was going to lead to her not getting that bonus and possibly never finding employment again. "Look, that's very touching. But it doesn't take away from the fact that Swartz's records are misleading and his—"

"Hey, his methods might not be by the books, but they work."

"Oh—so the end justifies the means?"

"Sometimes," Danny said.

"Well, that might be okay in Walker world, Danny, but

somehow I don't think Granny's Grains CEO would consider that a worthy slogan to sell his cereal," she retorted as she turned the key and the station wagon's engine sputtered to life.

"He wants to sell cereal, professor," Danny yelled as she started to pull out of her parking space, "tell him to quit wasting his time on words and start making something that doesn't taste like sugared cardboard."

HANNAH ROSS WAS the most deluded woman he'd ever met, thought Danny as he watched the station wagon drive away. It was like she thought life was supposed to be run by rules like that silly contest of hers. And she got her nose out of joint every time something didn't quite fit. At the rate things were going, Hannah Ross's nose was going to be on sideways by the time she left Timber Bay.

He climbed into his truck and drove over to Sweet Buns, picked up sandwiches for lunch, then headed for the opera house. Lukas had the side door propped open. Just inside, Danny paused, struck again as he always was at the idea that he owned such a magnificent space. He laughed at himself and shook his head. Talk about being a romantic. It'd be more realistic to say that he was in hock up to his butt for a run-down white elephant that no sane person had called a *magnificent space* for at least fifty years.

The red velvet on the seats was rotted, as was half the wood in the place. The wiring was a mess and the plumbing had to be replaced. But all Danny had to do was take the sweeping marble staircase to the balcony and look down on the stage and the words of Longfellow carved in the arch above it and he knew the place was worth saving—and that it was his job to do it. "*And when she had passed it seemed like the ceasing of exquisite music.*" It choked him up a little every time.

He wondered what Hannah Ross would make of that. A '57 Chevy and an opera house. She'd probably come up with some article in a journal that would say he fit the profile of men whose mothers only made waffles on Wednesdays. In Danny's opinion, the professor had a thing or two to learn. One of them being that she was never going to be able to stuff him into a neat little box and stick a list of ingredients on his forehead.

"Yo, Danny! Quit your daydreamin' and get up here with those sandwiches."

Danny looked up. Lukas was leaning over the balcony, a grin big enough to see from this distance on his boyish face.

"If you want me to work free on this heap of junk you're going to have to feed me."

Lukas took a lot of feeding. Which was one of the reasons Danny had taken Molly up on her offer to critique her latest sandwich creation. It meant a free lunch.

Molly, Lukas's kid sister, owned Sweet Buns, the coffee shop and bakery next to the old Sheridan Hotel. Unlike Lukas, who was still a bachelor, Molly had married young, become a mother young, and had been widowed young. The two of them had been squabbling about one thing or another ever since Danny had met them, but they were tight as a pair of leather pants on a rock star and Lukas was head over heels in love with his niece Chloe.

Bag in hand, Danny ran down the aisle to the lobby of the opera house, then took the stairs two at a time to join Lukas at the balcony railing.

"What'd Molly dream up today?" Lukas asked as he unwrapped his sandwich.

"Sprouts and goat cheese on wheat germ bread."

Lukas groaned. "She still experimenting with that health food stuff, huh?"

"Looks like."

"Tell her I don't appreciate being a guinea pig."

"Hey, she's your sister. You tell her. Anyway, the price is

right. And she threw in a couple of her cinnamon buns to sweeten the deal."

Lukas's boyish face lit up at that. "Good, we'll need something to wash down the taste of those sprouts. Hope you got large coffees."

"I did," Danny said, handing him one. "House blend."

"Ahhh," Lukas moaned after taking his first swallow. "Girl might not know what kind of sandwich to make a man but she sure knows her coffee."

"What have you been up to all morning?" Danny asked.

Lukas talked about the intricately carved moldings he was restoring while they ate. Danny always got a kick out of how wired Lukas could get when he talked about wood. Danny was the carpenter, the builder. But Lukas was the craftsman, the artist. He'd first taken up a knife to whittle when he'd been five years old and hadn't stopped since. Molly joked that if you needed to find Lukas, all you had to do was follow the wood shavings. He'd gone from whittling to carving. From carving to restoring. With Danny's practical building know-how and Lukas's artistic talent, they'd been a natural to form Timber Bay Building and Restoration together. Just like they were a natural to restore the opera house—and, if they got a crack at it, the Sheridan Hotel.

"Anything on the answering machine when you were back at the shop earlier?" he asked Lukas.

"One or two things—but nothing from old lady Sheridan."

Danny shoved the rest of his sandwich back into the bag, making a mental note to tell Molly to go back to the drawing board on that one.

"You know," Danny said, after taking a gulp of coffee, "my Ma always said that bad deeds come back to haunt you. I never should have busted Gavin Sheridan's nose."

"Ancient history," scoffed Lukas, downing the second half of his sandwich in one bite. "She wants that hotel renovated, we're the best around. Some of the same craftsmen worked on both the opera house and the hotel. Since we're already renovating this place, it only makes sense for old lady Sheridan to hire us. She might be unsociable but she's not stupid enough to let the fact that you rumbled with her grandson back in grade school interfere with business."

Agnes Sheridan had been Danny's nemesis ever since he'd climbed over her wrought-iron fence and stolen lilacs from one of her bushes when he was nine years old. He could have sworn the coast was clear but the old lady had come out of nowhere, grabbing him by the ankle and pulling him out of the overgrown bush so he'd landed with a thud on the ground in front of her. She'd gotten the chauffeur to stand watch over him while she called the cops who came and took Danny down to the station, gave him a talking to, and let him go. No big deal, really. Except the old lady's grandson, who lived with her at the time, had witnessed the whole thing. The next day he'd blabbed all over school that Danny had been picking flowers for a girl. Danny figured he was only defending his honor when he jumped the kid at recess.

"Agnes Sheridan is the type to hold a grudge," he said. "Starchy. A rule follower—just so long as she's the one to make the rules. Expecting people to fit a mold like a damn puff of cereal so she can stick them in a box and put them on a shelf and—"

"Whoa, Danny—cool it. I get the feeling you're no longer talking about the dragon lady. It's that cereal chick, isn't it? She's the one who's got you cranked."

"I swear, Lukas, you never saw a woman so full of illusions and delusions. I ran across her at the high school, bad-mouthing Swartz because he didn't fit her idea of Mr. Perfect Principal and then she had the guts to—" Danny broke off when he realized that Lukas was softly laughing.

"What the hell are you laughing at?"

"You, buddy. I haven't seen you this worked up about a

woman since Mary Jo Rumple showed up in eleventh grade English in those red high heels and pink anklets."

"Your analogy sucks, pal. That was a purely sexual response to those high heels. This thing with Hannah Ross has absolutely nothing to do with sex."

"Uh-huh," Lukas muttered into his foam coffee cup.

"Get real," Danny scoffed. "I can't get worked up about anyone with that much starch in her back. I like my women soft and ripe. Hannah Ross is neither."

Except, Danny thought to himself, when he'd seen her in her pajamas last night, with the lamplight all soft in her hair, and her mouth relaxed in a smile. She'd looked plenty soft, and ripe enough to pick. But he wasn't about to tell Lukas that. And Danny sure as hell wasn't going to tell Lukas how he'd tossed and turned half the night, wondering what the professor would be like with some of that starch washed out of her.

He stuffed his empty coffee cup in the bag and stood up. "Let's get down to the stage and take a look at that floor before you leave. It's a rare afternoon I get to spend over here, I'm not gonna waste it talking about the professor."

As they went down the balcony stairs together, the first sounds of distant thunder rumbled toward Timber Bay.

6

A SPEAR OF LIGHTNING SPLINTERED the sky on the other side of the bay as Hannah let herself into the Walker house. She followed the comforting fragrance of chicken and herbs into the kitchen to find Kate Walker stirring something on the stove.

"There you are, dear," she said, just as if Hannah walked into her kitchen every afternoon. "Have you had lunch?"

"No, I haven't. Whatever you're making in that pot smells like heaven."

Kate beamed. "It's my mother's chicken and dumpling soup. But it won't be ready until dinnertime. There's some cold meat loaf. I'll make you a sandwich."

"You're busy, Kate. I can do it if you show me where everything is."

"If you don't mind my saying so, you look a bit undone, dear." She held out a chair and pressed Hannah into it. "You just sit right down and rest while I get your lunch."

Hannah had grown up doing for herself. If she had soup, it came out of a can. If she had a sandwich, she made it herself. It felt so good having someone take care of her that Hannah decided to let it happen. The irony wasn't lost on her that it was the mother of the man who was making her come undone who was offering her comfort.

"How did your interview with Mr. Swartz go?" Kate asked as she put a plate holding a meat-loaf sandwich on thick, white bread and a mound of potato salad that looked homemade on the table in front of Hannah.

"It wasn't what I expected."

Kate sighed, but not unhappily. "Things seldom are," she said.

"You really think that?" Hannah asked as she raised the sandwich to her lips.

"Well, of course. You surely don't think that I set out to spend my life with a man who steals people's fences, do you?"

Hannah couldn't help it. She started to laugh. "Kate, there's no one like you."

"And there's certainly no one like Henry, either," Kate said. "But, you take the good with the bad, the rain with the sun. It all comes out the same in the end."

Hannah put the sandwich down and grabbed her notebook and started to scribble. She wasn't exactly sure if what Kate had just said fit the Great American Family image. But she wanted to remember it. She was going to have to find a new angle on these people. She was going to have to bend their image, albeit as subtly as possible. So subtly that Pollard wouldn't even notice.

It occurred to Hannah that talking to people outside of, but close to, the family might help her get some ideas. "Kate, did Danny or Sissy have any friends that spent a lot of time here while they were growing up?"

"Hmm—Lukas McCoy, for one. He was here as often as he was home, I'd say."

"Danny's partner?"

Kate nodded. "They've been best friends since grade school. The boys used to find out what both Lukas's mother and I were serving for dinner before they decided where to eat. If it was liver and onions night here, you'd find them at the McCoys'. If it was fish night there, they'd be over here."

It sounded like Lukas McCoy could be useful. But there was no way Hannah wanted to risk running into Danny anytime soon. "Any idea where I could find Lukas this afternoon, Kate?"

"I think Danny said Lukas was going to be at the opera house all day."

"With Danny?"

Kate shook her head. "I'm pretty sure Danny plans to be at the high school all afternoon."

That was all that Hannah needed to hear. She pushed her chair back and started to pick up her empty lunch dishes.

"Oh, just leave those dear and shoo! Go ask your questions so you can be home in time for dinner."

Home in time for dinner. Hannah liked the sound of that. "I wouldn't miss that soup for anything. Thanks for lunch, Kate."

She was almost to the front door when Kate called, "As long as you're going over that way, why don't you stop at Sweet Buns and pick up some cookies for dessert?"

An errand. The normal simplicity of it made Hannah feel all warm and cozy inside. No one, as far as Hannah could remember, had ever asked her to stop and pick up anything for dessert before. It was such a little thing, but it made Hannah feel absurdly hopeful that maybe she hadn't been completely wrong about the Walkers, after all.

Storm clouds were rolling in from the bay and the temperature was noticeably dropping as Hannah drove down Sheridan Road. She turned right on Miller Street and pulled up in front of the boarded-up opera house. That Danny Walker owned it still puzzled her. So maybe he liked opera. So did a lot of people. But they didn't, at the age of thirty, become obsessed with an old theater. Obsessed enough to put everything they had into it.

The '57 Chevy fit. The opera house didn't.

Hannah got out of the station wagon and started looking for a way inside. She found an emergency exit toward the back of the building propped open with an old orange crate.

She expected the place to smell musty and dead. But, despite the tattered red velvet theater chairs and crumbled plas-

ter, there was the smell of reawakening in the air. Paint, tur-
pentine, sawdust. The buzzing of a power saw made her turn
her head and look up at the stage.

He was bent over a length of wood resting between two
sawhorses. He'd taken off his shirt and Hannah could see the
muscles in his arms flexing as he worked. Sawdust sprayed
off the blade making him look slightly out of focus—like a vision. And what a vision he was. But it wasn't Lukas McCoy.
It was Danny Walker, shirtless, up on that stage and he could
have easily sold tickets for the performance because he
looked that good.

What was the matter with her? She was feeling downright
shallow. She barely knew him. And she could barely stand
him. But here she was, practically drooling because the guy
looked good with his shirt off.

The saw ripped through the wood and half of it fell to the
floor with a crash. Danny held the other half of the board in
his fist as he straightened and stretched an arm upward to
push his hair back. The movement made every muscle in his
stomach ripple ever so slightly—and made Hannah break out
in goose bumps. Her gaze moved up his body to his chest—
tanned and toned, and up to his shoulders—solid, his
throat—strong, his mouth—quirked, his eyes—*looking at her.*

Busted.

She opened her mouth to say something but her mouth had
suddenly gone dry as the sawdust Danny was brushing from
his chest. She licked her lips and tried again.

"Your mother said you wouldn't be here."

He cocked his head quizzically. "Then why did you
come?"

She couldn't remember. She searched her mind like a computer searches a database and came up with nothing. All she
could seem to do is stand there, getting a kink in her neck
from looking up at him.

Amusement glittered in his blue eyes. "I don't think I've ever seen you speechless before," he said.

"I'm just surprised to find you here. That's all."

He leapt off the edge of the stage, landing lightly on the balls of his feet, close enough for her to smell the sawdust on him. "Then who did you expect to find?" he asked.

"Your partner."

He frowned. "What do you want with Lukas?"

What was she supposed to answer to that? That she was desperate to find a new angle for the Great American Family? He'd never get off her back if she admitted to him that she had problems. Big problems. "Do you know where he is?"

"Yeah. He's over at The Church of the Holy Flock."

"Thank you," she said and turned to leave.

He stepped in front of her. "What do you want with Lukas?" he repeated.

"That's none of your business."

"It's my business if what you want with him is to find a new winner for your contest. Uncle Tuffy won and you're not taking that away from him."

"I wouldn't do that," she said indignantly. "I chose your family and I'm standing by my choice—despite certain—um—unexpected findings." Least of all that Danny's father had some sort of strange form of kleptomania.

He took a step closer to her. "You're a real fan of the expected, aren't you, professor?"

"I think most people are, Mr. Walker."

"If that's true, then that's pretty sad."

"Sad?"

"Sad," he repeated, taking two steps this time, bringing him close enough to put his hands on her upper arms. "The unexpected is so much more exciting," he said as his fingers caressed her. She barely had time to shiver and he was swinging her around so that she was facing the rows of seats sweeping back to the doors that led to the lobby and the box seats that curved out from the sides of the balcony above.

"Take a look at this place, Hannah. Don't you find it unexpected in a little town like this? Look up there—" he stretched out his arm and pointed to the ceiling.

Hannah looked. It took a moment but then she saw it, faintly beneath years of dirt and neglect. The domed ceiling was a mass of painted vines, flowers and birds. She gasped. "Wow—it's beautiful."

"And unexpected?"

"Yes—um—unexpected." But not nearly as unexpected as the hard warmth of his chest against her back and the sureness of his hands on her shoulders.

He swung them both around this time to face the stage again.

"Above the stage are carved the words of a poet," he said, pointing again, and she felt his excited breath against her cheek as he brought his head down next to hers. "The first time those words were ever read, Hannah, they were unexpected. Once this place held dozens of people all hearing the same voice, the same music for the first time. Imagine the excitement in a town of rough loggers and mill workers at the opening of this place and the world it brought to them."

He pulled her more tightly back against him and she thought she felt his actual lips against her cheek now as he whispered, "This place has secrets, Hannah."

He was like a pied piper weaving a spell with words instead of music. "What kind of secrets?" she asked like a dutiful follower.

He let go of her but only long enough to grab her hand. "Come on. I'll show you."

He ran with her up the aisle to the lobby and down a flight of half crumbled stone stairs to the basement. They followed one corridor then another before she remembered that she was no rodent, happily, and haplessly, being led to the sea. She tried to twist her hand out of his.

"Let go of me," she demanded. "How dare you drag me off like—like chattel!"

He laughed. "You're not willing enough to count as chattel, professor. Chattel wouldn't try to dig her heels in like you are."

"How observant of you. Now let go of my hand!" she managed to demand in between pants for air.

"And I'm pretty sure chattel doesn't talk, either," he threw over his shoulder at her.

"Tough. This chattel is going to start screaming any minute."

She opened her mouth to let out a howl when he pulled her into a storage room at the end of the corridor and let go of her hand. She slumped against the wall, trying to catch her breath. The fact that he was barely winded wasn't helping her mood.

"This had better be good, Walker."

"Watch," Danny said.

It was about all Hannah had the strength to do anyway. While she watched, Danny leaned on a shelf and the whole wall moved to reveal a heavy, medieval looking door.

Hannah pushed herself away from the wall. "A secret door? Where does it go?" she asked as she grabbed the doorknob. It wouldn't turn. She rattled it, but it was no use.

Danny took her by the shoulders again and spun her around to face him. "Why, professor, you surprise me," he said, his amused gaze dancing over her face. "So eager to explore the unexpected."

She sniffed. "I would think that most people would be curious about a secret door," she said defensively.

"Any statistics on that, professor?"

"You're the one who dragged me here against my will. The

least you can do for my trouble is to tell me where the door goes."

He cocked his head as he studied her. "The boys in the neighborhood must have had one heck of a time with you, Hannah Ross. I bet you had a braid down your back and drove them crazy with your stubborn single-mindedness."

"Wrong on all counts," she told him. "No braid. No boys. No neighborhood. Now are you going to tell me where that door leads?"

He laughed. "All right, professor. That door leads to a tunnel that runs clear under Sheridan Road."

"A tunnel?" she asked, hating the fact that she sounded so eager.

Danny shrugged. "But you wouldn't be interested in that. Not with the way you're so in love with normal. I mean, there's certainly nothing normal about having a secret tunnel running all the way under the main street of a town. In fact, it's probably downright Un-Great American Family-ish."

Hannah eyed him. What a scoundrel he was. She shrugged. "You're probably making it up, anyway."

His eyes glittered. "Wanna bet?"

"Ever been in it?"

"Lots of times," he boasted.

She ran her fingers along the door. "Liar. This looks like it was sealed a long time ago."

"It was."

"Then you couldn't possibly have been in it."

His eyes danced and his mouth quirked. "Oh, but I was. It's not sealed at the other end. Come on." He held out his hand. "I'll show you."

This was asking for trouble and she knew it. But, hell, she had so much trouble right now what was a little bit more? She put her hand in his.

Again they ran the corridors and up through the lobby and theater and outside where a fine rain had already started to fall. They ran down the half block of Miller Street that ended in Sheridan Road and Hannah thought her heart might burst from her chest. She didn't know if it was beating so fast from the running or from the feel of Danny's rough hand enfolding hers. They dodged honking cars as they ran across the road to the old Sheridan Hotel, then skirted the side of the building until they came to a low stone wall that bordered the overgrown, tangled gardens behind it.

Hannah gasped when Danny put his hands on her waist and lifted her clear over the wall and placed her on her feet on the other side. Then, with a hand flat on the top of the low wall and his arm braced, he leapt over, took her hand again, and started for the wide, stone steps that led to a tiled terrace and double helpings of French doors at the back of the hotel. Danny led her up the steps and over to an empty flower urn to the side of the terrace. He let go of her hand, squatted down, and pulled up a loose tile. There was a key lying in the hollow underneath. Danny picked it up, carefully replaced the tile, and stood.

"Come on," he said, taking her hand again.

"Wait! What are you going to do?" she demanded, trying to dig her heels in but finding it impossible on the wet tiles. Danny easily pulled her along after him.

"The other end of the tunnel is inside the hotel."

"So we're breaking and entering?" Why was she surprised? He was, after all, the son of a wishful salvager.

He held up the key. "We have a key so we're just entering—not breaking."

"With that kind of logic, I'm assuming you were the kid on the block who got away with murder," she said dryly.

His grin was wicked. "Not murder but plenty else."

"Well, you may have been a bad boy, but I was a good girl. I don't go into locked places that don't belong to me."

"Come on, professor, be a little bad for once," Danny cajoled in a voice that might make a saint falter. "Nobody is ever gonna have to know."

Hannah could just imagine how Mr. Pollard's jowls would shake if he had to bail her out of jail. Even if she managed to somehow make the Walkers look like they were supposed to, Pollard would never go for her becoming a lonely statistic in the nearly crime-free town. This was no time to become a bad girl.

Then again, how often was someone like her offered the chance?

Hannah took a quick look around. There was nothing beyond the stone walls but rough, rocky shore. Not a soul in sight. Just the tangled gardens stretching down to a ramshackle pier. The fierce wind off the bay was blowing the storm ashore. Thunder rolled closer and lightning flashed over the bay, filling the air with urgency. Yet Hannah still wandered in the valley of indecision. She imagined that this was what being the neighborhood Goody Two-shoes felt like. Afraid to explore. Afraid to take a chance. But tempted. Yes, very tempted. She bet that for every Goody Two-shoes there was someone like Danny Walker who wanted them to do something they shouldn't.

There he stood, ragged hair blowing in the wind, a light mist of rain glistening on his bare chest, challenging her with a lifted brow and a wicked grin.

How could she resist?

"All right," she said, "let's go. But only because it's raining," she added stubbornly.

He laughed like a pirate and unlocked the door just as the first stab of lightening hit the rocky shore.

"This place must have been really beautiful," Hannah whispered as they crossed the marble floor of a ballroom.

"There's talk that the old lady who owns it might restore it," Danny said, his voice echoing off the high ceiling. "Lukas and I would love a crack at it, but so far we haven't even been able to get a meeting with the dragon lady."

"The dragon lady?"

"Agnes Sheridan. The fire-breathing town matriarch. Got a face like a dragon and a personality to go with it."

"Gee, Walker, you don't think it might be because of your arrogance and your bad attitude that you haven't been able to get a meeting, do you?"

Danny tossed her a lethal grin. "I usually have no problem charming the ladies, professor. You're here, aren't you?"

"The tunnel is the draw here, Walker," she said dryly, "not your dubious charms."

Danny threw back his head and laughed. She vowed to ignore the flutter the sound of it made in her belly in favor of noticing architectural details as they crossed the lobby to the hotel restaurant. A crown molding here, a curved staircase there. Lots of old, carved wood and yellowed linen in the dining room. The kitchen was big and old-fashioned. Danny opened a door on the far side of it and flicked a light switch to reveal a set of stairs that disappeared into the gloom of the basement.

"Watch your step. They're kind of steep," he said as he started down.

Hannah followed. Once in the basement, Danny opened another door then pulled a small aluminum flashlight from his pocket and turned it on. The small circle of light swept over wooden casks and rows of dusty bottles lying on their sides in heavy oak racks.

"The hotel's wine cellar?" Hannah asked in disappointment.

"Wait," Danny said. He reached out and touched one of the racks. It swung open, revealing a twin to the door in the opera house. Only this time when Hannah reached to turn the knob, the door opened.

The small circle of light from the flashlight was lost in the gloom beyond.

"There's a lantern hanging on the wall just a ways up." He took some wooden matches from a box on a shelf by the door. "Wait here, I'll go light it."

She heard his footsteps on the floor of the tunnel, then the scratch and hiss as he struck the match. When he lit the lantern and its glow fell over the walls and floor, Hannah gasped. The plastered walls and ceiling of the tunnel were covered with paintings of vines and flowers, obviously done by the same artist who'd done the ceiling in the opera house.

"This is incredible," she said as she stepped inside. "But who on earth built this? And why?"

"The weather can get rough up in this part of Michigan, especially in the winter. The old-timers talk of years that the snow came up to their roofs. And the cold—the wind off the bay can be fierce as a gale." The flicker of the lantern played over his face as he talked about snowstorms and tornadoes and nights that were so cold that frost formed on the inside of windows. "Some say that was the reason the tunnel was built—to provide the players with a safe, warm passage to the Opera House from the hotel, where they all stayed. But others tell another story. And that's the one I believe."

"Tell me that story, too," she prodded, then bit her lip at how interested she sounded. But, why shouldn't she be interested? She was a sociologist, wasn't she? The study of society. Society equals people, she told herself. It was all academic and had nothing at all to do with the fact that Danny Walker had a deep lazy voice when he told a story.

"The hotel was owned by Carter Sheridan, who back around the turn of the century was one of the biggest lumber barons in these parts. He fell in love with a certain soprano from New York who was touring in a road company of *Carmen*. They say she had black hair that fell to her waist and the greenest eyes anyone had ever seen. Carter went to every performance and when the engagement was extended, rumor said that it was because Carter had arranged to pay everyone's salary in order to keep the show in town for two more weeks." Danny laughed softly and the lantern threw shadows across the walls of the tunnel. "Old Carter became a real patron of the arts. That troupe of players showed up in Timber Bay pretty regularly. The story goes that he had the tunnel built so when Carter's lover came to town, it'd be easier for them to meet without getting caught. He had the paintings done for her. So she would always walk in beauty."

Hannah sighed in a purely nonacademic way. "That's so romantic."

"It's also said," Danny went on, his voice so low now that she had to lean closer to him to hear, "that he once had a Persian carpet brought down here and scattered with fresh flowers so they could make love in the tunnel."

Hannah was speechless. Nearly breathless, in fact. It was the best story she'd ever heard in her life. And the way his eyes played while he told it. The way his mouth moved and his—

All of a sudden she became aware of what she was doing. She was gazing into his face, hanging on his every word, like a schoolgirl besotted with the neighborhood charmer. Which was probably the exact reaction he'd been going for. She stepped away from him and crossed her arms at her chest. "You made all that up," she said primly.

Danny shook his head and crossed his heart, which mostly only served to make her aware of the superb condition of his naked chest. "Nope," he said. "It's true. She had the man so tied up in knots that he eventually gave up everything he had and ran away with her. And that's how the legend got started."

"Oh, come on," she scoffed, "legend?"

"Legend," he insisted.

She wasn't going to give him the satisfaction of asking. But then she reminded herself that it was her duty as a representative of Granny's Grains to find out as much as she could about the town. She was only doing her job. "Okay—what legend?" she asked.

"The legend that says," he moved in closer to her and lowered his voice again, "if the tunnel brings two people together, they are destined to fall in love for all time. That's why, to this day, everyone in Timber Bay calls it the tunnel of love."

It was one of the most romantic things Hannah had ever heard. But she also knew it was pure baloney. Danny was a pied piper, all right, but she was no little mouse going for a midnight swim.

"How gullible do you think I am?" she demanded. "Just because there have been a few small glitches with the contest doesn't mean that I'm naive enough to swallow that an entire town believes in a tunnel of love!"

A sudden gust of wind buffeted the building and thunder cracked like a whip overhead.

Danny looked up at the ceiling and shook his head slowly. "Now you've done it. Haven't you ever heard that it's not wise to scoff at a legend?"

"Don't be ridiculous. That's just—"

There was a sudden draft and the flame in the lantern flickered and nearly died. In the eerie glow, something besides thunder crashed and Hannah jumped—right into Danny Walker's arms.

"What was that?" she whispered.

Now that she was up against him, the professor didn't feel all that starchy, thought Danny. The softness of a woman was under those tailored clothes. And lord help him if his artichoke-crusading sister ever found out, but Danny kind of liked the idea that the professor was trembling a little.

He only had to move his head an inch to have his nose buried in her hair. It smelled like lemons. Fresh and tart. Just like Hannah Ross herself.

She stirred a little in his arms and he could feel the heat of her skin through her shirt pressing into his bare chest. The blood started to rush through his body, making him wonder the kind of things he thought he'd never wonder about someone like her.

"Uh—shouldn't we go see what that noise was?" she asked in a throaty little whisper.

He pulled his head back so he could look into her face. "I kind of like it right where I am."

Her dark eyes widened. "What do you mean? What are you doing? Why—?"

He lifted her chin with his finger. "Anybody ever tell you that you ask too many questions?" he asked. And then he bent his head and kissed her.

She let it happen at first. Her mouth went all soft and pliant under his. She was a grown woman, but there was something sweetly innocent in the way she kissed him back.

And then, all of a sudden, it wasn't so sweet. It was like she'd come alive, her mouth taking over, the kiss becoming hers while her body wrapped itself around his just as natural as a vine on a pole.

Surprised, Danny opened his eyes. Her soft, dark lashes shadowed the pale skin of her cheeks. There was a light sprinkling of freckles on her nose. But there was fire in her mouth. It came on him strongly that he wanted to make her moan. To know what she would sound like if he touched her. He pulled her shirt out of the back of her khakis and started to slip his hand inside.

There was another crack of thunder and her eyes flew open. For a fleeting moment their gazes locked and then she tore her mouth from his and sprang away from him.

"What an original way to shut a woman up," she said testily.

"Is that what I was doing?"

"Isn't it?"

So she was going to pretend she didn't like it. Fine with him, he decided. The last thing he needed was to get tangled up with someone as uptight and upright as she was.

"Didn't exactly work, did it?"

She glared at him. "I suggest we get out of this place."

"Fine by me," he said, spreading an arm. "Ladies first."

Stiff as a board, she passed him and headed for the wine cellar. He was right behind her. When they got there, the door was shut.

"We left this door open, didn't we?" Hannah asked.

"That must have been what that noise was. The old place is full of drafts in this high wind. The door must have gotten caught in one of them."

Danny reached out to open it. It didn't budge.

"Here, hold this a minute," he said, and handed the flashlight to Hannah. He put his shoulder to the door and shoved. Nothing.

Behind him, Hannah gave an exasperated sigh. "Look, I admit I got caught up in your storytelling, but now will you stop fooling around like an eight-year-old and open that door?"

He gave a bark of laughter. "That was no eight-year-old boy kissing you, professor. And you sure didn't kiss me back like an eight-year-old girl, either."

"Oh, stop gloating and open that door."

He stepped aside. "Be my guest."

He watched while she tried the knob a couple of times and then tried pushing it the same way he had. Finally she turned around. "It won't open," she said.

"I know," he told her.

He saw it dawning in her eyes as she stared at him. "Are you telling me that we're trapped in this tunnel—together?"

"Afraid so, professor," Danny answered her with a grin. "We're trapped in the tunnel of love."

7

THIS COULDN'T BE HAPPENING, Hannah thought. She couldn't possibly be trapped in the so-called tunnel of love with Danny Walker.

"Do something," she demanded.

"What do you suggest, professor? I'm no magician."

"Oh no? You got me down here against my will, didn't you? Then tried to seduce me with all that fiction about legends and secrets and—"

"Against your will?" he cut in. "Oh, I don't think so. You were plenty willing in my arms a few minutes ago."

She had been, hadn't she? Face it, she'd been far too willing. And that was just one of the reasons she couldn't be trapped down here with him. *"Be a little bad, professor,"* he'd said out there on the terrace with the rain on his chest and the devil in his eyes. It'd be far too easy to be bad with Danny Walker. She had better keep in mind that he was a member of Granny's Grains Great American Family and that her fact gathering wasn't supposed to include how the subject kissed.

Although, already filed in the data bank in her brain was the fact that the subject kissed very, very well, indeed. Probably right off the charts statistically. But it wasn't exactly something she could put in her daily briefing to Pollard.

"Look, I think we better forget what happened earlier and concentrate on getting out of this place. So maybe you're not a magician. But you are a carpenter. Surely a carpenter can deal with a stuck door."

"This carpenter left his tool belt back at the opera house. I'm good with my hands, but not good enough to move a door that's made of iron."

Hannah decided that she wasn't going to think about how good he probably was with his hands. She crossed her arms. "Then what do you suggest?"

"Guess we have to wait to be rescued."

"Rescued? Are you serious? On the other side of that door is the wine cellar in the basement of an abandoned hotel! Who on earth is going to ever think to look for us here?"

"The professor has a point."

"And does the carpenter have a plan number two?"

He leaned against the door and shoved his hands into the pockets of his jeans. The action made them slip an inch or so lower on his hips. It didn't do anything for Hannah's peace of mind. She moved the flashlight up a few inches and tried to concentrate on his face. It wasn't hard to do at all.

"We'd probably be better off at the other end," he finally said after a few seconds of attractive brooding. "At least if we pound on the door at the opera house end, there's a chance Lukas will hear us. Come on."

Hannah peered into the tunnel. There had to be better playgrounds for her inner child than this. "It's an awfully long tunnel, isn't it?" And probably inhabited with spiders and other weird multilegged insects. Not to mention a bat or two. Or dozens. Didn't bats come in dozens?

Danny took the flashlight from her. "It's long," he said, "but the night will be even longer if we have to spend it down here."

Hannah didn't like the sound of that at all, so when Danny started walking she reasoned that it'd be worse to be left behind than to face that long dark tunnel. She took a swift look over her shoulder and then quickly caught up with him.

Even with the lantern, their movement as they started to walk cast ghostly patterns along the walls. Something small scampered across the ground in front of her and she gave a little yelp and dropped the flashlight. It went out when it hit the floor of the tunnel and she heard it roll away into the darkness.

"Steady, professor. Just mice. Probably more scared of you than you are of them."

"I assure you that I am not afraid of a mouse. I was just startled, that's all."

He laughed softly. "Okay, then let's get moving again."

Hannah peered into the gloom, trying to see if there was an army of mice waiting to crawl up her pant leg. "Um—shouldn't we try to find the flashlight?"

"Nah. It probably broke when it hit. The lantern gives off more light, anyway."

She hesitated and he glanced at her.

"Don't go on many adventures, do you professor? Just you and your notebook and that tape recorder, gathering bits and pieces of other people's lives."

He made her life sound pretty lame. "I consider running this contest an adventure," she said defensively as she started to walk again.

He laughed softly. "Well, considering the family you chose to win, it's probably more of an adventure than you bargained for. But what about when you were a kid?"

"What do you mean?"

"You must have explored an old vacant house that everyone thought was haunted or scaled the fence of the meanest man in town with your buddies to steal apples or climbed out your bedroom window on a warm summer night to meet someone in an alley."

"My childhood wasn't like that," Hannah told him as she looked furtively about for anything that scampered, climbed or flew.

He glanced at her again. "No? Well, what did you do for fun, then?"

"Fun?" Hannah echoed as she peered into dark corners for any sign of watching eyes.

He laughed softly and it struck her how often he laughed—and how much she liked the sound of it. "Yeah," he said. "Fun, professor. Surely you've heard of it."

"Well of course I had fun. Twice a week I was allowed to go

to a friend's house. She lived in a real neighborhood. But we usually stayed in the yard."

"Couple of little girls sitting on an old blanket, having a pretend tea party, huh?"

"Close. We used to play library."

Danny hooted and the sound echoed from beyond the glow of the lantern. "You wild thing! And when you and your little friend weren't playing library?"

"I took piano lessons and read and my father and I sometimes played chess."

Danny clucked and shook his head. "Professor, you might have a load of degrees on your wall but I'd say your education has been sadly lacking. Good thing you wound up in the bedroom next to mine, because I'm just the man to teach you all that you've missed."

She gave him a sideways look. "How comforting to know that the fact that we're trapped underground hasn't affected your arrogance."

He gave her a crooked grin. "It's not arrogant if it's the truth."

"So far, I'm not impressed, Walker. I think I could have continued to miss the experience of being trapped in a tunnel and somehow gone on with the rest of my life."

"The adventure isn't over yet, baby," he drawled. "You just might be happy that you came, after all."

"I see I was wrong. Your arrogance has been affected. It's even worse."

He stepped in front of her and she had to put her hand on his chest to keep from bumping into him. "It's not arrogant if it's the truth," he said again.

His chest was hard under her palm, his skin golden in the flame of the lantern. Oh, she bet he had plenty to be arrogant about. He started to lower his head to hers. Mustering the kind of willpower she usually reserved for holding a difficult pose in yoga, she pushed him away and started walking again. "Your mother is making chicken soup for dinner, and I intend to be there for it."

"Rejected for a bowl of broth," he said sadly as he came up behind her. "I think the magic of this tunnel is wasted on you. Your deprived childhood, no doubt. Last night I heard you tell Susie that you grew up on a college campus."

"Westbridge College. My father is a professor there."

"And your mother?"

"She died when I was four years old."

"Rough," Danny said. And it also explained a few things, he thought to himself. No wonder Ma in her apron looked so good to Hannah. "Are you close to your pop?"

Hannah laughed softly. "What?" Danny asked.

"*Pop.* It just sounded funny, that's all. I can't imagine addressing my father that way."

"Addressing?" To Danny, that seemed like an awfully weird choice of words. "What about talking?" he asked her. "Don't you ever just talk to him?"

She made a noise in her throat. "It's hard to explain."

"Try," he coaxed.

"My father is a very insular man. He only really comes alive when he's behind a podium. When he's not lecturing, he spends most of his time in his study, writing, poring over books, thinking. We'd sometimes go days without exchanging a word. Even when I was a young child—"

As she talked Danny got a pretty clear image of what Hannah's childhood had been like. The ivory tower of academia was no place for a kid. And nothing at all like his childhood had been. His parents and their friends had been all over him. Questions. Hugs. Cookies. Sometimes he'd hated it, but most of the time he'd soaked up the attention like a kid should. Like it was his due. Yeah, his father was a little strange and his mother was a little dizzy. His Uncle Tuffy was both strange *and* dizzy—no little about it—and his sister Sissy was headstrong and as stubborn as they came. But he wouldn't change all their noisy eccentricities for anything. Because along with them came warmth and caring and love. It was the foundation he stood on, no matter how wobbly it could sometimes be.

"Your father sounds like a real block of ice."

"Oh—no," she said quickly. "I didn't mean to imply that. I know that he loves me. It's just his way."

"Well, I guess I ought to be able to understand that. I've been saying the same thing about my father most of my life."

"Because of the wishful salvaging?" she asked.

Danny stopped walking.

She knew about Henry. The knowledge landed almost like a punch to his gut. He didn't know why it hit him like that. Everyone in town knew about Pop. What was one more? But Hannah was an outsider. An outsider sent here to pry and to judge.

"If you're planning on using that information I'd think twice about it," he said as he started walking again.

"You can't think that I would do that."

"Why not? Everything we do goes into that notebook of yours, doesn't it? Like we're a bunch of crated rabbits you're observing in a laboratory?"

"That's ridiculous. The company intends this whole thing to be positive—and that's exactly why I'd never use it. It's not exactly a Great American Family trait, is it?"

He snorted. "Right. Silly me. Perfection is the name of the game here, isn't it? And old Henry is far less then perfect, isn't he?"

"Danny, that's not fair. I've just told you that I've got an eccentric father, too. I'm not naive. I know that nobody's perfect. But your father isn't exactly the image Granny's Grains is going for."

"You picked him."

"I was misled."

"I wouldn't brag about that, professor. It only proves my theory of how easily these things can be manipulated. For all you know, Jane Doe in Topeka feels like having a little fun when she fills out a survey. She's never actually played golf. But she checks a box, just for the hell of it, and already the statistics on female golfers in Topeka are skewed."

She sighed. "Interesting example, Walker. But that's why studies allow for a margin of error."

"If I allow for a margin of error your back door doesn't close right."

"Look, I'm really not in the mood for debate. How much farther is it to the other end?"

"Typical. When losing an argument, change the subject."

"Getting out of this tunnel *is* the subject, Walker. The *only* subject. Now where is that damn door?" she asked as she grabbed the lantern out of his hand and held it up high as she started to walk faster.

"Why professor," Danny said behind her, "how you talk. I don't think the folks at Granny's Grains would like the fact that the professor curses."

They'd like it even less if they found out she'd been trapped with a half-naked man in Timber Bay's so-called tunnel of love, thought Hannah. And they'd probably really hate it if she murdered him just to shut him up. Which was just what she was considering when the lantern's light swept over an old rusted iron door.

Hannah thrust the lantern back at Danny, strode up to the door and started to pound. Seconds later she pulled back and shook out her stinging hands. "Damn, that door is hard."

"Shhh," Danny said and put his ear to the door.

"Hear anything?" Hannah asked.

He shook his head, then started to pound on the door with his fists. It was hard not to notice the way his muscles bunched and worked. After all, he wasn't wearing a shirt. How could she not notice? She was trained to observe humanity.

Suddenly, Danny let out a bellow. "Luuukaaaas!" he yelled in a way that made Hannah think of loincloths.

This was ridiculous. To get her mind off beefcake, she started to pound and yell, too. A few minutes later, they both gave up and leaned against the door.

"What now?" she said in a voice that sounded a little hoarse.

He looked at her. "We wait. We'll know if he heard in the next fifteen minutes or so."

He dropped to the floor next to the lantern. "Pop a squat," he said. "Might as well be comfortable."

"Um—" Hannah peered at the floor. It was some sort of stone—plenty of crevices for creepy little things. "I think I'll stand."

He shrugged. "Suit yourself."

She hadn't really realized how warm it was down there until she was standing still, waiting. Warm and damp. Her shirt was starting to stick to her back and she could feel a tiny bead of sweat trickling down her forehead. She wondered if it was still raining outside. She hadn't heard any thunder for awhile. In fact, it was almost too quiet. Like the world out there had disappeared—which meant there would be no one left to rescue them.

"Things like this just don't happen," she burst out in a panic. "There's got to be some other way out of here."

Danny got to his feet. "I hate to break it to you, professor, but this is a pretty good example of what real, normal life is like. Surprises pop up all the time."

"Well, this is one surprise I can do without," she retorted.

He tweaked her nose. "Oh, sweetheart, it's never a good idea to turn your nose up at life's surprises."

She batted his hand away. "Just find another way for us to get out of here."

"Anyone ever tell you that you're rough on a guy's ego?"

"Let me clue you in—burying me alive is not a way to get me to help stoke up your already giant ego."

"How about if I get you out of here in time for that chicken soup?"

"Then you're my hero. In the meantime," she said, getting her notebook out of her shoulder bag, "we might as well get some work done."

Danny groaned. "I'm starting to hate that notebook."

"I need to know a few things about your father. Positive things."

"Like what?"

"You're a good storyteller. Tell me a story about something you did together when you were a kid."

"Something that'll make him worthy of being Granny's Grains Great American Dad?"

"You needn't be so cynical. Help me make him look good."

"Fair enough. If you want to see Pop at his best, then you need to see him at work. He can scrap an old lawn mower or boat motor down to nothing and find uses for most of the parts. Keeps everything neat as a pin, labeled and shelved. He knows his stock like the back of his hand. You've got a vacuum cleaner from 1955, Pop probably has the part you need to fix it. And hell, if you can't fix it, he'll do it for you. 'Course, some day, if you leave it out on the porch for anything, he might just resalvage it, too."

Hannah laughed. "Is he good at fixing things?"

"He's a tinkerer. Loves to tinker with old appliances people throw out. Toasters, mixers, that kind of stuff. If he can get it going again, he donates it to the Church of the Holy Flock for their annual rummage sale."

This was more like it, thought Hannah as she scribbled.

"I used to love hanging out down there when I was a kid. Climbing all over the piles in the yard behind the shop, looking for hidden treasure. Pop used to make us grilled cheese sandwiches on an old hot plate and then he'd leave me alone to figure out how to take an engine apart and put it back together again. We made this really crazy go-cart together once—"

It's a good thing Hannah had turned on her tape recorder because she'd totally forgotten about the notebook in her hand. She was too caught up in listening to Danny, in watching him as he talked about the man he clearly loved despite his faults.

"—we had this old manhole cover that—"

He broke off and she waited for him to continue. Instead he grabbed the lantern. "That gives me an idea. Wait here."

He took off running back the way they came. Hannah

wanted to run after him but he quickly disappeared into the darkness. It was so quiet, she could hear her tape recorder whirring. She reached into her purse and shut it off. She started to lean against the wall, then remembered the possibility of ugly little creatures. Just as she thought she felt something run over her foot, the glow of the lantern reappeared and a grinning Danny with it.

"There's a manhole cover a ways back. The way I figure it, it should lead up to Sheridan Road, just around the corner from the Opera House. Come on, professor. Let's see if we can get it open."

Hannah gladly followed.

He pointed out the manhole when they reached it, then put the lantern down and grabbed her around the waist.

"Hey! What are you doing?"

"I'm hoisting you up so you can see if the cover is loose. Unless you wanted to try hoisting me up."

She eyed his bare chest and the smooth muscles of his arms. There was no way she was hoisting him anywhere.

"Okay," she said. "Hoist away."

He lifted her as though she weighed nothing.

"Can you reach it?"

"A little higher—"

"That better?"

"Ugh! There are spiderwebs up here!"

"Be brave," Danny cracked.

She closed her eyes and willed herself to think of fresh air, then she thrust her hands up through the spiderwebs.

"That's it!" she called down to him as her fingers hit the manhole cover. "Hey—I think it's loose!" she yelled, excitement surging through her. She could feel the cover give ever so slightly. "I need a couple of more inches, Danny."

Danny laughed. "I never had a woman complain before, professor."

She looked down at him. "Think you could get your mind off your physical attributes long enough to find a way to get me closer so I can give it a harder push?"

"How's this?"

Hands still at her waist, he lifted her up and swung her back behind his head and sat her with an unceremonious plop on his shoulders. Afraid of falling, she grabbed hold of the first thing she could find.

"Ouch! Um—professor, do you think you could let go of my hair?"

"Oh—sorry," she said. She let go of his hair but immediately lost her balance again. Her arms flailed out and she grabbed the next closest thing—his head.

"Watch it, professor. You're about to gouge out my eye."

"Oh—sorry." She forced herself to move her hands from around his face and put them on top of his head for a moment to steady herself. Then she reached for the manhole cover again. This time she was able to push it up enough to clear the opening and shove it several inches over. A bright shaft of light streamed down on her.

"Got it!" she yelled in triumph. "And look! The storm's over! The sun's out!"

Without warning, Danny put his hands on her waist again and swung her back over his head and into his arms.

"Way to go, Hannah!" he said, grinning at her. "We might make an adventurer of you yet."

He put her down and she tried to ignore the feel of her body sliding against his. A couple of jumps and he was able to grab hold of the edge of the opening and pull himself up. The manhole cover screeched as he pushed it aside the rest of the way.

"Come on, Hannah," he said, holding his arm down to her while he perched on the rim. Lord, he looked good up there. The sunshine on his shaggy hair, his blue eyes flashing like sparklers out of his dirt-streaked face, grinning like he'd just conquered the world. "Take your hero's hand, baby, and I'll make you fly."

Laughing, she put her hand in his.

"Hold tight," he said as he engulfed her hand with his hard, rough one. Then he hoisted her up, grabbed her waist with his other hand, and settled her beside him on the edge of the manhole.

The clean rain-washed air felt wonderful on her face. "We're free!" she cried.

"Time for the hero to collect his reward," Danny said.

He pulled her up against him and covered her mouth with his own. She was so startled at first that she didn't protest—and after a moment, she didn't want to protest. Maybe she was going to like Danny's idea of an adventure, after all. His hot mouth, the warm sun, the clean breeze off the bay. It just seemed right somehow.

He pulled his mouth away and she opened her eyes. His bright blue gaze held hers for a long moment before she noticed something. "Look what came out to welcome us," she said as she pointed at the sky. Out over the bay was the most beautiful rainbow Hannah had ever seen. "It's like the heavens are putting on a show for us," she cried.

"You two are putting on an even better show!" came a shout from behind them.

Hannah turned her head so fast she thought she'd get whiplash. "Oh, no," she muttered.

More than the rainbow had come out to welcome them. People were lined along the sidewalk on Sheridan Road like they were expecting a parade. What looked like half the town had witnessed their escape from the tunnel.

And their kiss.

8

HANNAH DECIDED to take refuge in Sweet Buns. She ducked under the green-and-white striped awning, slipped in the door, then shut it quickly behind her like she was the village monster and there was a mob at her heels. Which, of course, when she peered over the green-and-white checked café curtain covering half of the door, there wasn't. Most of the people had already dispersed. She had no idea where Danny had gone.

"Can I help you?"

Hannah whirled around. It crossed her mind to ask the young woman behind the counter if she could please help Hannah get her dignity back. She decided to ask for cookies instead.

"Uh—yes. I need some—uh—cookies."

The blond woman grinned. "I know the feeling. I always eat sweets when I'm stressed out, too."

Hannah came away from the door. "It's that obvious?"

"Well, yes. But I have to confess that I was out there along with everyone else admiring that spectacular rainbow when you and Danny crawled out of the manhole."

Hannah grimaced. "Is there anybody who didn't see?"

"A few. But they'll all have heard about the manhole incident by dinnertime. Have a seat. I'll get you a cup of coffee—on the house."

The little shop was a friendly refuge, with its light oak floor and little oak tables scattered here and there. A comfortable-looking love seat was tucked into the bay window. A coffee table in front of it held an assortment of magazines and news-papers. At the back was a counter with stools and a display case filled with baked goods.

It was exactly the kind of place where she and Lissa liked to spend Sunday afternoons.

The woman behind the counter put a thick, white ceramic mug in front of her and filled it from the coffeepot in her hand. The warm scent of fresh-brewed coffee steamed up from the mug. Hannah immediately felt calmer.

"This is great coffee," she said after taking her first sip.

"Thanks. How about a sweet bun with that, Hannah?"

Hannah looked up sharply. "You know my name."

The young woman laughed. "Relax, I'm not psychic. My brother works with Danny. I'm Molly Jones." She put out her hand and Hannah shook it.

"You're Lukas's sister?"

"Right. Now I'm going to get you one of my famous good-for-whatever-ails-you sweet buns. You look like you could use one."

Hannah watched Molly put the coffeepot back on the burner behind the counter and move over to the display case. She was large-boned and soft-looking. She'd probably been considered chubby when she was younger. Now she was what Hannah would call voluptuous. Earthy in a natural, cheerful way. She wore her pale blond hair short and looked right at home in the green cobbler's apron she wore over jeans and a white T-shirt. She used tongs to place a huge bun slathered with frosting on a plate that matched the mug, and set it down in front of Hannah. It smelled of cinnamon and comfort. Hannah hadn't known she was hungry but she eagerly picked it up to taste it.

"This is delicious," she said, talking with her mouth full. "But I'll still need those cookies. Kate asked me to bring some home for dessert."

Home. Is that how she thought of the Walker's house, despite the fact that they kept falling short of her ideal? What she'd told Danny was true. It was how a family handled its problems that showed their strength as a unit. But somehow, she didn't see either Henry's wishful salvaging or Sissy's revolving-door marriage as making good cereal-box copy. Which reminded her—

"Molly, if this isn't a bad time, I'd like to talk to you about the Walkers."

"Excellent time, actually. Not a lot of customers this time of day and my brother took my little girl to the park."

"I'd like to talk to him, too."

"They'll be back soon." Molly topped off Hannah's cup then poured herself one before she came over and leaned on the counter. "What's on your mind?"

"I just wanted to find out how you feel about the family. Did you spend much time there growing up?"

"I tagged along when Lukas would let me. It was a fun house to be around. Kate and Henry are a little—um—odd, but they used to cater to us kids. We used to sit on the front porch in our wet suits after swimming and eat Kate's sugar cookies by the dozens. Kate was the only mom in town that didn't make us take off our snow boots in the winter before we could go in the house. She'd serve us hot chocolate while the snow would melt in puddles on the floor."

"So there was a sense of freedom?"

"Oh, yeah. They made you feel special. And they knew how to appreciate a kid's imagination."

"What do you mean?"

"Have you been over to Henry's junkyard yet?" Molly asked.

"Well—no," Hannah admitted. She was still dealing with the fact that Henry wasn't exactly a steel magnate.

"We used to go over there on Saturday mornings when I was a kid. In the winter, we'd stay in the shop and explore the inventory like we were looking for buried treasure. We usually found it, too. Henry would always let us take some little thing home with us."

Yeah, thought Hannah, since he'd probably stolen it in the first place.

"In the summer, we'd turn the piles of junk in the yard behind the shop into just about anything we could think of. An old Chevy would become an ambulance and we'd rescue people from an earthquake. Once we found a couple of old cameras so we scoured the place like we were news people, reporting on some disaster. I don't think I was ever bored when I was a kid. And that was partly due to the Walkers."

The bell over the door jangled and Molly's face lit up. "There's my little pumpkin!"

Hannah looked over her shoulder. A giant of a man had just come in. He was carrying a small child against his shoulder, his massive hands gently stroking the little girl's back. Molly came out from behind the counter and held out her arms.

"Come to Mama, pumpkin. Did you have fun with Uncle Lukas?"

"She sure did, didn't you sweetie?" Lukas said as he handed the toddler over.

So this was Danny's partner, thought Hannah. He had the body of a college football player and the face of an angel with dark blond curls falling over his wide forehead and a deep dimple in each cheek.

"This is Chloe," Molly said as she brought her over. "Chloe, say hi to Hannah."

"Hi!" the baby said—or close enough to it.

Chloe was chubby and blond and all smiles. "How old is she?"

"Almost a year."

"She's adorable."

"She's my precious pretty," Molly cooed. "I'm gonna go

upstairs and put her down for her nap. Lukas, keep Hannah company and watch the shop."

"Hey, I haven't got all day!" Lukas called as Molly disappeared into the back of the shop.

"Oh, have a bun and chill," Molly called back. "Hannah wants to talk to you about the Walkers, anyway."

Lukas grinned and shook his head. "That woman takes advantage of me all the time. Like I've got nothin' better to do than hang around here and pour overpriced coffee."

While he talked, he ambled behind the counter and poured himself a cup, then took a sweet bun from the display case. It looked small in his huge fist. One bite finished off half of it.

"So you're Danny's cereal chick," he said while he chewed.

Hannah nearly choked on her own bite of bun. "Excuse me? I'm not Danny's anything."

Lukas grinned and his dimples got deeper. "Danny tells me you're a big believer in statistics and numbers. Hate to break it to you, Hannah, but odds are in favor of you being Danny's."

"What do you mean? What odds?"

Lukas shrugged and stuck the rest of his bun in his mouth. "When the tunnel brings two people together they are destined—"

"Stop right there. The tunnel did *not* bring us together. We got trapped down there, that's all. The tunnel had nothing to do with it."

"And the kiss?" Lukas asked as he licked frosting off his fingers.

Hannah groaned. "Don't tell me you were out there, too?"

Lukas shook his head. "Didn't actually see it for myself. But I heard that it was pretty sweet."

Sweet was not the word Hannah would have used. She felt a blush rising up her neck and into her face at the memory of Danny's mouth on hers. She was appalled when her body started to react. Well, she just wasn't going to let it. She sat up straighter on her stool.

"That whole legend thing is ridiculous," she stated. "And I'm surprised that in the twenty-first century anyone would give it any credence. We were trapped down there, for heaven's sakes! All we could think about was finding a way to get out of there before we—before we suffocated!" Okay, she was laying it on pretty thick. They hadn't actually been afraid of suffocating, but still, the idea that it was all fun and games—well, okay, maybe some of it had been fun. Toward the end, she'd been feeling a little like she was on an adventure. And bursting through that manhole and feeling the sun on her face and seeing the rainbow—and the kiss. Yes, the kiss had certainly been fun—

The bell over the door jangled again and Tuffy Walker came bustling in, baggy clothes flapping around him as he walked.

"They told me you'd be in here, Hannah."

Hannah started to ask who *they* were but what was the point? Everyone in town seemed to know just about every move she made.

"Henry told me to tell you that he can probably get you a ring for next to nothin'!"

"A ring?" Hannah asked.

"Yeah. I just told them all down at the tavern that you and Danny will be engaged soon!" Tuffy's gnomelike face creased into a huge, gap-toothed grin. "Welcome to the family, Hannah!"

HANNAH PARKED the Granny's Grains station wagon in front of the Walker house, cut the engine and banged her forehead against the steering wheel a few times while she berated herself. What had she been thinking? *Bang.* Was she out of her mind to consider for one minute that anything that happened after she'd been dragged into that tunnel was fun? *Bang.* She wasn't in Timber Bay to have fun! *Bang*. And she sure wasn't here to fool around with the local beefcake. Her forehead was starting to hurt and self-flagellation wasn't really her style so she leaned her head back on the headrest and stared up at the roof of the car.

Her behavior with Danny that afternoon had *unprofessional* stamped all over it. How could she have let him taunt her into what was quite possibly illegal behavior? How could she have let him hold her hand while he told his stories in a voice that did more for her than her last boyfriend had managed to do for her throughout the entire relationship? How could she have let him kiss her? More than once?

And now half the town had them practically engaged! All because of some crazy legend.

She lowered her head, looked at the Walker house and sighed. "Never judge a family by its front porch," she murmured.

She finally got out of the car, grabbed her bag of cookies, and headed up the front walk and into the house. As usual, she found Kate in the kitchen.

"Here are your cookies, Kate," she said wearily, setting the bag from Sweet Buns on the table.

"Why thank you, dear," said Kate. "You seem upset. Is something wrong?"

She hadn't intended to say anything. But she wasn't used to coming home to anyone asking her if something was wrong. It caught her off balance. "Yes, Kate," she admitted. "Something's wrong. In fact, just about *everything* is wrong!"

Kate smiled sweetly and patted her arm. "Well, supper is almost ready. I'm sure you'll feel better after you've had a bowl of soup."

"Good as that soup smells, Kate, I'm afraid a bowl of it isn't going to help solve this problem."

"Well, what is it, dear?"

Suddenly, she felt uncomfortable. Kate was, after all,

Danny's mother. Hannah couldn't exactly tell her how appalled she was at the prospect of people thinking she was involved with her son. Still, she needed an ally. "Kate, I'm not sure how to say this, but there seems to be a rumor floating around town. I don't know who started it—or how it got started, but—"

"Well, I know how it got started," Kate interrupted cheerfully. "It started because you and Danny were in the tunnel together and—"

Hannah groaned. "Don't tell me you just happened to be downtown, too, when that damned rainbow came out!"

"Well, no, dear. I was right here all afternoon making my soup. But Linda from the bookshop called about a book I'd ordered and—"

Hannah threw up her hands in exasperation. "Does the whole town know about this?"

"Well—" Kate began, but just then the back door burst open and Sissy and Chuck, arms around each other and beaming, came in. Hannah was dumbfounded, but Kate just took it in stride. "Oh, I'm so glad you made up before supper, Chuck. I know how you love my soup," she said.

Okay, thought Hannah as she slumped into a kitchen chair. One problem solved. But how on earth was she going to get through this dinner without dying of embarrassment? Briefly, she thought about holing up in the station wagon and eating cereal for supper. But maybe she didn't have to do anything that drastic. After all, Sissy and Chuck were so wrapped up in each other that they probably hadn't heard about the kiss. There was no telling what Kate might come out with, but Hannah hoped that now that she knew that Hannah was upset about the whole thing that she wouldn't bring it up during dinner. Henry would probably be behind his paper again. Hopefully, Uncle Tuffy would be in the living room with his cartoons. And that left Danny. Who never seemed to miss an opportunity to embarrass, taunt and drive her generally insane. She wondered what Pollard would say if she threw a bowl of hot soup into the face of the son of the Great American Family? Whatever he'd say, she was sure it would be a deal-breaker as far as successful completion of this project was concerned. She'd have to find a less felonious way of dealing with Danny.

She was still trying to come up with one as she eyed Danny suspiciously through the steam rising from her bowl of soup during supper. He was being a little too pleasant for her peace of mind. A little too—well, *normal.* He was chatting with his niece and nephew about their swimming lessons and discussing baseball scores with Chuck—when Chuck wasn't busy playing kissy-face with Sissy, that is. Was it possible that Danny hadn't heard about Uncle Tuffy welcoming her to the family?

She had just taken a bite of dumpling when Danny said, "Hannah—"

She braced herself. Here it comes, she thought.

"—you live in Chicago, right?"

Was this some sort of trick question? Hannah scanned her mind for pitfalls but came up empty. "Yes," she answered warily.

"Are you a Cubs fan?" he asked pleasantly.

"I'm afraid I don't follow sports," she said.

He just smiled at her, said, "I see," then turned back to Chuck and a lively discussion of someone who pitched for the Cubs in the '80s.

Hannah narrowed her eyes. What was going on? Why was Danny being so nice? She thought sure he'd take advantage of every opportunity to tease her about the legend. Or to make sure that the whole family knew there'd been more than one kiss. But there he sat, acting—well, acting normal. It didn't bring her any peace of mind, though. Danny acting normal was somehow more sinister than Danny acting like the devil.

Or maybe Hannah was just being paranoid. After all, Hannah thought as she ate, Sissy and Chuck were practically necking over their soup bowls so that problem was solved. And Andy and Susie were being total angels. She'd be able to present Mr. Pollard with a complete, multigeneration family that was perfectly intact. So maybe her luck was changing and Danny had decided to look elsewhere for his entertainment. And if he was willing to act like nothing had happened between them, then the whole legend thing would die down before the rest of the Great American Family crew arrived in a few weeks.

She felt herself relax a little. Everything was going to be just fine. And tomorrow was Wednesday. Kate's card club. She was really looking forward to meeting Kate's friends and listening in on their conversations. She was pretty sure women playing bridge in the afternoon was nearly a lost art. Witnessing the scene would be practically anthropological.

Suddenly, Hannah felt good enough to ask for seconds.

LATER THAT EVENING, Hannah sat at the desk in her room, composing the daily e-mail report for Pollard. It was a struggle. She'd decided that all communications with anyone at Granny's Grains would first have to be forced through a filter to rid them of everything that didn't fit with *the image.* Thus, the opera house made it in, but the tunnel of love didn't. Molly's coffee shop was in. Tuffy's engagement announcement was out. The rainbow made it. The kisses, most decidedly, did not.

Because the day had been riddled with unmentionables, Hannah heavily hyped Kate's bridge club tomorrow, an activity that should really have been saved for Wednesday night's report. Just a little borrowing that she was hoping to pay back with interest when she reported on her lunch with the mayor tomorrow. Ed Miller sounded like a perfectly pleasant, perfectly normal man when she'd set up the date on the phone so her hopes were high on that score.

She closed with a short list of possible photo ops and hit send. Then it was time to make sure the coast was clear to head to the bathroom. One of the downsides of charming old houses was that they generally only had one full bathroom. Hannah had decided to start showering at night in order to keep out of the family's way. But first she had to make sure she wasn't going to run into Danny. She tiptoed over to the wall that separated her bedroom from his and put her ear to it. Silence. Carefully, she eased the bedroom door open a few inches. The hall was empty. She listened. There was only the sound of Henry's faint snoring behind his and Kate's bedroom door. Kate, she knew, was downstairs sniffling her way through an old Bette Davis movie. Danny was probably out, doing whatever bad boys did on chilly summer nights. She grabbed her pajamas and toiletry bag and made a dash for the bathroom at the end of the hall.

The water was deliciously hot and soothing but, mindful that this was the only bathroom upstairs and that she still wanted to avoid Danny, Hannah didn't linger. She dried herself with one of Kate's fluffy green towels, quickly slathered on some lotion, then pulled on her pajamas.

She wiped the steam from the bathroom mirror and towel dried her hair, then brushed her teeth. She rinsed her brush and started to open the door to leave the bathroom when she noticed a bottle of men's cologne on the shelf next to the sink. Was it Danny's?

Well, she thought with a sniff, what difference did it make if it was?

She'd never smelled cologne on him, though. Most of the time he smelled like sawdust and fresh air. But she supposed that when he got dressed up to go out on a date, he probably wore cologne. With a curiosity she knew she should resist, Hannah went back to the sink and picked up the bottle. It was only half full. And why not? Danny Walker probably had women all over the place. And he probably stood in this very spot, shaving and finger combing his sexy hair then splashing on cologne. They'd smell it on his neck when he held them close to dance. Or on his cheek when they cuddled with him at the movies. Or on their pillows the morning after—

Okay, now she *had* to smell it.

She opened it and raised it to her nose.

"Like it?" said a voice behind her.

Her eyes shot up to the mirror over the sink. Danny Walker was standing behind her, a big, knowing grin on his face.

She put the cap on the cologne and stuck it back on the shelf. "Oh, is it yours?" she asked indifferently. "I thought maybe it was Kate's."

"Ma doesn't usually wear men's cologne."

Hannah looked at the bottle. There it was right on the label—and not even in very small print—*cologne for men*. Busted. Again.

"I could wear some to bed tonight if you're planning on a visit."

Her head shot up and their eyes met in the mirror. "Don't be absurd," she said stiffly.

"I can guarantee you that there won't be anything absurd about it," he said as he put his hand on her upper arm in a soft caress that sent a shiver down her spine.

She shrugged his hand back off. "Would you mind taking your colossal ego and getting out of here? What will people think if they find us in here together?"

"Oh, I think they'll understand—" his grin widened "—seeing as how we're practically engaged."

Hannah gasped and turned around, which was probably a mistake given how close she now was to him. Close enough that if he'd been wearing any of that cologne, she would have had no problem getting a whiff. "You talked to Uncle Tuffy, didn't you?"

"He's been a busy little guy," Danny said, enjoying the view from up close. He liked the way her brown eyes flashed darkly when she got all geared up for a fight. She was wearing the same pajamas Danny had seen her in the night before. He'd had women put on all sorts of things for him that they thought were sexy—from lace to leather to nothing at all. But somehow the sight of Hannah in those men's pajamas got to him.

When he'd first seen her sniffing his cologne through the partially open bathroom door, he'd intended to tease her a little. After all, he'd been a very good boy all the way through dinner. She couldn't have handed him a better opening than being caught with her nose to the bottle of his cologne. Hard to ignore such a gift. But, now that he was close to her, now that he could smell her clean fresh skin and the lemon scent coming from her wet hair, he thought the time might be better spent.

Hannah had other plans.

"If you do anything," she said in an angry whisper, " to perpetuate this—this ridiculous story, I'll—I'll—"

He lifted his hand to her hair and pushed his fingers into the damp, tangled strands. "You'll what?" he asked, fixing his gaze on her mouth.

"I'll—I'll make sure that you won't see box one of that year's supply of Super Korny Krunchies!"

He laughed softly while he brushed his thumb over her bottom lip. "You'd be doing us a favor."

She flicked her head away from his thumb. "I mean it, Danny. This foolishness about the legend and the tunnel has got to stop. Right now. You'd better make it clear to everyone that there is absolutely nothing going on between us."

"Isn't there?" Danny surprised himself by asking. Because right now it definitely felt to him like there was something between them. Just like in the tunnel, he wanted to drag her body up against his. He wanted to feel her mouth under his.

Feel her respond to him—feel that hot, swift change she went through when he had her in his arms.

"Of course there isn't! How could there be? I mean—you're part of The Great American Family. What would it do to the image if anyone found out that—"

Danny threw up his hands in mock horror. "What was I thinking? We can't forget about the image."

"Make fun of it all you want, Danny, but this is my job and I can't have anyone think there is anything going on. You got that?"

"Got it," he said dutifully.

"Thank you," she said brusquely before brushing past him and leaving the bathroom.

He poked his head out the door. "A word of advice, professor," he called after her. "It might help the cause if you didn't stand around sniffing my cologne."

He laughed softly when she slammed her bedroom door. But lying in bed an hour later, he was no longer laughing. He kept thinking about how a droplet of water from her hair had pooled in the hollow of her neck. He kept thinking about how she smelled. How those damn pajama sleeves hung over her hands.

Finally, he threw back the sheet covering him, got out of bed, went over to the window and opened it. The night was cool, as June nights in the UP often were, but the sky above had cleared. No clouds in sight, just a blue-black sky thickly frosted with stars.

He wondered if, in the room next to his, Hannah had her window open. Wondered if she was looking up at the same stars as he was.

And then he wondered what he was doing, standing there naked, thinking about the last woman on earth that he should want.

9

HANNAH THREW OPEN her bedroom window and let the warmth of the morning inside. Birds were singing, the sun was out. It was a lovely day for a bridge party. Unfortunately, Hannah's mood wasn't nearly as lovely.

She hadn't slept well at all the night before. She kept hearing Danny's laugh when he told her to keep her nose out of his cologne. She seemed to have lost some brain cells since arriving in Timber Bay. Because she knew for a fact that she'd never, ever gone around sappily sniffing a man's cologne bottle. Any man.

Was there something to the legend of the tunnel of love, after all? Could her strange behavior be due to some sort of spell?

"Nonsense," she scoffed as she turned away from the window. She didn't have time for legends and spells. Hannah dealt in reality. At least, she did before she came to Timber Bay, she reminded herself uncomfortably.

There was a phone next to her bed. Maybe she should call Lissa. She could use someone to talk to. Someone to offer support. Someone who would keep reminding her how unprofessional it was to fantasize about the son of Granny's Grains Great American Family.

She started to reach for the phone, then snatched her hand back. What was she thinking? Lissa would probably tell her to go for it. No, Lissa was definitely not the person to give her a dose of reality. Better to put her hopes on the Honorable Ed Miller.

Hannah had a late-morning appointment with the mayor and she wanted to shoot some preliminary photos of downtown and the town square before she met with him in his office at City Hall. If that didn't make her act like a professional, nothing would.

She threw open the closet door and looked at her meager selection of clothes. She wished she had something more feminine to wear. She pictured Kate's friends in flowered dresses and hats although she really had nothing to base this on except old movies. What did the modern woman wear to a bridge club afternoon? She shrugged. Didn't matter, really. She had a choice of khakis, her black pantsuit, or jeans. She'd never been frivolous about clothes. There was no frothy, flowered dress hanging amid the button-downs and T-shirts. Oh well, she thought as she grabbed the pantsuit. It was a good choice for her meeting with the mayor. It would just have to do for the bridge club, too.

After she was dressed, she repeated her surveillance routine of the night before before going out into the hall. Avoiding Danny was even more crucial this morning. She managed to get downstairs without running into him.

She found Kate arranging flowers at the dining room table. Hannah was relieved to see that they were perfectly normal daisies. She told Kate that she wouldn't be home for lunch, but that she'd be back by two in time for the card club, then headed out on foot. Downtown Timber Bay was only a few blocks from the Walkers' house and City Hall was right on the square. Hannah figured she wouldn't need the company wagon at all that day. It would be a relief to not have children cheer and adults jeer at the flying ear of corn painted on the side.

Family sounds spilled from the open windows of the houses as she passed. Bikes leaned against porches and curtains blew through open windows. So different from the sober campus where she'd spent her childhood. The regulation venetian blinds on the windows of the austere row houses tended to stay closed and the people behind them tended to keep their noses buried in books instead of in each other's business. Since moving to Chicago, Hannah lived in a big, bright studio apartment. Cheerful compared to Westbridge College, but still nothing like the Walkers' neighborhood.

She spent about an hour using a digital camera to snap pictures that she later planned to e-mail to Granny's marketing department. Then she headed back to the town square and City Hall.

The mayor's office was at the back of the first floor of the Federalist style building made of the same redbrick as the courthouse. He had a view of the bay from his office window. Boats sailing in the distance blended with the nautical decor in the office.

The mayor was a big man with a sailor's tan and only a slight paunch showing beneath his polo shirt to mar his athletic body. They shook hands then chatted about the town and what his vision was for the future. How it was built on solid families and was a great place to raise kids.

"Speaking of families, you couldn't have chosen a better one for your contest. The Walkers are the salt of the earth. Salt of the earth," Ed Miller said.

"Then they are generally well-thought-of in town?" Hannah asked cautiously.

"Hell, yes! Danny Walker is a local hero in my book!"

Hannah nearly choked. "Danny?" she managed to croak.

"He stepped right up to the plate when the town council rejected the idea of funding the opera house's rehabilitation. I don't mind telling you that it was a disappointment to me. One of our hopes of surviving as a town is to attract tourists. The opera house, I felt, would have been a gleaming jewel in our crown. But now, thanks to Danny Walker, that hope is alive again. He's a fine young man—"

With some astonishment, Hannah listened to the mayor of

Timber Bay sing Danny's praises. She jotted down catch-words in her notebook. *Industrious. Talented. Generous. Kind.*

Could this be the same Danny Walker who had delighted in goading her, teasing her, and tormenting her since she hit town?

"—his partner, Lukas McCoy, is quite talented, too," the mayor was saying. "As a team, they could restore the Acropolis. Make it look good as new."

Restoration, Hannah scribbled in her book. She looked at the word and it reminded her of something Danny had told her. "Mayor, someone told me that the Sheridan Hotel might be restored, as well. Is there any truth to that?"

The mayor chuckled. "I've heard the rumors, too, but I'd be the last to know if they're true. Agnes Sheridan hasn't spoken to me since I refused to be coerced into helping get the properties adjoining her estate condemned. She's been trying to get her hands on those houses for a couple of decades now. Some fool notion about tearing them down and adding the land to the Sheridan estate. As if she needed any more space, living up there alone as she does."

Hannah scribbled in her notebook: Ethical mayor.

"Is that a job that Timber Bay Building and Restoration could handle? In your opinion, I mean?"

"Absolutely. I have nothing but faith in those boys—"

Hannah was foolishly pleased. The mayor segued into a discussion of fishing and boats and ended with a standing invitation to go sailing with him and his wife.

By the time Mayor Miller had to leave for a lunch appointment, Hannah's stomach was starting to growl. In an effort to avoid Danny, she'd skipped breakfast and now she was starving. Sweet Buns was only a few blocks away so Hannah started walking.

Ten minutes later, the bell over the door rang as she opened it and went inside. There were people sitting at the counter, so Hannah chose a table at the front. She was a little worried that the town might still be speculating about the manhole in-cident. This way, if they talked about her, at least she wouldn't be able to hear it.

Molly came out of the kitchen and spotted her right away. She gave a little wave as she served a customer. She refilled coffee cups, then came over to Hannah's table.

"Hey, Hannah. Nice to see you again. Are you here for lunch?" she asked.

"Yes. And I'm starving," Hannah told her.

"I'm featuring a great chicken salad sandwich with al-monds served with homemade apricot chutney on fresh-baked whole-grain bread."

"Sounds wonderful."

"Iced coffee with that? Today's special is hazelnut."

"Sold again."

"Okay. Coming right up."

Molly stopped at the only other table occupied to see if they wanted anything else, then filled an order at the counter be-fore she went back to the kitchen. Hannah felt a little self-conscious sitting there by herself so she pulled her notebook out and went over her notes from the meeting with the mayor.

Ed Miller was definitely going on the list of people she was going to recommend that Pollard meet. In fact, it might be a good idea to have Pollard meet Mayor Miller first, before he met the Walkers. Once the mayor had sung their praises, it would be a lot easier to make Pollard think that the Walkers were the perfect image to sell his cereal. What problems she couldn't fix or conceal would be tempered by the Honorable Ed Miller's praise.

The bell over the door jangled and Hannah looked up from her notes in time to see Danny Walker shut the door behind him. She held her breath as he walked back to the counter and slid onto a stool. Miracle of miracles, he hadn't seen her.

Should she try to sneak out now, before he did? That would

mean sticking Molly with an unpaid order. She liked Molly too much to do that to her. Maybe if she hid behind her notebook. She opened it and raised it to her face. This might work. After all, if Henry could eat behind the evening paper, Hannah should be able to handle it.

"I'd recognize that notebook anywhere."

Hannah lowered it to find Danny pulling out a chair. "Don't bother sitting down if you're not going to behave yourself."

He paused and cocked his gorgeous head. "Define *behave*."

"Behave in this instance means not making any moves or uttering any words that will make anyone think there is any truth at all to this particular installment of the legend."

He pretended he was thinking it over but Hannah knew she hadn't a hope that he'd just go away.

"Deal," he said and sat down.

Hannah put her notebook down. She should have driven a harder bargain.

"So, what have you been up to today?" Danny asked as he craned his neck to try to get a peek at her notebook.

She closed it. "I had a meeting with Ed Miller."

"How did it go?"

"It went well. He seems perfectly normal."

Danny laughed and the people at the counter turned around at the sound. Hannah felt encouraged when they lost interest almost immediately. Apparently, talk about them had died down.

"Well, congratulations, Hannah," Danny said. "You've finally found something normal in Timber Bay."

Hannah relaxed a little and smiled. "He'll be an asset, I'm sure."

"People around here think so."

"He had good things to say about you and Lukas, too."

Danny shrugged. "Ed's pretty cool."

Molly came out of the kitchen and headed their way, tray in hand.

"Is this nonpaying customer annoying you?" she asked as she put Hannah's order down in front of her. "I'll have him tossed out if he is."

"Hey," Danny said, "I've already been warned."

"Good. Glad she's not letting you get away with anything. I'll have your sandwiches ready for you in a few," she told him. "Hannah, you let me know if you need anything else."

Hannah picked up the sandwich and took a bite. "Mmm."

"You like?" Danny asked.

Hannah nodded as she chewed.

"Molly's a great cook as long as she stays away from the goat cheese."

"I like goat cheese."

He grinned. "You would. So what did Miller have to say about me?"

"Stop fishing. You don't need the reassurance. I did, however, ask him if he knew anything about the hotel being restored."

Danny raised his brows. "Really?"

Hannah nodded and took a sip of her iced coffee. "Apparently there's some bad blood between him and Agnes Sheridan. He didn't know a thing about it."

"Huh—just about everyone in town has some bad blood with the dragon lady."

"He did say that you and Lukas would be the ones for the job, though."

"He's a fan of the opera house. Tried to get the city to fund it."

"He told me," Hannah said with her mouth full. The sandwich was too good for decorum.

"I'm heading over there as soon as I get those sandwiches. Hoping to put in a couple of hours. We got in a shipment of oak today. Really beautiful. Lukas can hardly wait to get his hands on it."

"What is he going to do with it?"

"Some of the crown moldings and rosettes in the lobby need replacing. He loves that kind of stuff. He's more of an artist than a builder."

"Yet, you're the one who bought the opera house."

"I couldn't restore it without Lukas, though. But then, I couldn't do much without Lukas."

"How long have you two been friends?"

He told her about how they'd met in grade school when Lukas had come to his rescue. "That was the first time he backed me up, but it sure as hell wasn't the last."

Danny launched into an anecdote about Lukas, and, once again, Hannah got so caught up in it that she completely forgot to be paranoid about what anyone in the place thought of them sitting there like that. By the time Lukas was helping Danny from the roof of a girl's house where he'd climbed when her parents came home early, Hannah was laughing and shaking her head.

"So now I'm even more puzzled about that opera house."

"What do you mean?" he asked. Then, "Oh, I get it. Doesn't fit the rest of my profile, huh?"

"No, it doesn't." She took a last sip of iced coffee, then rested her chin on her fist and said, "Tell me why you bought it."

At first she thought he wasn't going to answer her. He ran a hand into his tangled hair and gave her a little half grin. "Only if you promise to behave," he said.

"Define *behave*," she said.

He laughed softly. "Now that I think about it, maybe I'd like it better if you didn't behave."

Those goose bumps shot up her spine again. She decided to laugh them off. "Shut up and tell me why you wanted to own the opera house."

He grinned at her and sat back in his chair. "Because there's magic in the old place—and the world can always use more magic. And because it has a certain tradition that deserves to be preserved. And because I went to New York when I was eighteen and saw *La Bohème* at the Met and never got over it."

"You like opera?"

"Yeah. I like opera." He gave her a grin. "But don't go jumping to conclusions. I like rock and Sinatra, too."

She smiled back at him. "You seem to make it a point to defy description."

"It's a gift, professor. You should try it sometime."

Honestly, when he was like this, she could have sat there all day. It was disconcerting to realize just how much she might like this side of Danny Walker. She picked up her glass and fiddled with the straw. "Um—was the New York trip with your senior class?"

He shook his head. "Summer after I graduated, I bought one of those train tickets that lets you travel all over, with stopovers along the way. I hit NYC, Boston, Philly and Newark. Just to see what was out there. I spent a week in NYC. Stood in line in the rain to get cheap tickets to just about everything I could. Walked the streets. Ate off the hot-dog and knish carts. It was great. I loved it. But by the time I got back to Timber Bay I knew one thing for sure."

"What's that?"

"This is home for me."

She looked into his eyes, those glittering blue eyes, and knew that he meant it. And why not? Wasn't Timber Bay exactly like the kind of town she'd wished she'd grown up in? Okay, so maybe the fantasy turned out to be flawed, but those flaws could also be endearing and—

Hannah's musing was interrupted by the jangle of the bell over the door followed by raucous, hoarse laughter.

"So it's true what I hear. The tunnel has finally accomplished what no girl in Timber Bay was ever able to do single-handedly! Land Danny Walker!"

Danny groaned. Talk about a mood breaker. Gertie Hartlet of Hartlet Homes Realty, cigarette dangling from the side of her mouth, and, from the smell of it, fresh from a three-martini lunch at Belway's had instantly put the starch back in Hannah's spine.

"You must be that cereal gal everyone's talking about." She took the cigarette out of her mouth long enough to use it to point at Danny. "This kid has already been through every girl in town," she said, ash spilling onto the table like dirty snow. "So you better watch him, girl. He's gonna be hard to hold onto—legend or no."

"I have no intention of holding onto him," Hannah said primly as she dug into her purse, threw a ten-dollar bill on the table, pushed back her chair and stood up. "If you'll excuse me, I'm going to be late for Kate's bridge club."

"Bridge club!" Gertie exclaimed as Hannah headed for the door. "Ha! Is that what they're calling it these days?"

Oh boy, thought Danny. Hannah was in for another big surprise. He'd better stop her. He took off after her and caught up with her half a block away.

"Hannah—wait! There's something you need to know."

She kept on walking. "Oh, you're a big help," she said without looking at him. "Running out of there after me like this. Don't you have any idea how this looks after what that woman said in there?"

"Hannah, come on. Nobody pays any attention to Gertie Hartlet."

"I have a professional reputation to protect here, Danny Walker, and you're not helping. Now, will you please leave me alone?"

Oh boy, would he. He slowed down and let her walk away. She was in for a surprise. And she wasn't going to like it. But at the moment, Danny couldn't think of anyone who deserved it more.

When Hannah was sure she'd lost Danny, she sat down on the wide granite steps of the Timber Bay Public Library, took out her notebook, flipped to a clean page, and wrote: *Gertie Hartlet.* She was going to have to find a way to keep her away from Pollard because Hannah was pretty sure that Gertie was the kind of woman who couldn't be controlled. But how was she going to get rid of her? Nothing permanent. Just long enough to keep her out of Pollard's way. She wrote the word: *tunnel,* then quickly scribbled it out with her pen. Weird times called for even weirder measures but was she really considering locking a middle-aged woman with a serious smoking habit in the tunnel of love?

Okay, she had been. But she'd stopped herself. That was the important thing.

"Chill, Hannah," she muttered. Things weren't bad enough to start committing felonies. She looked at her watch then jumped to her feet. Kate's bridge club had started ten minutes ago. She stuffed her notebook back into her shoulder bag and started to jog down Sheridan Road.

How could she have let one little thing make her forget the bridge club? Danny, of course. He'd distracted her as usual. Only this time, to her disgrace, she'd thoroughly enjoyed it.

Until Gertie Hartlet had appeared in a cloud of smoke, that is.

Good thing she had, though, or Hannah might have missed the bridge club altogether. Proving once again that Danny Walker was just plain bad news. Even when he was being sweet and charming and entertaining and cute and—

"Oh, shut up," Hannah muttered. "You ought to be hanging your head in shame for getting so easily caught up in all that bad-boy charm."

It wasn't until she'd crossed the street in front of the Walker house that she noticed that the blinds were drawn and the front door was closed to the afternoon air. Very strange. She climbed the porch steps, paused a moment to catch her breath, and just as she was about to open the door, she heard a series of thumps from inside followed by someone crying "Ouch!" and someone else hissing, "Shhhh!"

What on earth was going on? She tried to turn the knob but the door was locked. She had to ring the bell a few times before Kate finally opened it a slice and peered out.

"We thought you might be Emma Baker," she said, her eyes darting left, then right.

"Who?" Hannah asked.

Kate opened the door a little wider and motioned for Hannah to come inside. As soon as she did, Kate shut and locked the door again.

"False alarm, girls," Kate said.

Hannah peered over Kate's shoulder but she couldn't see who Kate was talking to. The living room looked empty.

"Hannah, this is my card club," Kate said.

Hannah saw a card table and four folding chairs, but that was all. Perhaps a stronger word than dizzy was needed to describe Kate.

"Let me introduce you," Kate went on. "The one under the table is Connie—"

That's when Hannah noticed a head peeking out from under the tablecloth covering the card table. The woman slithered out and rose to her feet with fluid, effortless grace. She was thin as a sapling and was wearing a black leotard and short red tutu that matched the lipstick on her thin mouth and the headband holding her chin-length black hair back from a face that was probably close to sixty. "Constance Hilton," she said with a theatrically meaningful look in her over-mascaraed eyes. She produced a business card out of nowhere and held it out to Hannah. "Hilton Academy of Dance."

Hannah took the card. It seemed the academy offered lessons in ballet, tap and interpretive jazz.

"Have you ever considered ballet?" Constance Hilton asked. "Your legs look simply divine for it," she added with a sweeping gesture of her twiglike arm.

Ina Belway wiggled out from behind a wing back chair and got to her feet. "Oh, can it, Connie. Quit trying to drum up business. How ya doin', Hannah?" she asked.

Before Hannah could answer her, a voice from behind the sofa said, "Could someone please help me up? I've got a cramp in my leg."

"Oh, goodness, Clara!" Kate Walker exclaimed as she bustled over to the sofa. "Ina, give me a hand, please." Together they pulled the sofa out from the wall and helped Clara to her feet.

"Your muscle tone would improve if you took dance lessons," Constance Hilton trilled. She turned to Hannah. "Both Ina and Kate belong to the Happy Tappers adult tap dancing troupe. We're doing the *Wizard of Oz* for the Fourth of July pageant this year, you know. It will be great fun, but I can never entice Clara to join us."

"If you don't shut up about those dance lessons, Connie," Clara said as she rubbed her thigh, "I'm going to rip that damn tutu off your bony butt. I keep telling you I get enough exercise behind the lunch counter at Ludington's. You're never gonna see these feet in a pair of tap shoes, so just shut—"

"Now, girls," Kate admonished sweetly.

"Maybe we better stop hitting the floor whenever someone rings the doorbell on card club days," Ina Belway put in. "None of us is gettin' any younger," she added as she rubbed her back.

"And give Emma Baker the satisfaction of catching us playing cards every Wednesday afternoon?" Clara asked. "You know darn well," she said as she straightened the little peaked cap on her head and dusted off the ruffled apron that covered a good portion of the skirt of a uniform the color of bubble gum, "that she'd just love to blab the whole thing to the entire congregation down at the Church of the Holy Flock. So far, we've managed to keep our card games a secret despite the fact that that loudmouth Gertie Hartlet sometimes sits in. I'd just as soon keep it that way."

Hannah took out her notebook. "Playing bridge is against your religion?" she asked.

"Bridge?" Ina Belway snorted. "Who said anything about bridge? Poker is our game."

"Five card stud, dear," Kate added, with a sweet smile.

"Deuces and jacks wild," Constance sang out, punctuating her words by rising on her toes and spinning in place.

"Poker?" Hannah repeated. "You have a Wednesday afternoon *poker* club?"

And that's when Hannah noticed the poker chips on the table. And the bottles of beer. And the bowl of peanuts.

No watercress sandwiches, no lovely little hats, no china teacups.

Okay—so maybe now things were bad enough to start committing felonies.

10

HANNAH SANK INTO A CHAIR and Ina said, "Oh, oh. I think Hannah is disappointed in us again."

Kate's hand flew to her mouth. "Disappointed? Really?"

Hannah sighed. "Kate, the forms you filled out said you played bridge."

"You accusing Kate of lying?" Clara asked belligerently. "Kate doesn't lie."

"Indeed, not," Constance said. "Kate is the most honest person I know."

"Calm down, everyone," Kate said. "Hannah isn't accusing me of lying. She knows that Tuffy is the one who filled out the forms. Don't you, dear?"

Yes. Hannah had known that. Of course Kate wasn't a liar. Uncle Tuffy just got confused, that's all. Because Hannah was sure that the forms said bridge.

"I'll be right back," Hannah said, then took the stairs two at a time and went into her bedroom to find the original contest forms. She sat on the bed with a pile of papers and started to search through them.

On Kate's page, under hobbies and outside interests, it said, very clearly, *Wednesday afternoon card club.*

Hannah flopped back on the mattress, letting the papers fall to the floor where the breeze from the open window whispered through them. It almost sounded like they were laughing.

She'd seen *card club* and assumed bridge. She stared at the ceiling and groaned. She'd hyped the bogus bridge club to

Pollard like it was the frosting on the cake. But the fluffy white frosting that was supposed to hide all the flaws in the layers had slid off the cake to reveal a bunch of middle-aged women hiding their poker habit from the rest of the town. What a picture on a cereal box that was going to make. What else had she gotten wrong?

Plenty. She sat up. Hell, it would be easier to make a list of the things she'd gotten right. It'd certainly be shorter. It didn't really matter, though, because when Pollard found out the truth, Hannah was going to be toast. What on earth was she going to do?

The only thing she knew for sure at this point was that she had to go downstairs, admit she'd been wrong, and apologize to Kate.

There were hoots from the living room as she descended the stairs. Apparently, Constance had just won a hand with a royal flush. She was celebrating by pirouetting across the living room.

"Damn woman is like something on top of a music box," Clara grumbled.

"You're just a sore loser," Ina said.

"Kate," Hannah said from the doorway. "I just wanted to say that it was my mistake. The form says card club—not bridge."

"Oh dear, is this going to be a problem for you, Hannah?" Kate asked, her sweet face puckered with worry.

"Just a little glitch. Nothing I can't handle," Hannah said in what was probably the understatement of the decade. She watched Kate deal the cards as if she worked a blackjack table in Vegas. "I have some—um—some stuff to do," she mumbled.

"Fine, dear. See you at supper."

Hannah went back upstairs and changed clothes, then let herself out of the house and walked along past the library to the beach. She was looking for the sound of waves and solitude, but the place was crawling with screeching kids and screaming mothers who were begging them not to go out too far. She found an empty bench but the sun was hot and the noise only irritated her already lousy mood.

After a while, she wandered over to the drugstore and stared into the window. There was a sale on French milled soap. Buy one box, get one for a penny. There was a display of suntan lotion and a sign advertising the finest in boxed chocolates. She thought about going in, but there seemed to be too much happy bustle going on inside, so she kept walking. She turned the corner at Ludington Avenue and found herself in front of Belway's Burgers and Brews. How many people could be in a bar at this hour? She opened the door and went inside.

It was cool and dark—the perfect place to hide. She ignored the booths lining the left wall and took a stool at the end of the bar, her back to the door. The only other afternoon drinker was at the other end, the place so dim she couldn't make him out and hoped he couldn't make her out, either. She was relieved when she recognized Chuck Belway as the bartender.

"Hey, Hannah. What'll it be?"

"Um—" Hannah didn't usually go into bars or clubs. She wasn't sure what to order. Maybe just an orange juice. "Orange juice," she said.

"With vodka?"

"Um—" Was it a faux pas to not drink anything alcoholic in a bar? "Sure—I mean, yes. Vodka and orange juice."

"Kitchen's not open till four," he said as he set a frosted glass down in front of her. "But I can get you some chips or something."

She shook her head. "No, this is fine."

And it was, she thought when she'd taken her first sip. More than fine, in fact. Very thirst-quenching. She drank it surprisingly fast and ordered another.

"I'll be out back prepping. Give a holler if you need anything else," Chuck said before he disappeared again.

She was already feeling a little buzz from the first drink so she sipped this one and got her notebook out of her shoulder bag to help keep her hands occupied.

What was she going to report to Pollard about the card club? She'd hyped it pretty strongly to make up for the thinness of her last report. Now it had become one more thing she'd have to hide.

How did she get into this mess? Oh—right. She'd thought she'd known what she was doing. She'd thought that she could handle this. After all, it was only a contest. Talk about a humbling experience. Had there really been a time when she'd actually thought she was overqualified for this? What a dope. And then there was Lissa—because this was partly her fault, too. Lissa had encouraged her. Said it was Hannah's chance to give herself the perfect family. But the way things were turning out, her perfect family didn't just have feet of clay, they were wearing cement shoes. Nobody was going to come anywhere near walking on water. Especially not the sparkling blue, unpolluted waters of Timber Bay.

The second drink was going down too easily so Hannah slid off her stool and wandered over to the jukebox to pop in a few quarters. Over half the songs were by Elvis. Big surprise, given Chuck's pompadour. She picked a couple of mournful ballads. Back at the bar, she started to make a list of all the things that were positive about the Walkers. It didn't take much time. She needed two pages for the list of things that went against *the image.*

Maybe she should just head back to Chicago and throw herself on Pollard's mercy. Admit she'd screwed up. Forfeit the bonus. Of course, if she did that, she could wave bye-bye to her short, unhappy consulting career. Which wasn't necessarily a bad thing. Except she was pretty sure that she wasn't going to get a job in research when word of this mess got out. She'd probably be stuck waiting on tables the rest of her life. A dismal prospect considering the summer job she'd once had at a restaurant where by the end of the first week she'd owed more for broken dishes than her paycheck could cover.

The jukebox ran out of money, her glass was empty and she was just trying to get up the energy to leave when Chuck came out again and put a bowl of popcorn in front of her then refilled her drink without asking. She started to protest, then thought what the heck. A little vodka never hurt anyone. And the orange juice practically turned it into a health drink. She was digging in her bag for more change when a voice beside her said, "This is the last place I expected to find you."

Great. Danny Walker. "If you came here to remind me again of what a failure I am, I'm really not in the mood."

He took the stool next to hers. "Ma sent me looking when you didn't come home for supper."

Hannah hadn't thought she could feel worse, but she'd been wrong. "Oh great, not only is my job in jeopardy, but now I've upset your mother. This day just gets better and better. Tell her I'm sorry, okay?"

"Hey, she's not looking for an apology. She's worried about you. Have you been here all afternoon?"

"No. First I took a walk down to the beach. But the water was too crowded to drown myself in."

Danny laughed. "I don't think a game of poker is worth doing yourself in over, professor."

She picked up her glass and took another swallow. Chuck came ambling over. "Hey, Danny. Gonna have something?"

Hannah flapped her hand at him. "Sure, he'll have something. I'm buying him a celebratory drink. What'll you have?"

"Make it a beer, Chuck. Whatever is cold and on tap." He turned back to Hannah. "What are we celebrating?"

"The fact that you were right. I am in way over my head."

She swallowed more of her drink. "I don't think there's much of a market for a naive sociologist, do you? I'm thinking of asking Chuck if he could use a dish washer."

"Don't be so hard on yourself, Hannah."

She shrugged. "I thought I'd beat you to it."

"Did I ever tell you about—"

She held up her hand. "Please, not another one of your stories."

"You'll like this one. It makes me look like an idiot."

"Hmm, maybe you're right. That would definitely cheer me up a little."

Danny laughed. "Come on, let's take our drinks over to a booth."

The booths at Belway's were the originals, luxuriously curved and covered in orange pleather that screamed *cocktail lounge*. The witty ugliness of them suited her mood. And, what the hell, it was the same color as her drink. She took a seat and Danny slid in after her.

"I got my first carpenter job from Gertie Hartlet. She had a house on the market that wasn't selling so she figured if she rehabbed it a bit it might move. She hired me to fix the front porch and stairs. I totally screwed up. Didn't put enough joists under the new stairs. Gertie held an open house and bam! The first person went right through. Broke his ankle."

Hannah rolled her eyes. "You made that up just to make me feel better."

"Hey, I'm sharing my most humiliating experience with you and you're calling me a liar? You should have seen the poor guy. He cried like a baby. The funny thing was, he put in a bid, anyway. But he insisted on buying it *as is* so he could fix the damn stairs himself."

Hannah started to laugh.

"I spent the next three months working off the doctor bills."

She shook her head. "And they still let you be a carpenter in this town?"

"Town like this might not forget, but they forgive. Everyone makes mistakes, Hannah. Even chicks with master's degrees."

"Okay, okay. I get your point. But this isn't fixable like a set of stairs or a broken ankle, Danny. The only way your family is going to fit the image of the Great American Family that Pollard is expecting is if a parallel universe exists. I mean, they'd be perfect if I was writing a sitcom for cable TV but as for representing the Great American Family, they just don't cut it. They're just not *right.* There are too many quirks, too many imperfections, too many—"

"Enough!" Danny said. He slid out of the booth and held out his hand. "Come on, I've got an idea."

"Where are we going?" she asked as she eyed his hand warily.

"We're going to find some trouble to get into."

"No way, Walker. We've been there before, remember?"

"It'll do you good. And the rest of us, too."

"What does that mean?"

"It means maybe you'll go easier on the rest of us if you aren't so perfect yourself."

"I never said I was perfect, Walker."

"No, but you sure try to be the good girl, don't you?"

"You say that like it's a character flaw."

"It is."

She thought it over for as long as it took to drain her glass. "I guess I've got enough flaws already. Let's not add being good to the list," she said, then took his hand and let him pull her out of the booth and out to his truck.

By the time they'd gone a few blocks, Hannah was already starting to worry again. She had a feeling this caper was going to require a lot more vodka than she'd consumed.

"Um—Danny—this might not be such a good idea, after all."

"Don't worry. We'll start with something small."

"No, I mean it. I'm going to be in enough trouble with Granny's Grains as it is."

"Lighten up, professor. Haven't you ever heard that the biggest regrets are for the things you never did?"

"Easy for you to say. Your livelihood isn't on the line. I'm the one who would be taking all the risks here."

He gave her a grin. "Then we'll just have to find something to do that will spread the risk out evenly."

"How are you going to do that? Trouble rolls off your back. All the women in Timber Bay will still think you're adorable and ask you to rebuild their kitchen cabinets while I'm the one who will get stuck living on tips with no health insurance."

"Man, do you ever stop worrying?"

"No," she said stubbornly. Which was the truth. "Why don't we just go get a burger and fries? Heartburn is the only risk I'm really feeling up for."

Danny gave her a look. "Chicken."

Hannah gave him a look right back. "No, I said burger. See? I can live dangerously. Red meat is dangerous."

Danny laughed. "Very cute, professor. Humor might sustain you through this but it ain't gonna get you out of it."

"Out of what?"

"Shhh, let me think."

What they needed, Danny told himself, was something a little wild. Something that would loosen her up a bit without getting her arrested. Something that would be just as risky for him. It didn't take him long to come up with an idea. He felt his adrenaline surge the moment he thought of it. It was perfect.

"I've got the absolutely perfect plan that will be just as risky for you as for me. You're gonna love it," he crowed as he turned the corner and headed back to Sheridan Road. He drove all the way to the end then turned left. Parking around the corner was safer. He pulled up to the curb, got out, and went around to open Hannah's door. "Come on," he said.

"What are we going to do?" Hannah asked warily.

"You'll see."

"I just want it put on record that I'm getting out of this truck against my better judgement."

"Duly noted. Now get your butt out of that seat and let's go. The mosquitoes come out at dusk and they're going to be hungry."

She didn't want to take his hand so he let it go and they rounded the corner and started following the tall wrought-iron fence that surrounded the Sheridan estate.

"Wow, that is one wicked-looking fence," Hannah said.

"Wicked or not, we're climbing it."

Her mouth dropped open. "You're kidding, right?"

"Nope. Come on."

Hannah went closer and wrapped her hands around the fence to peer inside. "I can't see much through all these thick bushes and shrubs," she said. "Who lives here?"

"Dragon Lady Sheridan. My boyhood nemesis."

"Wait a minute—isn't she the woman who owns the ho-tel—the one you're trying to get the contract for?"

"That's the one," he answered.

"Look, I know a lot of people in Timber Bay are kind of—um—eccentric, but I don't think sneaking into the Sheridan estate is the way to go about getting business even in this town, Danny."

"You wanted to even out the risk, didn't you? We get caught, my job is on the line, too."

She looked slightly impressed. "Hmm, not bad, Walker."

"Thought you might like it," Danny said as he started to climb. Funny how the hand and footholds came back to him so easily, how his body knew just which way to turn to avoid being impaled by the spikes of wrought iron at the top of the fence. "Watch what I'm doing," he told her. "If you put your hands and feet in the same places you'll do fine."

"You're assuming that I'm just going to follow you over like a good little accomplice, aren't you?"

He swung one leg over the top of the fence and found the first foothold on the other side before he turned to look down at her. She had her hands on her hips and her spine was looking a little stiff again.

"The only thing I assume, Hannah, is that you're going to give me trouble every time. Now, come on," he said, holding his hand down to her.

She looked up and down the street before asking, "What are we going to do once we get inside?"

"We're going to steal some of the prettiest lilacs in town."

Hannah bit her bottom lip, worrying it with her teeth, but he could see that she was tempted.

"I've never done anything like this."

"That's the point. Come on, professor, let's be naughty."

This time, she grinned—wide and beautiful—and then she started to climb. He jumped down on the other side and watched her long legs as she tackled the fence with ease.

"Not bad, professor," he said when she dropped lithely to the ground beside him.

"Now what?"

"There's a huge lilac bush about halfway down the yard," he told her. "It's so overgrown it's like a tree. Every year about this time, it pops out the biggest lilacs in town."

"But won't someone be able to see us from the house?"

He threw her a grin over his shoulder. "If it wasn't dangerous, there'd be no point, would there?"

The bushes were thick and he held back branches here and there for her to duck around. When they reached the edge of the manicured lawn that swept up to the Sheridan house, Danny crouched low and motioned for her to do the same.

Behind him, Hannah gasped. "There must be at least twenty feet of open lawn before we reach that bush! What if she sees us?"

"Those heavy drapes on this side of the house are never opened."

"What about the rooms upstairs?"

Danny shrugged. "She'd have to be looking out the window on purpose to see through those lace curtains up there. As long as those curtains don't move, we're cool. Once we get to the bush, we'll stay on the far side of it. No one can see us there."

"You sure?"

"Getting cold feet, professor?"

"If you call me chicken again, I'm going to stick a branch in your eye."

Danny laughed softly. "That's the spirit. Now, come on, Hannah. Let's roll."

He broke from the bush and started to run, keeping as far left as he could. Halfway there, he glanced back. Hannah wasn't behind him. He hit the ground. "Come on!" he whispered as loud as he thought safe to.

"I can't—I'm caught!"

He looked back at the house. The bedroom curtains were hanging as still as a spider in an empty web. He got up but kept low as he ran back to the thicket. Hannah's hair was tangled in the branch of a Japanese barberry bush.

"Ouch!" she cried when he tried to free it.

"Hold still," he whispered as he gently tried to untangle the strands. Now that he had her hair in his fingers, he could see that it wasn't really light brown at all, but shades of wheat, honey and caramel all mixed together. It felt like silk in his fingers and the scent of it filled him even here among the flowering bushes. A mischievous thought crept into his mind: she was captive. He could take her into his arms right now and there wouldn't be a thing she could do about it. The idea sent heat into his blood. He tried to ignore it but it wasn't easy. The best thing was to get her free and get them out of the shelter of the bushes before he was tempted to give in to temptation.

"Hell with it," he said and snapped the branch off of the bush. "Let's take it with us."

Hannah laughed and this time when he ran out of the bushes she was right behind him.

She reached the lilac bush only a second after he did, burying herself against the fragrant branches on the side farthest from the house as she muffled her laughter with a hand over her mouth.

"What now?" she whispered.

"Start picking. As many as you can handle and still get back over that fence."

"The smell is incredible," she said as she reached up and snapped off a cluster of flowers just above her head. "I don't think the campus had any lilac bushes."

There were a lot of things that campus didn't have, thought Danny.

Hannah reached up again, grabbing for a plump bunch of lilacs on a higher branch, and her shirt came out of her chinos. There was a smudge on her backside and another one on her cheek and the sprig of barberry was still hanging from her hair. It was enough to get his body humming. But the grin on her face was what really got to him. She was having as much fun as that naughty little girl she was starting to look like.

But she wasn't a little girl. She was a woman. The sight of her on her tiptoes to reach the high branches with her clothes twisted around her body showed every bit of the woman that she was.

His blood started to heat and throb. This time he decided not to ignore it.

He put his hands to her waist and pulled her away from the

tree until her back hit his chest, then wrapped his arms around her from behind.

"Danny!" she squealed, and the sound of his name from her mouth finished the job that the sight of her had started. He grew hard with a speed that stunned him. He bent his head to the side of hers, opened his mouth on her earlobe and let his teeth graze across it.

"Danny!" she said again. Only this time his name from her mouth ended on a moan.

He spun her around so she faced him and pulled her quickly and roughly up against his body. For one moment he looked into her eyes, saw what he needed to see in her flushed face and rough breathing, then bent his head and covered her mouth with his own.

He tasted the orange juice on her tongue and felt the wild beat of her heart against his. He wanted to touch her, to hear that sound she made. He skimmed his hands up from her waist to the side of her breasts. Her mouth opened wider on his and he heard her moan once again. But the next sound he heard sure as hell wasn't coming from her.

"Young man, unhand that girl. And while you're at it, unhand my lilacs, as well."

11

DANNY HADN'T HEARD that voice in years but he would have known it anywhere. He unhanded Hannah, got to his feet, then helped her up.

"Well, well," Agnes Sheridan said, "if it isn't young Daniel Walker once again pilfering my lilacs. You have a new accomplice, I see."

Terrific, thought Danny. If he and Lukas had ever had a hope of getting the hotel job, Danny had just blown it, big time.

Lukas. Too late, he thought of his partner. It wasn't only Danny's own hopes he'd just flushed. Lukas had actually thought they stood a chance. When was he going to grow up? On the other hand, why did the dragon lady have to be such a hard-nosed snob? Maybe it was time someone asked her. And maybe, since he'd already blown it, Danny should be the one.

"Listen—" he began as he took a step toward her. Before he could really get going, Hannah put a hand on his arm.

"Danny, aren't you going to introduce me to Mrs. Sheridan?" She held out her hand to the dragon lady. "Mrs. Sheridan, I'm Hannah Ross. I'm sorry if we're trespassing, but Danny has tried several times to intervene on my behalf and schedule a meeting with you. You see, I am representing Granny's Grains Cereal of Chicago—I'm sure you've heard of us. We're about to launch a campaign that celebrates the Great American Family."

Despite the dirt on her face and the branch hanging from

her hair, Hannah still managed to have an air of dignity and authority. The combination usually brought out the worst in Danny, but he could see that it was bringing out the best in Agnes Sheridan. She smiled—thinly, but still a smile—and said, "Do go on, young woman."

"Well, since you are—uh—the matriarch of the most important family in Timber Bay, naturally it would be a benefit to us if we could get your views on—uh—family values."

Danny thought he was going to choke. The history of the Sheridan family wouldn't do a thing for the state of family values. But anyone could see that the old lady was eating it up like it was covered in cream. She turned to Danny.

"I'm surprised that you, of all people, would attract such an intelligent woman, Daniel." She looked Danny up and down and then sniffed. "Perhaps there are worthwhile talents there, after all. Aside, that is, from the talent for breaking my grandson's nose."

"Oh, but Mrs. Sheridan," Hannah began, "Danny and I aren't—"

Danny shut her up by putting an arm around her shoulders and beaming at her. "She certainly is something, isn't she, Mrs. Sheridan? And I'd be honored, Mrs. Sheridan, to discuss my worthwhile talents at architectural restoration with you sometime if you'd like."

"Oh, yes. The hotel. I understand that you and that rather large boy you're always with would like to do business with me. One or two things about your proposal intrigued me. Perhaps we should discuss it one day."

"Well, there's no time like the present, I always say," Hannah said heartily. "And I would love to stroll around your lovely garden, Mrs. Sheridan, if I may, while you and Danny talk business."

Agnes Sheridan's eyes glittered. "She must like you immensely, Daniel," she said, thumping him on the leg smartly with her cane. "Count yourself a lucky scoundrel. Now come along, I haven't got all night."

Danny hesitated. Was the dragon lady actually inviting him into her castle? Through the front door, no less?

"Go on," Hannah whispered as she gave him a little push. "Use some of that bad-boy charm to get that job."

"So you do see my charm?" Danny asked with a quirk of his brow and a twist of his lips.

Hannah laughed and Danny was hit with a sudden shaft of happiness, like the sun breaking through the clouds on a rainy day. The same feeling he'd gotten when they'd sprung out of that manhole. He grabbed Hannah by the shoulders, gave her a kiss on the cheek, then ran to catch up with Agnes Sheridan.

It wasn't until Hannah had sniffed the roses, run her fingertips along the daisies and was strolling under the willow tree that a horrible thought occurred to her. Mrs. Sheridan had probably been the only person in town who hadn't heard about the manhole cover incident, as Molly had referred to it down at Sweet Buns. Which made Mrs. Sheridan about the only citizen in Timber Bay who wasn't waiting to see if Danny and Hannah became a couple. So why had Hannah allowed the old lady to think that she and Danny *already were* a couple?

When Mrs. Sheridan had made the assumption, not hard to do considering the state she and Danny had been in when they'd been caught stealing her lilacs, her first instinct hadn't been self-preservation. Instead, she had instinctively done what she could to protect Danny. She'd tried to rescue him from doing or saying anything that would keep him from getting that contract.

Things were getting totally out of whack. On the one hand, she was plotting possible ways to turn the Walkers into something they weren't in an effort to hang on to some semblance of professionalism and on the other hand she was jeopardizing everything by helping Danny Walker.

Pollard was exactly the type of man who'd want to suck up to the richest woman in town. When he found out that the main street of town was named after the Sheridans, Pollard would be panting to ingratiate himself. If Mrs. Sheridan said anything about Hannah and Danny making out on the grounds of her estate when she met Pollard, Hannah would have to choose between having Pollard think she was unprofessional or telling him about the legend—which would definitely make Timber Bay look less than normal and make her look less than trustworthy and would lead to questions and disclosures and more questions and more—

Someone shouted her name and her head jerked up. Danny was running toward her, a huge grin on his face.

"You did it, baby! She's going to study our proposal!"

Before Hannah could react, Danny grabbed her and whirled her into a dance. "And not only that—she's going to stop by the opera house to check out Lukas's restoration work! We might just get that hotel contract after all, Hannah." He stopped spinning and pulled her body up against his. "And I owe it all to you," he said more soberly, more softly, with his blue eyes looking into hers in a way that just wasn't good for her. She stiffened and tried to pull away.

"Careful, Hannah," he murmured. "The old lady might still be watching. She thinks we're a couple, remember?"

"But—"

"Hush," he whispered—and then he kissed her.

All this kissing had to stop, Hannah told herself. But it was no use. His mouth was so sure, his kiss so warm, she was drowning in sensation. Before she knew it she was tangling her fingers in his hair, pressing closer to him, opening her mouth to his. And when his hands skimmed down her back and cupped her buttocks, a jolt went through her body that was sharper than anything she'd ever felt before in her whole life. It made her greedy. She wanted more.

And Danny, clever bad boy that he was, knew how to give her more.

He pulled his mouth from hers and kissed his way across her cheek and down her neck. His hands moved to her waist, glided across her midriff and up until she felt his thumbs pressing against her nipples. She cried out and then heard an astonished curse from Danny before he started to fumble with the buttons on her shirt.

Her eyes fluttered open. The house was too close.

"Danny!" she whispered urgently. "Someone will see us—"

He stopped long enough to take her hand and pull her behind a huge bank of hydrangeas. And then she was on the ground with him, the scent of earth mingling with the scent of Danny and the warmth of the sun on her face and the heat of his hand on the swell of her breast above her bra.

She'd never felt so wild. So damned turned on. If he didn't free her breasts from her bra soon she was going to burst. Actually explode.

She felt his hand move up under the back of her shirt. Felt his fingers at the clasp of her bra.

Yes! her mind screamed while her mouth still took from his. And then suddenly a shadow passed across her closed eyelids. She opened her eyes. A very tall, very uniformed man was standing over them.

He cleared his throat and Danny pulled his mouth from hers.

"Madam wishes for me to see you out the front gate," the man intoned. "She feels you might not be up to climbing back over the fence." He cleared his throat again. "I can wait until you're finished, if you wish."

With a huge shove, Hannah pushed Danny off of her and scrambled to her feet. "We're finished," she managed to get out around her heavy breathing. "Please," she said, mustering as much dignity as she could despite the fact that she was buttoning her shirt at the time, "lead the way."

She was already following him when Danny got to his feet and caught up with her.

"Hannah—" he began.

"Do not say a thing, Danny. Not one word," she told him as she marched resolutely behind the tall, funereal figure of Agnes Sheridan's chauffeur.

"I STILL DON'T GET how you managed to corner Agnes Sheridan yesterday," Lukas said. "And at her house, no less."

"What difference does it make?" Danny asked. "Like I told you on the phone last night, we met, she's interested."

Danny didn't care for the speculative look in his partner's eyes. He decided to ignore it and went back to measuring a length of wood for the repair of the stage floor.

"Does it have anything to do with Hannah?"

"Now why would it?" Danny asked indifferently while he pulled out his tape measure. Nothing indifferent about the little tripping of his heart at the sound of Hannah's name, though. It was all too easy to remember what her body felt like under his. All too easy to remember her response to him. All too easy to remember that moan in her throat. That—

"Ouch!" Danny pulled his thumb away from the board. There was a one-inch sliver of wood sticking out of the pad.

Lukas laughed. "You seem a little distracted, buddy. Something on your mind?"

"Just the job at hand. I want to get this floor repaired before Mrs. Sheridan shows up."

"I thought you might be thinking about how you had to climb the fence to take that meeting."

Danny scowled at his partner. Damn town was like living in a fishbowl and he wasn't exactly in the mood to swim around in crazy circles for everyone to watch while Hannah walked away from their tangled, panting moment in the grass as though it meant nothing to her at all.

"Word travels fast," Danny muttered. "Now what do you say you quit gossiping and help me get this place ready for the dragon lady's visit?"

Lukas laughed, obviously not put out at all by Danny's surliness. That was Lukas. He seldom got riled about anything. Danny managed to avoid further conversation by being noisy with the power saw and a hammer. When next he looked up, the dragon lady herself was standing in the aisle of the opera house, gazing up at the restored carvings over the stage.

"Who did this work?" she asked, her voice bouncing off the acoustics as she waved her cane at the carving.

"That would be me, ma'am," Lukas answered as he hopped down from the stage and held out his hand to her. "I'm Lukas McCoy, Mrs. Sheridan. And I'm pleased to meet you."

"Are you?" the old lady snapped. "Most people aren't."

Lukas grinned. "You want to restore the old hotel to its past glory. That makes you okay in my book."

"I'm so pleased you approve," Agnes Sheridan said frostily.

"Well, I hope you approve of us, too, Mrs. Sheridan," Lukas said without a trace of sarcasm. "'Cause I sure would love to get my hands on all that wood over there in the Sheridan Hotel."

"Suppose you show me around, young man, and we'll see about that."

Danny jumped down from the stage to accompany them but Agnes Sheridan warded him off with her cane.

"I've seen more than enough of you already, Daniel." She took hold of Lukas's arm. "Mr. McCoy will take me around."

Fine by Danny. He went back to sawing boards, knowing that once Lukas got going on the subject of wood he could dazzle even the dragon lady of Timber Bay. In fact, Danny figured that Lukas could handle just about anybody. He turned on the boyish charm and it worked every time. Except it wasn't really something that Lukas turned on and off. It was just Lukas. Seemed to come natural to him. Danny hoped it worked on Agnes Sheridan like it worked on everyone else.

Half an hour later he was pounding in the last board when Agnes Sheridan and Lukas came in from behind the stage. The dragon lady practically had stars in her eyes.

"Mrs. Sheridan has been telling me all about the shows that used to come here," Lukas said. "It must have really been something."

"You wouldn't have known the town, then," she said. "Full of the hustle and bustle of the timber trade. Swelling each weekend with the loggers from up north out to spend money and relax before going back to the camps on Monday." She stood on the stage and stared out at the rows of tattered velvet seats. "If you boys could make it what it once was," she said, "then maybe it could entice a man back, as well as it lured one away."

Well, imagine that, thought Danny. The old lady sounded as sentimental as a true romantic. Too bad the man she was talking about enticing back was her grandson, Gavin. He, like all the other Sheridan men, had fled Timber Bay for more cosmopolitan skies. Danny would just as soon he stayed there. In fact, he didn't like the idea that Gavin Sheridan would have anything at all to do with the hotel. Maybe he'd learned a thing or two from Hannah, because he diplomatically decided to keep his mouth shut.

Because of the extra time they'd spent with Agnes Sheridan that afternoon, Danny didn't make it home that night until after dark. His ma had kept a plate of food for him and he ate it hurriedly, leaning against the counter in the kitchen. When he went upstairs, there was no light showing under Hannah's door. He stood listening for a moment, raised his hand to knock, then pulled his hand back again like a kid who'd just been told not to touch a hot stove.

He took a hot shower, then crawled into bed. But he couldn't stop thinking about her. He laid his palm on the wall that divided them, then felt like an idiot and put both hands behind his head and stared at the ceiling. It had been a long time since he'd lost sleep over a woman. And he was pretty sure that Hannah Ross was losing sleep over him, too. He decided that, come morning, he was going to do something about that.

But, come morning, he checked her room to find the door wide open, her bed stripped and her laptop computer gone.

He raced down the stairs and into the kitchen.

"Where's Hannah?" he asked his ma who was at the counter, cracking eggs into a bowl.

"She just left for Chicago," his ma said. "French toast, dear?"

"Chicago?" Danny didn't think he'd ever felt his heart drop to his feet before. "Did she say when she'd be back?"

"Actually, she said she might not come back. But I wouldn't be too worried about that, if I were you. After all, she really has to come back, doesn't she?"

"She does?" Danny asked, hoping his ma had a good reason for believing it.

"Well, of course. How else could the legend come true?"

EXHAUSTED BY THE SIX-HOUR DRIVE, Hannah climbed the stairs to her little studio apartment in the Wrigleyville section of Chicago and let herself in.

When she'd moved into it last year, fresh from grad school, she'd seen it as bright and cheerful compared to the faculty housing at Westbridge. But, after living for a week at the Walker house, the place just didn't seem the same anymore. Maybe it was all those stacking cubes that held her books and papers. Or maybe it was her uncomfortable but trendy sofa from Ikea. Or perhaps it was the one lone window that looked out on an airshaft. Whatever. By Saturday morning, the walls were closing in. She called Lissa and arranged to meet for brunch.

"I don't know what I'm going to do, Lissa," she said over bagels, cream cheese and overpriced coffee at their usual place on Belmont Street. "Nothing is going as it was supposed to."

"The family is a real nightmare, huh?" Lissa asked as she slathered cream cheese on half a toasted bagel.

"Well, no. They're very sweet, actually."

"Then what's the problem?"

"Well, they're just wrong. The father owns a junkyard and has some weird form of kleptomania they refer to as wishful salvaging, the mother plays poker and tap dances, the daughter leaves her husband like every other week and the son—" She stopped. She didn't want to talk about the son. But Lissa's ears, as usual, perked up at the possibility there was an interesting male in the mix.

"The son?" she prompted.

"The son is a thirty-year-old bad boy who would drive a saint insane," Hannah said generically.

"Hmm, at least they sound interesting," Lissa said as she licked cream cheese off her finger.

"But they aren't supposed to be interesting. They're supposed to be normal!"

Lissa laughed. "Your idea of normal, right? Your vision?"

"What's wrong with that? It's half of America's vision, too."

"The only thing is, that kind of normal doesn't exist."

"Of course it does. Take your family—"

"You know," Lissa interrupted, "it ticks me off a little that you just never take me seriously about my family. It's like you're in a dream world when you walk in the front door. My family is *not* perfect. My mother drives me nuts. My brother is an egomaniac. My father—"

"Okay, okay. I get your point. But this time it's not just me wanting to exist in a dream world. I promised to produce *normal* for Granny's Grains and I've totally failed."

"Good," Lissa said before taking another shot of her double espresso.

"Good?"

"Yeah. Good. Maybe you'll get fired and you'll be forced to move on to something else."

"Hey, I've got nothing against moving on to something else. I'd *love* to move on to something else. Almost anything else. The question is, what?"

Lissa smiled. "How about that son who would bedevil a saint?" She settled her hand on her chin and looked expectantly at Hannah. "Why don't you tell me all about him?"

So Hannah told her about the talking hood ornament, and the tunnel—minus the legend, of course—then went on to the lilac incident—omitting the kisses, naturally. And by the time she was done, Lissa was laughing so hard she spilled coffee down the front of her T-shirt—and Hannah was beginning to actually miss Danny Walker.

"How brilliant am I? I *told* you that you'd find a playground for your inner child," Lissa bragged.

"Not to mention my inner liar," Hannah added, then told Lissa about the increasingly fictional e-mails she was sending to Pollard.

"I always said you could write fiction."

"Only you would make the fraud I'm perpetrating sound like an opportunity to explore a right-brained career change."

Lissa laughed. "Hey, whatever works." She started to gather up her things. "Listen, I have a shoot in about twenty minutes. A rock band from Peoria who think they're going to be the next Creed. I'm trying to talk them out of the usual roof and fire-escape shots. But listen, girlfriend, this is all going to work out. I promise. You'll pull it together. I have total faith."

The pep talk didn't stick and by Sunday night Hannah was completely torn. Should she march back to Timber Bay and try to make it work or should she crawl into Pollard's office in the morning, confess everything, and throw herself on his mercy?

Yeah, right. And then call a good lawyer.

And if she didn't go back, wouldn't that mean she'd never see any of them again? Including Danny? And why didn't that thought make her feel relieved?

The phone rang, interrupting her silent, angsty soliloquy. When she picked it up she was surprised to hear Kate on the other end of the line.

"Are you planning on coming back tomorrow, dear?" Kate asked once they'd said hello.

"I don't know, Kate. The thing is, there might be a little problem. I might have to meet with Mr. Pollard tomorrow to—um—talk over a few things."

"Oh, what a shame. Well, I hope you'll be back soon because we could really use your help."

"My help? Why, Kate? What's up?"

"It's the Eats for the Elderly program."

Hannah wrinkled her brow. "Eats for the Elderly?"

"Oh, I know the name is silly, dear, since we also deliver meals to anyone else who can't get out and about for whatever reason. Anyway, there seems to be a flu epidemic among the volunteers. There is just no one who can deliver the meals for the next few days."

"Can't you do it?"

"Oh, my—no. They haven't let me take my turn driving since I ended up on Mabel Weaver's front porch."

Kate had imparted this news so matter-of-factly that Hannah had to press her fingers tight against her mouth to keep the laugh rising in her throat from escaping.

"Anyway, Clara, who can't do it because she has to work, made the suggestion that you, Hannah dear, might be willing to help out."

"Oh, Kate—I don't know."

"Well, don't you worry about it, Hannah, dear. It's not your problem. Mabel will just have to open a can of soup. That is if the arthritis in her hands isn't too bad to use a can opener. And as for the rest, well—"

Hannah listened to Kate and thought about all the hungry elderly of Timber Bay gazing longingly at unopened cans. And wasn't the Eats for the Elderly program a perfect example of something The Great American Family would do? Maybe it wasn't too late to save the image, not to mention her butt. She still had three weeks before Pollard and the rest of the crew arrived in Timber Bay. It was worth a try.

"All right, Kate," she said into the receiver. "I'll do it."

"You will?"

Hannah took a deep breath and hoped she wasn't making yet another mistake. "Yes," she said. "I'll drive back tomorrow—on one condition."

"Of course, dear. Anything."

"You have to tell Uncle Tuffy—and everyone else—that there is no truth to the legend of the tunnel of love as far as Danny and I are concerned."

"Of course, dear," Kate readily agreed. Surprisingly readily, in fact.

And it was only much later that Hannah found out why.

12

SHADING HIS EYES from the noonday sun with his hand, Danny stood on Mabel Weaver's roof, looking for loose shingles. Sure enough—he'd been right. There were none. He and Lukas had just put a new roof on the place two years ago. There wasn't a damn thing wrong with it.

He sat down on the roof and raised his face to the sun—and thought about Hannah. Ever since she got back from Chicago, he kept running into her. Day before yesterday she'd been sipping a soda at Ludington's and chatting with Clara when he'd gone in to pick up something for his mother. Yesterday afternoon she'd been at the post office dropping off a package for one of her Eats for the Elderly clients when he'd been picking up mail for Timber Bay Building and Restoration. He'd run into her at Sweet Buns later in the afternoon and again at Sissy's when he went to pick up Andy for a ball game in the evening. She was everywhere—fitting into Timber Bay as though she belonged there. Everywhere, that is, except where he wanted her the most. With him. She'd been avoiding being alone with him like it was some new skill she'd brought back from the city.

"So how's it look?" Mabel yelled from below.

He stood up and walked to the edge. "Like new," he yelled down to her. "Just like I figured it would."

"Is that right?" Mabel said as he climbed down the ladder. "Hmm, I could have sworn I heard a couple of shingles rip loose last night. One of 'em even flew past my window."

Mabel Weaver had to be close to ninety. Her face was lined

and squished like an apple that'd been forgotten too long in the root cellar. She wore her gray hair wound around her head in braids and her hands were permanently cramped from arthritis. But she still had a twinkle in her eye and she still made sense—most of the time. In this case, Danny figured the old lady had been dreaming. The wind hadn't been up last night. He'd lain awake long enough to know that for a fact.

"Well, I don't know what you heard. But it wasn't any shingles blowing off."

"Hmm—" Mabel took a look at the old pocket watch pinned to the baggy brown cardigan she was wearing, "—maybe you better check the storm windows up in the attic. Could have been one of them."

"I took your storm windows down weeks ago," Danny reminded her. She didn't seem to be listening.

"What?" she asked absently, her attention taken with craning her neck back and forth to look up and down the street.

"You better come inside," she finally said.

"Why?"

"Why?" Mabel repeated with a look on her face like he was talking a foreign language that she didn't quite understand. "Uh—my cupboards. I'm thinking about having them redone."

Danny was surprised but he followed her up the front steps and into the house, anyway.

He was taking measurements in the kitchen when the doorbell rang. Mabel seemed surprisingly sprightly when she went to answer it.

"Well, look who's here," she said, as she came back into the kitchen. "And, my, doesn't that pot roast smell good!"

Danny turned around. Hannah was standing in the doorway, holding the familiar Eats for the Elderly insulated container. She was wearing another tailored shirt, pale pink this time, tucked into khakis. Well buttoned. Unwrinkled. And stiff as a two-by-four.

"Hello, Danny," she said, cool as if nothing had ever happened between them, while she put the container on the table and started to unpack it. Then she turned to Mabel and said, "Here's your lunch, Mrs. Weaver. I hope you enjoy it. I've got a lot of other stops to make. Goodbye."

She left quicker than she came. Mabel looked disappointed.

"Was that planned?" Danny asked.

"Planned? Well, of course. I get my lunch delivered every day."

Danny narrowed his eyes and studied her. "Yeah, but you don't get me over here every day on a wild goose chase."

"Just 'cause I'm an old lady doesn't mean I'm hearing things, Daniel Walker! Something flew past my window last night, sure as this meal is sitting here. Now, as long as you can't seem to find what it was, you might as well run along and let me eat in peace."

Fine by Danny. He had to make a stop at Shamus Cooper's house yet before he could break for lunch.

Danny pulled the truck to the curb in front of Shamus's big old brick house, cut the engine, and got out. The Sheridan estate was right across the street. He stared at the iron fence that bordered it and thought about the two messages he'd left with the dragon lady's housekeeper in the past week. They'd both been ignored. If she was going to turn them down, he wished she'd do it and put Danny out of his misery.

Or, at least, one of his miseries.

He started up the front walk but stopped in his tracks when the Granny's Grains station wagon came around the corner and parked behind the truck. He watched her get out, insulated container in hand. As soon as she spotted him he could see her spine stiffen. Maybe it was because of his frustration with the dragon lady or maybe it was because Hannah seemed so determined to be indifferent to him, but this time he decided he wasn't going to cut her any slack.

"Following me, professor?" he asked her with a grin.

"Don't be absurd," she said as she sailed past him.

"Seems like a pretty big coincidence the way we keep running into each other."

"The swelling of your ego is obviously cutting off the oxygen supply to your brain. Shamus Cooper is simply on the list."

She started up the steps. He was right behind her. While she rang the bell he leaned in close and put the flat of his hand against the doorframe. He took an audible sniff of her hair. She tossed her head as if she was tossing off something pesky—like a mosquito. It made him think about biting her ear.

He felt the blood rush low in his body at the thought. Felt himself start to swell beneath the zipper of his jeans. How the hell did she get to him like this? Because he might as well admit it. It happened every time he was near her. And what was even worse, when she tried to freeze him out it made him want to torment her, tease her like a bad little boy who was after the snootiest girl in the class. Anything just to get a reaction out of her.

Of course, *his* reaction had nothing whatsoever to do with being a little boy. Nothing at all.

"Your hair smells like lemons," he said with his nose close enough that her hair brushed his cheek when she shivered slightly.

He might have to kiss her. Right on the side of her neck.

Shamus Cooper opened the door and Hannah jabbed Danny in the gut with her elbow.

"I'm Hannah Ross, Mr. Cooper," she said, without missing a beat.

"I know who you are," Shamus said as he eyed Danny suspiciously. "Didn't expect the two of you to arrive together, though."

"We didn't," Hannah said pointedly. "It's merely a coincidence."

Shamus looked grumpy—which really wasn't unusual for Shamus, Danny knew.

"Well, you better get in here before my pot roast gets cold."

He held the screen door open for them and Hannah went in. Rubbing his stomach, Danny followed.

"What did you want to see me about?" he asked when they'd reached the kitchen at the back of the house.

"Huh?" Shamus had been hungrily watching Hannah set out his meal. "Oh! The storm window in the attic was flappin' all night. You gotta climb up there, boy, and fix it. I'm on medication. I need my sleep."

"I already took your storms down, Shamus."

"You did?" Shamus asked, poking his head out toward Danny.

The town seemed to be having an epidemic of storm window forgetfulness. "Absolutely, Shamus," Danny said. "End of April."

"Hmm. Then must be a shingle on the roof."

Danny laughed and shook his head. Along with old Shamus's pipe tobacco, Danny smelled a plot.

"Your roof is newer than Mabel Weaver's, Shamus. She was hearing phantom shingles last night, too. What are you two up to?"

"Aw," Shamus scoffed. "Can't an old man be forgetful anymore?"

Danny laughed. "Sure, Shamus. But I think you're hearing things, too."

"Aw, get out of here, Danny, and let me eat my pot roast."

Hannah decided it might be wise to try to beat Danny out of there. "I'll leave you to your lunch, as well, Mr. Cooper,"

Hannah said and headed for the front door. Unfortunately, Danny was right behind her.

"Danny, I wish you'd leave me alone," she said without breaking stride or bothering to glance at him. "Eats for the Elderly is the most wholesome, normal thing I've run into since I came to Timber Bay and now you're spoiling it by showing up wherever I go."

"Ha!" Danny hooted. "Now who has the huge ego?"

She stowed the empty thermal container in the back of the station wagon, shoved her hands into the pockets of her khakis, and finally looked at him. "You don't expect me to swallow that this is all pure coincidence, do you?"

"Of course not. We're being set up, baby."

"I'm not your baby—and what are you talking about?"

He took a few slow steps toward her. "Maybe you should try being my baby. You might like it."

"Would you like another jab in the stomach, Mr. Walker?" she asked him with as sweet a voice as she could muster considering her jaw was clenched. "Or maybe something lower?"

Danny laughed that soft, low laugh that made her stomach clench in a whole different way than her jaw.

"You're getting downright sassy, professor," he said as he reached out and ran the back of his fingers down her cheek. "I think I might like it."

Despite the fact that half of her body had just about melted, Hannah stepped away and glared at him. "Stop fooling around and tell me what you meant when you said this was a setup."

"Isn't it obvious? There is no flu epidemic, Hannah. I haven't got any proof—yet—but my guess is that Ma and some of her playmates were looking for a reason to get you back here and keep you busy."

"Why, for heaven's sakes?"

"So they could start sending me out on these bogus jobs

and we could keep running into each other. In other words, they're giving the legend a little push."

Hannah's mouth dropped open. "But Kate promised me. That was one of the conditions of my coming back. She promised that she would tell everyone that there was nothing going on between you and me and that there was absolutely nothing to the legend this time! She not only broke her promise but she actively tried to make that damn legend come true. How could she do this to me? How could she lie like that?"

"Hey, watch it. A guy doesn't like to hear his ma called a liar. Besides, don't you think your reaction is a little overwrought given what you turn into every time I take you in my arms?"

She gave him a look. "The legend involves the tunnel of *love*, Danny. Not the abyss of lust."

He gave her one of those lopsided grins that could break a girl's heart. "Hey, lust works for me," he said as he reached for her.

Hannah jumped out of the way just in time. "Don't you dare touch me right out here on the street after what you just told me about your mother setting us up. I can't afford to be involved in anything as ridiculous as a town legend, is that understood? You didn't win the contest because you flash my meters when you kiss me. You won it for being normal. Now would you please try to act like it." She looked up at the house where Shamus was peeking around the living-room drapes. "And that goes for everyone else in this town, too!" she yelled. When the drapes fell back into place, she turned back to Danny. "I came back from Chicago for only one reason. To do my job. I intend to make this contest work, Danny. So, please, just stay out of my way."

"SATURDAY NIGHT IS a stupid time for a business meeting," Danny grumbled as he shifted gears on the truck and shot up Sheridan Road toward the Sheridan estate.

"Man, you sure have been in a bad mood lately," Lukas said. "Ever since you and Hannah had that little spat out front of Shamus Cooper's house."

Danny shot Lukas a look. He'd never thought about living anywhere else but Timber Bay, but lately the whole small-town thing was strangling him. "Hannah has nothing to do with it," he snapped.

Lukas gave a short bark of laughter. "Oh no? Then how come you're not happier about this meeting? Seems to me the dragon lady wouldn't be inviting us into her parlor unless there was a good chance she was going to give us the contract on the hotel."

What Lukas said was true. He should be wild with anticipation, not grousing and complaining. And lying. Yeah, don't forget to mention lying, Danny thought irritably. And to his best friend, yet. Because his mood had everything to do with Hannah.

He pulled the truck to a stop just in front of the tall wrought-iron gates of the Sheridan estate. He got out of the truck and walked up to the intercom, pressed the button, identified himself, then got back into the truck to wait for the electronic gates to open.

"Boy, who would have thought it, Lukas," he muttered when the gates started to move. "Going in through the front gate."

Lukas had a huge grin on his face. "Yup. Truck and all."

Danny laughed. He was starting to feel some of the excitement he was supposed to be feeling. The excitement he *would* be feeling if it weren't for Hannah. She was causing him the kind of trouble he hadn't had over a girl since he was sixteen. He was sleeping fitfully. His work was suffering. He wasn't even sure anymore if what he felt about what Hannah had said to him was anger or hurt. Might have been hurt for all he knew because he'd never felt it before. Not connected to a woman, anyway. Danny was used to calling the shots—not being shot down and told to stay away.

"Hey, buddy. What ya' waiting for?" Lukas asked. "Gates are open."

"What?" Danny said. Then, "Oh—yeah. Well, then, let's get on with it."

"Full speed ahead, Danny boy. I can almost feel the wood from the hotel in my hands."

To hell with Hannah, thought Danny. This was his moment and he was going to enjoy it. He plastered a grin on his face, socked Lukas in the arm and drove the truck through the gates of the Sheridan estate. It was the first time he'd gotten inside without having to climb the fence.

LISSA HAD BEEN RIGHT. Hannah really was good at writing fiction. Her nightly reports to Mr. Pollard were so creatively finessed that she was tempted to put *docudrama* in the subject line. She'd stretched the truth about as far as it would go so tonight she sat at her notebook computer and actually made a few things up.

Like the Saturday-night bonfires at the beach and the Sunday evening singalongs on the Walkers' front porch.

Well, something had to take the place of *the bridge club that wasn't*, didn't it? After all, she was certain that someone, at some time had had a bonfire on the beach. And surely Kate or Uncle Tuffy had hummed a tune while swinging on the front porch swing. Besides, both events could be easily staged.

Hannah thrust her hands into her hair and hung her head in shame. Staging events. A new professional low. She hoped it wouldn't have to come to that. Pollard and the crew were due in Timber Bay in two weeks. If she stayed focused and coordinated everything tightly, she just might be able to pull off delivering what Pollard expected without having to resort to any actual playacting. If that happened, she prayed to the gods of research, she would never finesse any findings ever again.

A volley of sound suddenly hit the bedroom window and startled her. Hail? She went over to look but the sky was still an inky black. Not a cloud in sight.

"Hey!" someone said softly from below. Hannah looked down into the yard. Danny was standing beneath her window.

"What are you doing?" she hissed down at him.

"Trying to get your attention without drawing attention," he said. "Come on down, I've got something to tell you."

"Are you kidding? Absolutely not. Someone might see us. Now go away."

She had started back to her desk when there was another shower of pebbles against the window. She swung around again, stuck her head out the window, and nervously looked around to see if any of the neighbors were watching. She couldn't see anybody, but there were plenty of bushes to hide behind. If Danny was anything to go by, the residents of Timber Bay were old hands at doing all sorts of things in bushes.

"What do you want?" she whispered down to him.

"I've got some good news!"

Was it her imagination or had his voice gotten louder? And was that the sound of a neighbor's screen door opening?

"Danny, this is dangerous. Someone's going to spot us and get ideas. I can't afford to—" Her words ended in a gasp when he grabbed hold of a trellis of sleeping morning glories, swiftly climbed up to her window and crawled inside.

13

"ARE YOU CRAZY?" Hannah demanded.

"I thought we'd already established that," Danny said as his eyes wandered over her.

Suddenly her white cotton pajamas sprinkled with rosebuds seemed much too revealing. She was sure her rapidly beating heart—along with a few other things—was visible beneath the thin fabric. Where was her robe?

"What did you want to tell me?" she asked, hoping that he'd just tell her and then go away.

"I—um—" he cleared his throat. "You—you look beautiful, Hannah."

"What?" she croaked stupidly.

His smile was small and sweet—not like his usual grin at all. It made her tummy flutter. "You look beautiful with your hair all mussed, standing by the window, in those—um—flowered things."

She fought against every little flutter. "They're called pajamas and I hope that isn't what you climbed up here to tell me. We've been through this before. If you think you're going to come in here and sweep me off my feet—"

He laughed and shook his head. "Didn't anyone ever **tell** you, professor, that when a man tells you you're beautiful, it's not a bad thing."

"Well, maybe it isn't—normally," she said defensively. "But things are seldom normal around here. I just don't want you thinking that you can come up here with your charming bad-boy routine and—"

He strode up to her and clapped his hand over her mouth. "If you'd shut your mouth a minute, professor, you'd find out that I did not come up here to have my wicked way with you. I came up here to tell you that Lukas and I got the hotel job." Her eyes widened and he dropped his hand. "I just thought, since you helped us get it, that you'd want to know."

"You got the hotel job? Danny—that's wonderful!" Without thinking she threw her arms around him. "I'm so happy for you!"

He was wearing a white T-shirt and she could feel the heat of him under her hands and through the thin fabric of her pajama top. She started to pull away but he had his arms around her waist and he wasn't letting her go anywhere.

"Danny—" she warned.

"Shhh, professor. You still talk too much," he said. And then he kissed her.

And it felt so good. His mouth on hers. His body close. And the thought came to her that maybe she should just go for it. Who would blame her? Men like Danny Walker didn't crawl in a girl's bedroom window every day of the week. Who would know if she took him into her borrowed bed for a few hours of bliss?

There was a knock on the bedroom door and Hannah quickly pushed Danny away. This was exactly why she couldn't just go for it. In Timber Bay, there always seemed to be witnesses. And word would spread. And then the whole town would be talking and she'd never be able to control them all and someone would be sure to say something in front of Mr. Pollard and then—

"Hannah?" Kate asked sweetly from the other side of the door.

"Quick," Hannah whispered furiously. "Hide! Get under the bed," she told Danny, as she pushed him down onto the floor. He hit it with a thud.

"Are you all right in there, dear?" Kate asked with a worried tone.

"Yes, Kate! Of course! Be right there!" she trilled cheerily while she motioned frantically to Danny to get under the bed. It seemed to take him forever to wiggle under it. As soon as he completely disappeared, Hannah opened the door.

Kate came in and looked around. "I thought I heard voices."

"Oh, um, just the computer talking back. What did you want, Kate?" Hannah asked, hoping to distract her.

"Well, I'm afraid I have another little favor to ask of you. As you know, the Happy Tappers are performing the *Wizard of Oz* at the Fourth of July celebration."

"Yes, I know, Kate," Hannah said, noticing that Danny's elbow had started to protrude from under the bed. "You're the scarecrow," she said as she sat down on the bed and kicked Danny's protruding arm back under it with her heel.

Kate didn't seem to think she was acting odd. Well, why would she? thought Hannah, finally beginning to appreciate Kate's dizziness.

"That's right, dear. But something terrible has happened to the lion!"

"The lion? What lion?"

Kate looked at her like Hannah was the one who was dizzy. "Why, the Cowardly Lion, of course."

"Oh! Of course."

"Gardenia Swartz, the high-school principal's wife, was supposed to tap the part of the cowardly lion but she broke her ankle this afternoon trying out one of those electric scooters. So now we have no lion."

"What a shame."

"Unless—"

"Unless?" Hannah asked, a little distracted by the bed shaking slightly and the muffled sound of laughter coming from under it. She coughed, hoping to cover it up. Apparently, Kate hadn't noticed.

"Unless you'd be willing to take her place," Kate said hopefully.

"Me?" Hannah croaked. "But—"

"You are one of the few women of Timber Bay tall enough to fit into Gardenia's costume, Hannah dear."

Hannah didn't see the point in pointing out to Kate that she wasn't a woman of Timber Bay, so she just said, "But, Kate, I don't tap-dance."

"But you could learn! Constance could teach you. She's a wonderful teacher. Why, in no time she'd have you dancing like a cowardly lion should!"

The bed started to shake and laugh again and Hannah rose from it, put her arm around Kate's shoulders and led her to the door. "You'll have to let me think about it, Kate," she said. "Let me—um—sleep on it and I'll let you know in the morning."

"Oh, thank you, dear." Kate patted her hand. "It's so sweet of you to consider."

"You can come out now," Hannah whispered as soon as Kate was gone. "You almost blew it," she accused Danny as he wiggled out from under the bed. "What was so damn funny?"

"The image of Gardenia Swartz on a scooter—and then the idea of you tap-dancing in a lion suit—"

Danny started to laugh again and she glared at him until he stopped. "I'm glad you enjoyed your laugh, Danny, because there is no way you're really going to see me in that lion costume."

"Well," he said as he lay down on the bed and put his hands behind his head, "you might have some trouble convincing my mother of that."

That's when it hit Hannah. Slowly, she sat down on the foot of the bed. "Oh-oh...I told her I'd think about it, didn't I?"

Grinning, Danny nodded. "Yeah, you did."

Hannah raked her hands through her hair. "Another predicament. Why am I surprised? Well," she threw her hands up, "there's just no way I'm putting on a lion costume and tap-dancing down the yellow brick road. I'm a woman of science for heaven's sakes. I've done enough crazy things since I hit Timber Bay. There's no way I'm putting on that costume."

Danny shrugged. "Well I guess you'll just have to break it to Ma first thing tomorrow that you really had no intention of helping out the Happy Tappers and that you lied to her and that—"

"Oh, shut up," Hannah grumbled as she got to her feet and started to pace. "I feel guilty enough already."

"What do you care? Everyone in Timber Bay has let you down already. Just call it tit for tat."

She stopped pacing and narrowed her eyes at him. "Let me down?"

"Yeah. By not being perfectly normal. So what do you care?"

"Don't be ridiculous. Of course I care. I love your mother and I'm very fond of all the Happy Tappers. In fact, everyone in town has been very nice to me. Uncle Tuffy, your father, Molly, Lukas. I don't see what being normal has to do with it at all."

"Bingo," Danny said.

She gave him a look. "Okay, point taken, Danny. But even if I wanted to help them, I don't see how I could. It's bad enough I'm running this contest. If I start tap-dancing in a lion costume, no one will ever take me seriously as a researcher again."

"Hey, tell it to Ma."

"Come on, Danny. Be fair. It's not like I haven't helped them out before. I drove for the Eats for the Elderly. And just because it turned out that they hadn't really needed me doesn't mean—'' Hannah sat back down on the foot of the bed. "Danny, what if this is another setup?"

He frowned. "You mean Gardenia might just be pretending to have a broken ankle?"

"Why not? They made up the Eats for the Elderly flu, didn't they? If we could prove that this is just another ploy, then I wouldn't have to consider making a fool out of myself in a lion costume. But how are we going to do that?"

"We?"

"Yes, we. You got me into this mess this time so you're going to help me get out of it." She slapped him on the knee and tried not to look at the thigh above it, all bulging under worn denim and reclining at the moment on her bed. "Come on," she said, "there must be some brilliant caper scrambling around in that mischievous brain of yours."

Now it was Danny's turn to pace. He got off the bed and started to prowl the room. In just seconds, his head came up. His blue eyes were glittering. Hannah already knew that look.

"What?" she asked impatiently. "What did you come up with?"

"Wouldn't it be a hassle to have to pretend that you have a broken ankle all the time? Such a hassle that when no one was watching, you'd probably stop pretending."

"Makes sense. But if no one is watching, how would we ever know if she stops pretending?"

"We spy on her."

"Spy on her?"

"Yeah. The Swartzes live just through the alley. We could sneak over there and take a peek in their windows. See if we can catch Gardenia walking normally."

Hannah took a moment to wonder why the idea didn't strike her as absurd. Maybe she had been around Kate and the entire Walker family too long because the notion of peeking into someone's windows in the middle of the night seemed perfectly logical.

"Okay, you're on. Now, how do we get out of the house without anyone hearing us?"

Danny looked over at the window. "I think it's time to work on your education again, professor," he said.

Hannah had to get dressed so Danny stood facing the closet door, his back to the rest of the room, while she took off those sweet pajamas. The rustling sounds drove him crazy—guessing what she was taking off, what she was putting on, with every little noise. He was battling arousal and losing when she finally said, "I'm ready."

He turned around. The sight of her in jeans, a white shirt tied at the waist and scuffed white sneakers didn't exactly deflate anything.

"Something wrong?" she asked when he just stood there.

Other than the fact that he wished he was wearing a shirt with very long tails, nothing at all was wrong. "I'll go first," he said as he headed for the window, "then I can help you down if you need it."

The morning glories rustled as he climbed down within jumping distance of the ground. He landed on his feet, then watched Hannah, her feet sure, her body lithe and pliant, as she climbed out the window and down the trellis. She didn't need help so he had no excuse to touch her. But he wanted to. Oh, yeah, he did.

In the moonlight, they ran through the backyard and out the gate. They crossed the alley and stopped to catch their breath behind the Swartzes' garage.

"There's a huge fir tree in the side yard, right across from a living-room window," Danny whispered. "Head for it."

They ran for it, jostling each other as they tried to hide among the prickly branches. "I can't see much of anything," Hannah whispered.

"I think we're going to have to get right under that side

window to get a better look. On the count of five, I'll make a break for it. If it's clear you follow two seconds later."

He couldn't help but notice that her hair shimmered in the moonlight when she nodded. He could smell it, too, despite the fir. After they found out the truth about Gardenia, then he was going to bury his face in that lemon-scented hair, and untie that knot at the waist of her shirt, and—

"Danny, you're not counting," Hannah hissed.

He dropped into a crouch, counted to five under his breath, and made a break for it. Two seconds later, Hannah joined him under the window.

Together, they raised their heads to peer inside. When he took in the scene through the window, Danny almost lost it. Gardenia, who was a good five foot ten inches tall and outweighed her much shorter husband by at least fifty pounds, was scooting across the floor on her rear using only one foot because the other one was in a cast to just past her ankle. Mr. Swartz, sweating profusely, was behind her with his hands under her armpits, helping to steer her toward the stairs. His shirt was askew, tails hanging out, but his bow tie was still neatly in place.

Beside him, Danny could feel Hannah struggling to hold in her laughter, but it was too much for Danny. He couldn't hold it in any longer. He burst out laughing. Immediately, Mr. Swartz raised his head and looked right at the window.

"Run for it!" Danny whispered and took off for the alley. Hannah was right behind him. Once they scurried behind the garage they fell into each other's arms, trying to muffle their laughter against each other's neck.

"I can't believe we just did that!" Hannah gasped.

"Did you see the look on his face? I wonder if he wears that bow tie to bed," Danny got out around his laughter.

Hannah abruptly pulled away. "Well, I guess we've got our answer."

"Yeah," Danny said, wishing he was still holding her. "No way is Gardenia gonna travel that way unless she has to."

Hannah started to laugh again but a door slammed somewhere and they both suddenly sobered. "Come on," Danny said. "Let's get out of here."

He took her hand and started to lead her down the alley.

"Where are we going?" she whispered.

"It's a great night. Let's take a walk."

"Danny—" she warned.

"Don't start worrying. It's late. No one's going to see us."

The sky was beautiful and the breeze was sweet. Just a little walk. What would it hurt? So she let him hold her hand and they walked the silent streets and alleys of Timber Bay. He showed her where he went to grade school and where his favorite teacher lived. They walked past the library and she told him how much she loved books.

"You and your friend played library."

She was foolishly touched that he remembered. "Yes. Lissa. We're still best friends."

"Like me and Lukas."

"Yes," she said, although she'd never thought of it like that before. "Lissa is a lot different than I am, too."

They walked down to the beach and sat on the sand while she told him about Lissa and her life in Chicago.

"So you're a big-city girl, now," he said.

She shook her head. "Not really. I don't really belong there, either."

"Maybe you belong here," he said.

She felt such pleasure at the thought of that that she had to dip her head and not look at him. Finally, she got up and started to look for shells in the moonlight on the cool, wet sand at the edge of the lazy lapping waves. He got up to help her and by the time they started for home, she not only had a pocket full of shells, she knew his favorite movie, his favorite book and his favorite kind of ice cream. She also knew that she was falling in love.

DANNY DIDN'T WANT it to end. As a nondate, it was the best damn date he'd ever been on. He insisted they walk back down the alley, just because he knew it would take them longer. By the time they reached the back gate, the birds were already waking up. As soon as they went through the gate, he pulled her into the shadows behind the oak tree next to the garage. He put one hand up on the tree and leaned into her, nuzzling her neck with his mouth, loving the little gasp she made.

"Danny, I don't think—"

"Shhh," he said. And then he kissed her. Long and slow. It was sweet. Peaceful. He thought maybe he could spend the rest of his life doing it. When he finally stopped kissing her it was only because he wanted so badly to look into her face.

"We shouldn't be doing this," she whispered. "Someone might see."

He laughed softly as he reached down to unknot her shirt. "If you're going to tap-dance in a lion costume, I think we better work on overcoming that shy streak, baby."

She pushed him away. "Since I'm *what?*"

"Since you're going to—" Danny began but his words trailed off when he saw the look of horror travel over her face. "Hannah, we've found out that Gardenia's ankle is really broken. That means the Happy Tappers really need you to fill in."

"But—but Danny—I can't! I mean, what would Granny's Grains say? I'd feel so silly. How could I—"

"Oh man—there goes that spine of yours again. I guess I should have known that you'd be way too uptight to have that kind of fun."

"That's not fair, Danny. Didn't I just hide you under my

bed? Didn't we just sneak out the bedroom window to spy on someone?"

"Hide and sneak are the operative words, baby. And you're an expert at it."

She tossed her head. "Well, that's just ridiculous. What am I hiding from?"

"Life. That's why you picked research. You'd rather study it than live it. Out here on this side of your little notebook, life sometimes gets messy. Things don't fit into a multiple choice question on a survey form. People do unpredictable things—and sometimes they do silly things, like tap-dancing on the Fourth of July. But, let's face it, maybe it's better if you don't come over to our side of the notebook since you're too worried about your precious dignity as a researcher to even help out a friend."

He was getting to her, he could tell. The leaves from the old oak tree shadowed her face but he could see that she was steaming. One more push and she just might blow. Fine by Danny. "Oh, what's the use," he said, jerking his head dismissively. "Fourth of July is only about a week away. You probably couldn't learn to tap-dance by then, anyway."

That did it. She blew.

"Oh, you think so, huh? Well, you listen to me, Danny Walker," she told him as she poked a finger into his chest, "I can be as real as anyone else in this town can. And I can help out a friend, as well as anyone else, too. I'll learn to tap-dance, all right. And I'll be the best darn Cowardly Lion this side of Oz!"

She brushed past him and headed for the back of the house. Her back was stiff as he'd ever seen it and he could tell by the tilt of her head that her straight little nose was in the air. He figured it would take her until she got up to her bedroom to realize what she'd just done. He also figured that she'd be too stubborn to back out. Hannah Ross was going to play a cowardly lion in tap shoes. And Danny couldn't wait to see it.

14

THE SKY WAS BLUE, the sun was hot, and the smell of corn on the cob roasting over coals filled the air when the Timber Bay Marchettes, a drum and bugle corps of five, took the bandshell stage and started to massacre "The Stars and Stripes Forever." Danny grinned around a slice of watermelon and leaned against a sprawling oak tree to listen. He could see Uncle Tuffy up near the front of the stage marching back and forth like he was part of the show. And there was his pop, eyeing up an old motorcycle that someone had parked illegally on the sidewalk. Danny made a mental note to keep an eye on Henry before he started to scan the rest of the crowd.

He'd left the house just after dawn that morning to help set up the food booths for the Happy Tappers and Sweet Buns so he hadn't seen Hannah since dinner the night before. Not that he'd seen much of her for the past week, anyway. He was almost sorry he'd goaded her into tap-dancing because the damn lessons took up most of her time. Mostly, he saw her at mealtimes. And then she'd get his ma talking about Walker family life and the two of them would start giggling over some story his ma told about something he did when he was four and Danny would take refuge at the opera house, venting his frustration by ripping out rotten boards and tattered upholstery.

Last night, he and Lukas had run into Hannah and Molly at Belway's and they'd all had a burger together. They'd talked and laughed and had a good time, but then the women had gone shopping and by the time Danny had gotten home, Hannah had already gone to bed.

He threw his melon rind in the trash basket then started to scan the crowd. He wondered where she was now.

"Lookin' for someone, Danny boy?"

Danny stopped scanning. "Hey, Lukas, not really. Just trying to figure out what to eat next."

"Hannah's over at the Happy Tappers booth, dishing out pie."

Danny shrugged nonchalantly. "Not ready for pie yet," he said. "I'm thinking fried chicken or a hot dog."

Lukas chuckled. "Yeah, right. You might as well give in to it."

Danny grunted. "Lukas, I think the sun is getting to you. You're not making sense."

"I'm just saying that there's no point in fighting it since it looks like the tunnel has worked its magic again."

"Better not let Hannah hear you say that. She'll get spooked and then it won't matter if I feel like giving in to it or not."

Lukas shrugged. "So she's a little skittish. One of these days she's going to be heading back to Chicago and you will have missed the boat. That's not like you, buddy."

"I've caught that boat a couple of times, but she keeps tossing me back out. I just wish I knew—"

"Daniel Walker and Lukas McCoy! I hope you aren't planning on taking tomorrow off of work, as well!"

Both Danny and Lukas turned around to find Agnes Sheridan, dressed jauntily in a long navy-blue pleated skirt and a white blouse with a sailor collar. Her chauffeur was close behind, carrying a folded lawn chair and an umbrella despite the fact that a straw hat shaded the dragon lady's face.

"We wouldn't dream of it, Mrs. Sheridan," Lukas said agreeably. "I plan on taking out that rotted banister in the lobby first thing tomorrow morning."

"Good boy!" Mrs. Sheridan pronounced, then poked Danny in the chest with her cane. "Let's hope you plan on being just as enterprising, Mr. Walker. As soon as the place is completed, I plan on getting that grandson of mine home to run it. Now, come along, Hampton. I think I see a spot up near the stage." The chauffeur grunted and Mrs. Sheridan turned to Danny. "I haven't been to the festivities in years, but I want to see that girlfriend of yours perform."

"Wouldn't you know," Danny said as they watched her move toward the stage, the crowd parting for her like she was an aging Cleopatra, "making my dream come true is gonna lead to Gavin Sheridan coming home."

Lukas shook his head. "Nah, I don't see it happening. The Sheridan men leave. It's like a family curse or something. It'll take more than reopening the hotel to make Gavin Sheridan come home again. She was right about one thing, though."

"What's that?" Danny asked absently, his mind on looking for Hannah again.

"Even she knows that Hannah and you belong together."

HANNAH CUT A PIECE of peach pie, placed it on a paper plate, and handed it to Ina Belway.

"This is my second piece," Ina said, "but Kate makes the best peach pie this side of Georgia so who's counting?"

Hannah's tummy did a slow roll. "I don't know how you can eat, Ina. I'm so nervous I could hardly get any breakfast down this morning."

"Aw, honey, you're going to do great. You've got the steps down pat."

Hannah wished she could be as sure. She felt way out of her element—and not just because of the tap-dancing. There was also her new dress. Self-consciously, she tugged on the straps again. Was it her imagination, or was the neckline lower than it had been when she'd tried it on at Whittaker's Department Store last night? Despite the flared skirt that fell to midcalf, Hannah felt practically naked in the red sundress. Why on earth had she let Molly talk her into buying it?

"What does a guy have to do to get service around here?"

Hannah looked up. Danny.

"What can I get you?" she asked primly while she smoothed some already smooth paper napkins.

His soft laughter shot through her like heat lightning. "If I were to answer that," he said, "it would have nothing to do with pie."

She shot him a look. Which was probably a mistake, because instead of withering him, she was close to withering her own composure when she saw that his blue chambray shirt was open over a pair of jeans that rode a little low on his hips. His chest was nearly as tan as his face. Smooth and hard and—

"I get the feeling, Hannah, that you're not thinking about pie right now, either."

She forced her gaze from his chest to his face. He was giving her one of his best, knowing grins. Okay, so he was right. That didn't mean she was going to let him get away with it. "Did you want that slice of pie on a plate or on your face?" she asked him sweetly.

Danny threw back his head and laughed. "Feisty, I like that. Hope you're just as feisty when it comes time to go up on that stage."

"Still think I might not have the nerve, huh?"

"I think this is one Oz that is going to be missing a lion. He's too cowardly to show. In fact, I'd be willing to bet all the hot dogs you can eat that he doesn't."

"Don't be ridiculous. I'm not betting with you."

"Afraid you'll lose, huh?"

She narrowed her eyes. "You really think I'd let the Happy Tappers down at the last minute? That's pretty insulting, Danny."

He shrugged. "So take the bet. Prove me wrong."

She had to admit to herself that as busy as she'd been she missed this—this sparring, this flirting. Danny was so good at goading her into things. And she always ended up enjoying it. Why fight it?

"Okay," she said. "You're on."

Out of the corner of her eye she saw him raise his hand and reach out. He looped a finger around the strap of her dress where it had fallen down her arm and gently replaced it on her shoulder. She shivered. Oh yeah, buying the dress had definitely been the right move.

"See you in Oz," he said. And then he turned and walked away.

THE SHADOWS WERE STARTING to lengthen by the time the Happy Tappers took the stage. Danny had found himself a spot to stand off to the side of the band shell. An old recording of the song about the yellow brick road started to spit weakly from the ancient speaker system. It was nearly obliterated by the sound of tap shoes when Gertie Hartlet, in the role of Dorothy, clicked onto the stage.

There were snickers here and there from the audience, and no wonder. As far as Danny was concerned, Gertie was ushering in a whole new era of miscasting. In a ruffled pinafore and a cigarette hanging out of the side of her mouth, she looked like a Salvador Dali version of the little girl from Kansas. Danny's ma, who'd coveted the role herself, let it slip at the supper table one night that the only reason Gertie got the part was because she had a Cairn Terrier named Scruffy who looked just like Toto.

Gertie tapped to the center of the stage then looked back, clearly surprised when she realized she was out there all alone. She took the cigarette out of her mouth just long enough to whistle.

Scruffy burst out onto the stage and ran to the edge where he took up the kind of stance you'd expect to see on a bulldog and started barking at the audience. The audience laughed but Danny was too busy looking toward the wings, waiting to see if Hannah was going to be more cowardly than the lion.

The audience started to clap as the three other principal dancers skipped out onto the stage, arms linked. His ma, as the Scarecrow. Ina Belway as the Tin Man. And Hannah as the Cowardly Lion, tapping her way down a fake yellow brick road for all of Timber Bay to see. His heart started swelling and he could feel a huge grin stretching his mouth wide. For half a second he thought about checking to see if anyone was watching his reaction, but he didn't want to stop looking at her that long.

She was dressed in a furry pale gold lion suit. The ears were attached to a hood that covered her hair, but her face was uncovered. She looked scared to death. But she was up there—doing it anyway.

Mercifully, the Happy Tappers had chosen to do only one scene—the one where Dorothy and Toto meet the scarecrow, tin man and lion in the woods. Each cast member had a few lines to say, not that anyone could hear much dialogue over Toto's running commentary. Constance Hilton had crawled out onto the stage in hopes of unobtrusively calming Toto down but Gertie, who never saw anything wrong with Scruffy's behavior, reacted with a mixture of bawdy laughter and heavy coughing.

Constance finally succeeded in getting Scruffy to shut up in time for the last line to be recited. The music started up again and the foursome started back down the yellow brick road. It was a short trip. Scruffy decided that Kate should stay put and grabbed hold of her pant leg in his mouth. Some of the scarecrow's stuffing showered out across the stage. Hannah slipped on a piece of it and down she went, landing on her shapely fanny with a thud. Scruffy was on her immediately, licking her face and wagging his tail eagerly.

Danny held his breath for a second and poised himself to

run for the stage. But it was clear in an instant that Hannah wasn't hurt. Her head was thrown back, her mouth wide with laughter, while she tried to evade Scruffy's tongue.

Man, she looked beautiful. There wasn't a trace of fear left on her face. And not a trace of embarrassment, either. She looked happy and so much more carefree than when she first came to town. She seemed to fit right into the chaotic production on the stage—just another one of those slightly daffy, anything for fun, Timber Bay women. Danny knew in that moment that he loved her.

INA BELWAY HAD BROUGHT a couple of bottles of champagne from the tavern and everyone backstage was toasting and congratulating each other on getting through another Fourth of July show. The way everyone acted, you'd think they'd just pulled off a perfect concert in Carnegie Hall, thought Hannah. Everyone was just *so* pleased. *So* happy. *So* relieved it was over. And nobody cared a fig that Hannah had literally stopped the show by the seat of her pants.

"Hey, Hannah!" Ina called over to her. "I don't remember there being a love scene between the lion and the dog in the script!"

Gertie laughed so hard at this that she started coughing and actually had to take the cigarette out of her mouth before she could stop. Ina started yelling at Gertie to keep her cigarette away from Kate's stuffing and Kate became all flustered and started apologizing for her stuffing causing so much trouble. Adding to the confusion, Scruffy was trying to attack one of the stuffed crows from the Oz set and Constance was pirouetting about as she demonstrated how she wanted to do *The Wizard* with the ballet class next year.

Next year. And Hannah wouldn't be there. All these people had become her friends. But soon she'd be saying goodbye to them. Suddenly the gaiety and chaos made her a little sad. Or was it the champagne on an empty stomach? She needed food—and she needed fresh air. She finished changing and left the stuffy little dressing room at the back of the band shell and shut the door quietly behind her. Danny was waiting for her, hot dog in hand.

"I hope you don't think that that one dinky dog is going to settle our bet."

He grinned and shook his head. "No way. I'm going to take you on the gourmand's tour of the Timber Bay Fourth of July festivities. Sky's the limit. You can even have your pie à la mode." He stopped grinning. "I'm proud of you professor," he said quietly.

"Why?" she asked, tossing her head, feeling suddenly giddy, "because I proved you wrong?"

"I think I might just like it when you prove me wrong," he said.

"Then hand over that dog, loser. I'm starving."

Danny watched her eat it, and she didn't give a damn if there was mustard on her chin or relish in her teeth. The hot dog was the best thing she'd ever tasted. "More, please," she said.

Danny held out his hand to her. She looked at it, then back up into his eyes. "The whole town is here tonight, Danny. You think it's wise for us to hold hands?"

"This isn't the kind of night to waste on wisdom. It's a night for magic."

The sky over her head was filled with stars and she could hear the gentle movement of the water and the far-off sound of the calliope from the carousel the Church of the Holy Flock brought in for the festival. There was the smell of popcorn and peaches and the ebb and flow of hundreds of voices—talking, laughing, having fun. Magic, yes. She'd been neglecting her job while she'd learned how to tap-dance and there was a mountain of damage control to do before Pollard and his crew came to town in a week. But wouldn't tomorrow be soon enough to come back down to earth? Didn't she deserve tonight?

"Come on, professor," Danny cajoled in that charming, bad-boy way of his. "Quit giving me trouble."

She cocked her brow at him. "I thought you liked trouble."

He grinned. "Yeah, but only if we get into it together. Take my hand and I'll show you how wonderful a small-town Fourth of July can be."

She took his hand.

They ate burgers and corn on the cob and pie à la mode. They stuffed cotton candy into their mouths and licked the stickiness from their fingers. They tried their luck at winning a huge stuffed octopus and made each other laugh hilariously when Danny tried to ring the bell of the he-man machine with a mallet.

"Hmm," Hannah said, "I think you reached the *please don't kick sand in my face* level."

"Hey, that last shot was way out of the *wimps are us* range! I made it all the way to the *don't pick a fight with this sucker* level," he boasted, sticking a finger in her face. "And that means you, professor!"

She laughed. Why would she want to pick a fight with him? She'd never had so much fun in her life!

"Never mind your muscles, what are we going to eat now?" she asked, eyeing the caramel apple in the hand of a woman passing by.

"I like my women insatiable," Danny teased. "But the fireworks will be starting soon. Come on."

He took her hand again and they skirted the crowd until they reached the sidewalk, then started walking toward the hotel.

"We're not breaking and entering again, are we, Danny?"

"Nope." He fished a key out of his pocket and held it up. "I've got my own key this time."

She laughed and followed him up the two shallow stairs

that led to the front door and waited for him to unlock it. He led her inside. The boards had been taken off the windows and the light from a street lamp out front cast a glow across the lobby.

"It really is beautiful," Hannah said in an awed whisper.

"Wait till you see it when Lukas and I are finished with it."

"What will you work on next?" she asked as she ran her fingers over the restored carvings on the hotel's front desk.

Danny walked over to the gracefully curved staircase and ran his hand along the banister. "This, I think," he said. "I'll feel safer using it after it's been restored." A quick smile touched his mouth. "Besides, Lukas can't wait to get his hands on it."

"You're as eager as he is," Hannah said, smiling gently at him.

"Guilty," Danny said. "For me, it's not so much the wood, though."

"What is it?" she asked him.

"For me, it's the idea of making something beautiful again. Restoring it to some kind of order—to its original purpose. My grandfather used to tell me stories about this town. His old man, my great-grandfather, had been a logger. The last in a line of them. Grandpa remembered when some of the country's wealthiest businessmen used to stay in this very hotel."

"And went to shows at the opera house?"

He gave her a quick grin. "Yeah. I sound like a damn romantic, don't I?"

"I suspect that's exactly what you are, Danny Walker."

He laughed softly. "When I was a kid, as far as I could tell, my grandfather was the most stable person in the family. If things got too insane, he'd sit us kids down and tell us tales of logging in Timber Bay. The old man sure knew how to tell a story."

So that's who Danny learned it from, thought Hannah as

she watched Danny stroll around the lobby, running a hand on the desk, rapping on a wall, peeking under faded rugs.

"The place always sounded like it was magic to me, then."

"And you want to re-create that."

"Yes," he said as he walked slowly toward her. "For myself. And for others."

"I think you're probably very good at creating magic, Danny," she said softly.

He raised his hand toward her mouth, stopping just short of touching her. She fancied she could feel some sort of current of connection between them, something she'd never felt with any other man. If he didn't touch her soon, she was going to beg him to.

There was the sound of an explosion overhead and Danny said, "They're starting. Come on." He grabbed her hand and ran with her through the dining room to the kitchen and up a back flight of stairs to the second floor.

As they ran down a hallway Hannah managed to ask, "Where are we going?"

"The roof!"

Hannah bit her lip. "The roof?" she croaked.

"You bet! It's the very best place to watch the fireworks."

She was about to ask if they would have to climb out a window to get there when he pulled open a door at the end of the hall to reveal a narrow staircase. Despite the lack of light, they climbed quickly.

"These attic rooms were once used as bedrooms for hotel workers who were brought in from the city," Danny told her as they hurried through a series of long, narrow rooms. Shapes of old trunks and stacked boxes loomed here and there out of the darkness. The place smelled musty and it was unbelievably hot. Hannah could feel sweat forming between their hands and a trickle of it ran between her breasts.

Danny opened another door and they went up four more steps and then through another door and onto the roof.

The air was cool and fresh and light against her sweat-dampened skin. Overhead was a sky of deep bluish black with stars glinting thickly across it.

"There's a low wall all the way around the roof so it's safe to go closer. Come on."

She allowed him to lead her over to the waist-high wall at the back of the hotel. Out on the bay, small motorboats with their engines stilled waited in anticipation.

There was a small lean-to—just a roof of worn canvas stretched over the corner of the wall to form a triangular-shaped cave. Danny bent into it and drew out a bedroll. He untied it and smoothed it out. "Just in case you get cold," he said. She shivered again, but it had nothing to do with being cold.

Suddenly there was a burst of color overhead. Hannah looked up and gasped.

Danny watched her face. He didn't think he looked up at the fireworks in the sky even once. The better show was the one in Hannah's eyes. She had never looked more alive—or more beautiful. One of the tiny straps of her sundress had slipped again and the neckline scooped just low enough to glimpse the top of her breasts when she moved a certain way. As he watched the pinks, golds, blues and greens wash over her joyful face his heart banged against his ribs as if it would explode and the blood rushed through him hot enough to light a firecracker.

"Hannah," he whispered hoarsely. Miraculously, over the sound of the fireworks, she heard him. She turned her head and looked into his face. She gazed at him for a long moment and he watched the look on her face change from joy to something that smoldered. But, this time, he had to be sure.

"Tell me what you want," he said in a voice that was ragged with need.

"I want you to touch me, Danny," she said.

15

AT FIRST, IT WAS ENOUGH—to just touch her. Her arms, her face, her neck, her shoulders. But when she closed her eyes and moaned, he knew he had to have her mouth. But he wanted to take his time. To savor. He kissed her forehead, her eyes, the curve of her cheekbone and the straight, serious line of her nose. Then he kissed her stubborn chin and her soft, graceful neck.

"Are you—um—" she said, her voice catching in her throat in a way that made his body throb "—are you going to make me ask you to kiss me, too?"

He smiled into her neck. "I thought that's what I was doing?" he whispered. "Kissing you." There was the burst of color overhead and he nipped the side of her neck with his teeth.

She gasped and moaned. "My mouth, Danny," she murmured roughly. "Kiss my mouth."

Quickly, he pulled her up against him and took her mouth with his. The kiss was as wild and free as the fireworks bursting above them.

"Not one bit of starch tonight, professor," he murmured against her mouth as he ran his hands down her back.

"Show me more magic," she said.

He smiled briefly against her lips and then kissed her again. And again. And again. Her mouth was so pliant, so open to him. Even his dreams hadn't been like this.

Reluctantly, he left her mouth and pulled back to look into her face. Her lips were dark and wet and a little swollen. Her hair was mussed from his hands and the wind. And the look in her eyes—he raised his hands to her face and tugged back her hair. Yes. It was there. She wanted him as much as he wanted her.

The people below them gasped as bright gold and blue lit up the sky and Danny hooked a finger in the strap of her dress and gently tugged it off her shoulder. The dress dipped lower and he cupped her breast in his palm until it swelled up over the soft fabric. He lowered his head to trace the curve of it with his tongue. She shivered slightly and he reveled in it. He wanted her to shiver. He wanted her to tremble. He wanted her to cry out. And all for him.

He found her nipple under her dress with his thumb and she threw back her head and moaned.

That's all he needed. He tugged her dress down until her breast was completely bared. It was softly rounded and pale, the nipple puckered and pink. He grazed it with his teeth then sucked it. Grazed it, then sucked it. And she started to move restlessly in his arms, shoving her hands into his hair to hold him there at her breast. He reached down and gathered the skirt of her dress up into his hand until he could feel her bare leg just below the edge of her panties. He worked his fingers up under the edge and touched her. She gasped and bucked and pulled his head away from her breast so that she could have his mouth. Have his tongue. He touched her again beneath her panties and felt how soft she was, how wet she was. It made him crazy to know that she could want him that much. Here on the rooftop with the whole damn town below them and the fireworks bursting above.

It made him feel like all kinds of a man.

And then he felt something else. He felt Hannah's hands at the zipper of his jeans, tentative at first and then quickly sure of themselves. She unzipped and tugged his jeans open and then he felt her warm soft hand touch him and he gasped and gritted his teeth against the pleasure that was as intense as pain.

"Am I—?" she asked. "I mean, I've never—"

He looked into her face. "Angel," he said, "if you were doing any better I'd be dead right now."

The sound of her soft laughter rocked him and he grew harder. Her eyes widened. "Oh, my," she said.

He grinned. "Lions and tigers and cairns, oh my," he said and then he started kissing her again and moving his hand against her where she was wet and slick and womanly. She moved and bucked against his hand. He thought he'd burst when she wrapped her fist around his hardness and moved it in rhythm with her hips. He couldn't take much more.

"Tell me you want me," he demanded. "Tell me you want me inside of you."

"Yes," she said. "I want you inside of me."

There was no stopping it then. With a quick movement, he had her down on the bedroll and was pushing her dress up and her panties aside. He thrust into her and she wrapped her legs around him and took him deeper, holding him while he thrust wildly over and over, crazy with want for her, but not so crazy that he didn't know that what he felt for her and what he wanted from her was so much more than this.

But first—*this*.

He put his hands at her waist and rolled her over with him until she was on top, straddling him. He reached up and yanked her dress the rest of the way down to her waist and put his hands on her breasts, teasing and pinching the nipples until she started to move wildly on him. Her face was beautiful to watch—the surprise there. The wonder. The need.

And then there was no more watching. He became as consumed as she was. He put his hands at her waist and thrust himself higher into her. And they made magic.

HANNAH COULD HEAR the distant sounds of car doors slamming and people laughing. The explosions in the sky had stopped around the same time the explosions in her body had ceased. Now she lay in the circle of Danny's arm, her head on his chest, her hand on his stomach. She felt warm and pleased. She stretched against him.

"That was amazing," she said.

He laughed softly. "You mean the fireworks?"

"There were fireworks?" she asked with exaggerated innocence.

He laughed again and held her closer. "I like your powers of concentration, professor."

"And I like your little hideaway up here. Do you come here often?" she asked him teasingly.

"If you're asking if I've ever done this before—made love up here—the answer is no. I've been coming up here since I was a kid, but it was always alone."

She raised herself on her elbow and looked down into his face. She didn't like the thought that there might be others after her, but she laughed lightly and said, "So I'm the first, huh?"

Without warning, he pulled her down to him and rolled her over, reversing their positions.

"The only, Hannah," he said. And then he made love to her again. This time slowly, carefully. And then he walked her home along a deserted Sheridan Road, holding her hand all the way. There was no one to see. And maybe it didn't really matter anymore even if there was.

DANNY LAY IN BED and listened to the sound of the shower running. Naked under the sheet, he moved restlessly, thinking about Hannah's breasts with the water streaming off of them. He knew it was Hannah because he'd lain in bed until he was sure that everyone else had woken up and gone down for breakfast. He had a plan.

He threw the sheet off, got out of bed, and padded over to the door of his bedroom. He opened the door a crack then stood still to listen. The phone started to ring and he glanced back at it on the bedside table but after two rings, it stopped. His ma must have answered it in the kitchen. That should keep her busy for awhile. He slipped out of his bedroom.

"Danny! Is that you up there?" Kate called from the bottom of the stairs.

Oh yeah, it was him all right. Naked as the day he was born. He spun swiftly around and promptly stubbed his big toe on the doorjamb. He gritted his teeth and hopped back to his room on one foot.

"Danny?" his ma called again.

"Yeah, Ma? What is it?"

"Lukas is on the phone."

"Okay, thanks," he called then shut the bedroom door and hobbled over to the phone at the side of the bed.

"This better be important, pal," he said into the receiver as he sat down on the edge of the bed and started to rub his throbbing toe.

"Important as it gets, Danny boy. Mrs. Sheridan wants to see us pronto."

"What about?"

"Beats me. But she sounds mad as hell. She wants to see us at her place. I'll meet you there. It'll save time."

The shower stopped and Danny's body took notice. "Put her off until this afternoon," he said, his mind on catching Hannah wrapped in nothing but a towel.

"Put her off? Danny, are you nuts? This is the biggest contract Timber Bay Building and Restoration has ever had. I'm not gonna risk it by telling the dragon lady we can't make it 'cause you haven't eaten breakfast yet."

What Danny had in mind to eat wasn't breakfast. But it was more than the fact that he wanted to taste Hannah again. He needed to talk to her. When they'd gotten home the night before, they'd necked like a couple of teenagers in the front hallway. Then they'd heard a noise in the kitchen and Hannah had run upstairs and vanished behind her bedroom door while Uncle Tuffy, his pudgy hand wrapped around a stack of sugar cookies, waylaid Danny in the living room and talked his ear off about the day.

He needed to see her. Because things had been left unsaid last night. Important things.

But there would be time. This was business and he owed it to Lukas to be there.

"I'll be there," he said, then hung up the phone and reached for his jeans.

HANNAH DRESSED in a hurry, wishing she had another dress to put on. Maybe she should ask Molly if she'd like to go back to Whittaker's. There had been another dress on sale that she'd liked. Danny liked her in a dress.

God, she sounded so sappy. So in love. But how could she not love the man who'd given her a childhood in just a few weeks? But it was more than that. She liked who she was when she was with Danny. Almost like he completed her. Hannah groaned. How sappy was that? So much for being a woman of science. Lissa was going to get an enormous kick out of all of this. Hannah thought about calling her but she couldn't wait to see Danny so she ran out of the guest room, down the stairs, through the living and dining room, then stopped at the kitchen door to catch her breath. He was probably behind it right at that moment, eating pancakes, waiting for her.

She pushed open the door.

"Hannah, dear, there you are! I saved some pancakes for you. Sit down and I'll heat them in the microwave."

Hannah felt a major letdown when she saw that there was no one else in the kitchen. She only half listened to Kate chattering as she morosely pushed a pancake around on her plate. She was barely aware that the kitchen windows were open to a glorious July morning. She didn't hear the bees buzzing or see the butterflies fluttering by.

"Well, you seem to be in a pout, dear. Anything I can do?" Kate asked.

Yes, she thought to herself. You can tell me why Danny wasn't just dying to see me this morning. Out loud she said, "Guess I ate too much at the park yesterday."

She wanted to ask where Danny was, but she thought it would be too obvious. Yeah—like the sweet-faced woman puttering at the sink would even for a minute think Hannah had been up on that roof doing—well, doing *it*. Still, she couldn't bring herself to open her mouth and ask.

The garbage disposal grumbled and Kate started to take her apron off. "Oh," she said as she drew something out of the pocket. "I nearly forgot all about this. I took down this phone message day before yesterday but things have been so hectic around here that I forgot all about it."

Kate handed her the paper and Hannah unfolded it. What was written there shot her out of her chair and onto her feet.

"But, this says that Mr. Pollard and the crew will be here tomorrow!"

"Yes, dear. Is that a bad thing?" Kate asked with a concerned look on her face.

Bad? Oh, yeah. It was bad. It was very, very bad. She was supposed to have a week left to work everything out. Now she had less than twenty-four hours!

Hannah was trying not to panic when the back door burst open and Susie and Andy came running in, followed closely by their mother. "We're baaaack!" Andy cried.

"Not again?" Kate asked.

"I'm sorry, Ma, but there is just no way I can live with that man," Sissy said.

And, just like that, the situation was no longer bad. Now it was a full-blown disaster.

"So, NATURALLY, when I talked to Gavin and he said—"

Danny was absorbed with trying to balance the smallest teacup he'd ever seen on his knee and wondering what the dragon lady would do if he spilled the foul-tasting contents on the thick floral rug under his feet, but his head jerked up when he heard the name. "Gavin?" he asked.

Mrs. Sheridan inclined her head. "My grandson. I think you remember him, Mr. Walker."

"Yeah, I remember him. And as far as I remember, he wasn't exactly working in a quarry."

"No," Agnes Sheridan conceded. "But he oversees all aspects of two of the world's finest hotels. I assure you he knows what he's talking about."

"In this case, he has no idea of what he's talking about."

The old lady's spine went rigid, giving an added inch or two to her scrawny frame.

"Mrs. Sheridan," Lukas quickly put in. "What Danny means is—"

"I think we can let Danny talk for himself, Mr. McCoy."

"The marble we need to match the bar top has a very limited availability," Danny told her. "The price we quoted you is the current price and no one—not even your grandson—can get you a better one."

"We'll see about that," Agnes Sheridan said as she picked up the receiver of the old-fashioned dial telephone at her elbow.

"You're gonna blow this job, yet, Danny boy," Lukas hissed out of the corner of his mouth.

"You surprise me, Lukas. I didn't think you liked being called a liar any more than I do."

Lukas gave him what was, for Lukas anyway, a stern look. Lukas didn't do stern so well, despite his size. His dimples generally got in his way. "There's ways of dealin' with this stuff, Danny. You don't have to go chargin' in like a bull with his balls in a harness. There's such a thing as—"

Danny had stopped listening as soon as Agnes Sheridan uttered the word *padding the bill*. He set the china cup on the table beside him, hopped to his feet, walked over to the old lady and jerked the receiver out of her hand.

"I'd think twice about calling me a liar, Sheridan," he barked into the phone. "And if you can find that marble at a better price than I quoted there'll be no charge. And if you can't, then I suggest that you get off our backs and let go of your granny's skirts." He slammed the receiver down. Behind him, it sounded like Lukas was going to choke. Danny squeezed his eyes shut. *Lukas*. He'd had no right to make a gesture like that without consulting his partner first. But, damn it all! Nobody was going to call him a liar.

He turned and looked Lukas straight in the eye. "Sorry, but this has to be said." Then he turned to the old lady again. "We've got a contract, Mrs. Sheridan. And there was nothing in the fine print that said we have to get your grandson's approval for anything that we do. When we're finished with

The Sheridan Hotel, it'll be time enough for him to have his say in running it. Until then, I intend to honor our contract. We quoted the going rate for the marble. It's already been ordered on your say-so. You aren't planning on going back on your end of the contract, are you, Mrs. Sheridan?"

The dragon lady stared him down with those steely gray eyes of hers but Danny refused to blink.

"Don't like having your honor questioned, do you?" he asked her.

"No, Mr. Walker, I do not."

"Neither do I. Now, I've got someone to see."

"What is more important than this job, Mr. Walker?" she demanded.

What the hell, he thought. Hadn't he just given a nice little speech about the truth? He might as well try telling it himself. "Hannah," he answered.

There was a smile glittering in the old lady's eyes but she wasn't about to let it reach her mouth. "Then, by all means, you're dismissed, Mr. Walker."

Danny couldn't help it. He let out a bark of laughter. Then, grinning, he took Agnes Sheridan's withered white hand, raised it to his lips, and kissed it. "I appreciate that, ma'am," he said.

Now it was her turn to laugh. Danny was sure he'd remember the sound forever.

When he pulled up in front of his parents' house, he was relieved to see the Granny's Grains station wagon. Hannah was home. But any hope he had of catching her alone ended when he walked into the house and found the living room full of people. Sissy and Chuck, Ina, Gertie, Constance Hilton in her tutu, his parents. They were having some sort of meeting and it must be an important one, thought Danny, because his father had a suit on that hadn't been worn in the past two decades.

"All right," his sister Sissy was saying, "I'll go back to Chuck—"

"Aw, honeybunch," Chuck cried happily from the other side of the room.

Sissy shot him a look to chill. "I'm doing this for Hannah and Uncle Tuffy. For them, I'll pretend we're a happy couple."

"You think you're that good an actress, Sissy?" Ina Belway drawled.

"Don't start with me," Sissy snapped at her mother-in-law. "If your son wasn't so stubborn I wouldn't have to keep leaving him!"

"Seems to me that he wasn't so stubborn until he married you."

Sissy gasped and Kate quickly interjected. "Maybe while Mr. Pollard is here, we should pretend that Ina and Sissy aren't related."

"Well," Ina said, "isn't that cozy? As soon as a celebrity comes to town, the in-laws get cast aside and your family gets all the glory."

"Excuse me, Ina," Hannah said, "but I don't think that the CEO of Granny's Grains qualifies as a celebrity."

Ina paid no attention. "You just want to make sure that yours is the only family that gets on that cereal box, Kate Walker!"

"Why—I never!" Kate exclaimed. "I was only trying to be helpful."

"I suppose you'd like Susie and Andy to pretend they never saw us before if they pass us on the street, too!"

Danny had never, ever known his ma to have a fight with anyone. Let alone Ina.

"Ma! Ina!" he said, getting between them before they could start pulling hair. "What is going on? Why on earth would the kids pretend they don't know you?" he asked Ina. Ina clamped her mouth shut and glared at Kate. "And why is Pop all trussed up like a Thanksgiving turkey in a suit?" The room was silent so Danny turned to his ma. "Ma? What's going on here?"

"Maybe I better explain, Danny," Hannah said.

"Yeah," Danny agreed grimly, "maybe you better."

Was it fair, thought Hannah, that the first time she got to see Danny after those rooftop fireworks he was glowering at her? Where was the sweet afterglow? The dreamy looks? The whispered endearments? The furtive touches? Didn't she deserve any of that? And things were only going to get worse after she explained what was going on. Danny had the kind of moral code that all good rogues had. He definitely dwelled in the no baloney zone. What she had to say, he wasn't going to like one bit.

"You've heard me mention Randall Pollard, Danny," she began. "He's the CEO at Granny's Grains." She paused but Danny didn't say anything. "Well, anyway," she went on, "he's coming to Timber Bay tomorrow with the photographer and the advertising people."

"Yeah. So?"

"Well—for some reason, Mr. Pollard seems to believe certain things that might not be entirely true."

"Really?" He leaned in the doorway like he was settling in for a nice long chat. "Such as?" he asked.

He wasn't going to make this easy for her, thought Hannah. "Well, it's a little complicated—"

"Oh, don't be silly, Hannah," Kate interrupted before turning to Danny. "It's quite simple, really. Hannah's boss expects a perfect family so we're going to pretend to be one," Kate said reasonably—like people asked her to be something she wasn't on a pretty regular basis. Hannah was definitely starting to love that quality in Kate—the ability to take anything that came along in stride.

Danny, on the other hand, didn't look like he was taking this news in stride at all. But before she could explain to him that it wasn't as bad as it sounded, Clara came bustling in, her pink apron flying. "I just talked to Gardenia. She's going to teach us to play bridge. She thinks we can learn enough by tomorrow to fake it."

Danny came away from the doorway. "Fake," he repeated.

"Danny, maybe we should talk alone," Hannah whispered.

"Let me get this straight," he went on like he hadn't heard her. "You're asking everyone to pretend to be something they're not just to make you look good?"

"Hannah didn't ask us to, Danny," his father said. "Kate volunteered us."

"And you're letting them do this?" Danny asked her.

"I have to do *something*, Danny," Hannah said. "And it will only be for a few days. If I don't pull this whole thing off, I can kiss my career goodbye. What will it look like if I can't even run a simple contest?"

"It will look like you can't run a simple contest," Danny said flatly.

"Listen—I'm willing to admit that I made some mistakes— mistakes that should have been corrected earlier. But this is not entirely my fault, Danny, and you know it."

"She's right about that," Ina said.

"And she did a wonderful job as a substitute lion," Constance Hilton trilled.

"Lots of people owe Hannah favors, Danny," Gertie Hartlet said, the cigarette hanging out of the side of her mouth bobbing with every word. "It's only right we help her out when she needs it."

There was a murmur of assent from everyone in the room.

"And it's not much different than playing a part in a pageant," Kate said.

"And what part do you see me playing, Hannah?" Danny asked.

"You don't have to play any part," she quickly told him. "But—uh—there is something I need to ask you to do." She glanced around the room. Everyone was still with waiting. "When we're alone," she added pointedly.

"Coffee in the kitchen," Kate sang out and everyone reluctantly followed her from the living room. Hannah really, really loved that woman.

"So what do you want me to do?" Danny asked as soon as they were alone.

"Nothing much," she said offhandedly, hoping to set an inconsequential tone. "I just don't want you to let on to anybody that we're—uh—well, that we're—"

His mouth twisted wryly. "I think the word you're looking for is lovers."

"Okay, yes—that's the word—the one I don't want you to say. Say you understand, Danny," she added quickly. "Please. I'm on shaky ground here, already. What would it do to the image of the Great American Family if it got out that the representative of Granny's Grains was running around on rooftops having sex with the son?"

Danny grinned. "I guarantee you'd get a lot of press."

"This is not a joke, Danny."

He was suddenly sober. "No, it's not." He walked up to her and ran his hands up her arms. "We were special last night," he said with a quiet kind of intensity that made her absolutely melt.

"Don't you think I know that?" she asked, as she reached out to cup his face with her palm.

"Then don't hide it. And don't ask my family to pretend to be something they're not."

She dropped her hand. "Danny, try to understand. I'm the one who sold the company this idea. I've worked hard, but still everything went wrong. Your family is almost as special to me as you are, but I need to be able to pull this project out of the toilet or I'm going to be in big trouble."

He let go of her and paced over to the windows, stood thinking for a moment, then turned and started walking back toward her. Hannah started to feel hopeful. Maybe she'd reached him. Maybe he'd understood.

And then Kate came into the room.

"Hannah, dear, I just wanted to let you know that Molly called back. It's fine with her for Tuffy to stay over there for a few days. She says she'll do her best to keep him from coming home while Mr. Pollard is here."

Hannah felt a horrible flush climb up her neck. "Thank you, Kate," she croaked.

She couldn't look at Danny until she knew Kate had gone back to the kitchen.

"So you're going to hide Uncle Tuffy away, too. Pretty funny, Hannah, considering he's probably the only one in town who actually eats your lousy cereal."

Hannah gasped. "Cereal! I almost forgot! I've got a carload of it to pass out."

"Setting the stage for your little farce, huh?"

"I'm not happy with this, either, Danny. But if I can make it work, I'll never have to take this kind of job again. Now, I've got to saturate the town with Super Korny Krunchies before Pollard gets here." She headed for the front door.

"Well, don't expect me to eat any of it!" Danny yelled after her.

That was definitely not what she'd hoped Danny would be saying to her on the *morning after*, Hannah thought as she raced out to the company station wagon. He was acting like a disappointed little boy.

"Now who isn't dealing in reality?" she muttered as she turned the key and the engine chugged to life. She didn't have the time to deal with him now, but just as soon as this damn contest was over, she would make Danny see reason.

Wouldn't she?

16

DANNY WALKED into Sweet Buns at nine o'clock the next morning.

"A little early for your coffee break, isn't it, Danny?" Molly asked him.

"Ma's busy helping Hannah so I'm a hungry man in search of a little breakfast." He slid onto a stool. "I'll have a—" Danny suddenly noticed that the bakery case was empty. "Hey—where are all the sweet buns?"

"Sorry. Got a late start today after helping Hannah last night. Here," she said as she pushed a box of cereal in front of him, "this should tide you over for awhile."

Danny picked up the box. Super Korny Krunchies. "Since when do you serve this stuff?" he asked.

"Got it from Hannah. She figures that the more boxes of it that Mr. Pollard sees the less he'll be inclined to ask any questions that could get her into trouble."

"She'll be in trouble enough when the entire town dies of malnutrition," Danny muttered as he read the nutrition label on the side of the box.

Molly put a hand on her hip. "You know, Danny, you could go a little easy on her. She's wedged between a rock and a hard place."

Danny put the box down. "Yeah, but she crawled in there all by herself."

"Everybody makes mistakes."

"So you think how she's handling this is a mistake, too?"

Molly shrugged. "Maybe. But who am I to judge? She's a friend who needs help, so I'm helping."

Danny grunted. "Where do you have Tuffy stashed, anyway?" he asked.

"He's out in back, playing with Chloe. She's gonna love having him all to herself today."

"That doesn't make banishing him from his own home right," Danny said. He slid off the stool. "I'm gonna head over to the drugstore for some eggs."

But at the drugstore it was pretty much the same story. Clara was over at Gardenia's learning to play bridge and the only thing available at the lunch counter was Super Korny Krunchies.

Next, Danny headed around the corner to the Belways' tavern. There were the usual four or five third shifters at the bar, drinking their breakfast. He could see Ina back in the kitchen so he headed that way. With any luck she'd take pity on him and fry him a couple of burgers.

"Sorry, Danny," Ina said. "I'm just on my way out. Gotta get over to Gardenia's. But, here." She shoved a box of Super Korny Krunchies into his hands. "Have a bowl of this—on the house."

Danny threw the box on the bar and left. But he couldn't get away from Super Korny Krunchies. The grocery store had a big display in the window. Stan the barber was standing out in front of his shop eating a bowl of the stuff. The dime store promised a free box with every purchase and the park seemed to be full of kids eating it right out of the box.

Stomach still empty, Danny walked back to the hotel. Lukas was sitting on the stairs in the lobby, bowl in hand, spoon to mouth—and a box of—you guessed it—Super Korny Krunchies sitting next to him.

"Traitor," Danny grumbled.

"Man's gotta eat, Danny boy."

"What's happening around here? Has everyone in Timber Bay given up cooking?"

Lukas shook his head. "Everyone is too busy helping Hannah."

"Whole damn town has gone crazy. Letting Hannah force them into pretending to be something they're not."

"Easy, Danny. She's not forcing anybody," Lukas said between crunches.

"I believe in owning up to your mistakes, Lukas. Always have. Hannah screwed up, she should own it."

Lukas shrugged. "Day's not over yet," he said before taking another spoonful of cereal.

Why was everyone going so easy on Hannah? Or should the question be why was Danny being so hard on her? Was it really a matter of ethics? Or was it because he didn't like the feeling that maybe if she thought Ma and Pop and Sissy and the rest of the town weren't good enough, she wouldn't think *he* was good enough, either? Damn it, he wasn't used to this kind of thinking—to wondering if he measured up, if he was enough just the way he was. He'd never been short on ego. But he'd never been in love before, either.

"That stuff any good?" Danny asked as his partner poured himself another bowl.

Lukas shrugged. "Grows on you after four or five bowls."

"Well, you might as well hand it over since it appears to be the only food left in the whole damn town."

"DID THAT FLOWER just move?" Hannah asked.

She was out in the greenhouse with Kate, stuffing silk flowers into all the carnivorous plants.

"They generally only move when they're eating, dear," Kate answered.

Hannah watched the plant out of the corner of her eye. "They don't like silk, do they?"

Kate laughed. "Don't be silly, dear. They're not vegans, you know."

Yes, Hannah knew. And that was exactly why they had to be camouflaged. Hannah hoped they didn't resent having to be daisies for the day.

She hoped Kate didn't resent any of this, either. "Kate, does this pretending bother you? Do you resent me for asking?"

Kate looked at her. "Why no, dear." She patted Hannah's cheek. "You know how fond I am of you. I'm happy to help you any way I can. Besides, it's fun to pretend sometimes. Just like tapping down the yellow brick road."

Yes, thought Hannah. Except that had only lasted fifteen minutes and then it was over. The participants got out of their costumes and dispersed to their own lives. But that's not what Hannah wanted to happen this time. She wanted more than her fifteen minutes on stage with the people of Timber Bay. And especially with the Walker family. All of them. Including Danny. *Especially* Danny.

She looked at her watch. Pollard and the crew were due to arrive soon. She hoped the poker—um—bridge club was on their way. Meanwhile, she had a few more things to check on.

Yes—in the kitchen the plate of cucumber and watercress sandwiches was ready for the bogus bridge club.

Yes—in the living room the card table was set with a tea service instead of beer bottles and poker chips.

Yes—Chuck and Sissy were sitting on the front porch swing, Chuck serenading Sissy with his guitar. Susie and Andy were dressed in their Sunday best, sitting on the top step, halfheartedly singing along. She'd told Pollard that the singalongs happened on Sundays, but the family scene was a nice touch and a perfect photo op. Pollard couldn't help but be impressed when he arrived. As long as none of the Belways blew from the tension, that is.

Sissy was on edge, Chuck was clueless as usual, Susie kept complaining about her shoes but otherwise was taking it gamely. But Andy was downright unhappy. It got worse when some boys around his age went by on bikes. They slowed down, recognized Andy, and started to heckle him like they were in the front row of a comedy club on amateur night.

"You just ignore them, Andy," Sissy said.

The boys did a U-turn on their bikes and shouted a second round of insults.

Andy's scowl deepened. "By the time this day is over everybody is gonna think I'm a supergeek. I won't have any reputation left by the time I start fourth grade."

Hannah felt worse than ever. Along with everything else, was she trading in the dignity of an eight-year-old so she could keep a job? She was considering letting Andy off the hook when two luxury vans pulled up in front of the Walker house. Hannah took a deep breath and walked down to the curb to meet them.

Pollard's executive assistant got out of the driver's seat of the first van and went around to open the passenger door. After some struggle, Randall Pollard emerged. He was beaming.

"The town, Miss Ross, is perfection! And this house! You seem to have done a splendid job, Miss Ross. Splendid."

The head of marketing got out of the back seat, took a look around and said, "The color of the shutters will have to go. And we'll need more flowers in that border."

The photographer climbed out of the second van, surveyed the scene briefly, and started to unload his equipment. "I thought I told you I didn't go for this artificially setup stuff," he said to the head of marketing. "I'm a serious feature photographer. I worked under Geraldo Rivera. This is crap."

Pollard's jowls quivered. "I don't think we need to use that kind of language. It hardly befits the image of the Great American Family or the image of Granny's Grains. We are a company that was built on—"

Pollard launched into one of his values and ethics speeches and Hannah did her best to tune it out. She tuned back in when she heard her name mentioned.

"Just ask Miss Ross. Of course it's real. That is, after all, the whole point. Right, Miss Ross?"

"Of course. The family often gathers on the porch to— um—sing." Right now, though, it looked an awful lot like they were arguing. Hannah thought she heard the word *artichokes*. Luckily, Kate came out of the house in time to distract Pollard.

"Kate! Please, come meet Mr. Pollard of Granny's Grains. This is Mrs. Walker, Mr. Pollard."

Pollard rubbed his hands together. "Yes, yes. Most impressive—a wonderful picture she makes," he said as if Kate were a walking billboard.

Kate, of course, hadn't let Hannah down. In one of her pastel housedresses and a crisp apron, she was perfect. She came lightly down the stairs and walked out to the front sidewalk to shake Pollard's hand.

"Such a pleasure, Mrs. Walker. It's not often that a man gets to meet a woman who still embodies all the traits of my dear sweet grandmother, the founder of our company. I'm sure you would have had so much in common. She was such an unusual woman."

"Oh," Kate said, a pleased smile on her face, "did she play poker, too?"

"Excuse me?" Pollard asked while Kate looked totally mortified at what she'd just said and Hannah tried to dream up an explanation for it. Luckily, another distraction came along.

Exhibiting excellent timing, the ladies of the bogus bridge club came up the walk. And quite a distraction they were, too. Wearing an odd assortment of suits, hats, gloves and shoes, they looked more like they were going to a costume party than if Constance had been wearing her tutu and Clara had been in her uniform.

"Here's my po—uh, bridge club, now," Kate said.

Kate was introducing them to Pollard when, in a squeal of tires, the Walker Salvage truck pulled into the driveway. Henry, wearing the same truly awful suit jacket he wore at last night's meeting, but over his usual dirty coveralls this time, got out of the truck, ran to the back, let the tailgate down then pulled out an intricate wrought-iron table, weathered but still beautiful. He crouched low and dragged it down the driveway then disappeared into the garage.

"Who was that?" Pollard demanded.

Hannah was saved from answering by another squeal of tires. This time an enormous gold Cadillac pulled to the curb. Leaving the engine running, Gertie Hartlet, the ubiquitous cigarette hanging from her mouth, got out.

"Where is that damn fool?" she demanded. "Where did Henry take my table?"

Hannah squeezed her eyes shut, placed the pads of her fingers against her forehead and pushed. She wasn't sure if she thought the pressure would help the pounding in her head or if she was hoping to block an artery so she could lose consciousness. Neither happened. She opened her eyes and prepared to face the music.

"You'll find Henry—and your table—in the garage, Gertie," Hannah said wearily.

"I don't want to make trouble, Hannah, but that man could try the patience of a saint," Gertie said. "And you know I'm no saint. On the other hand, you make allowances for people who save your dog from drowning." She shrugged. "Nobody's perfect."

"Henry saved Scruffy from drowning?" Hannah asked in surprise.

Gertie took a drag off the cigarette then pulled it from her mouth and blew smoke up over Hannah's head with a skill Hannah couldn't help but admire. "It was right out there across the street. Winter—bay had frozen over. Henry was out there ice fishing when Scruffy fell through the ice. Damn fool Henry dove in like he was some sort of seal or something. I thought they were both goners and then up pops Henry with Scruffy in his arms." Gertie shook her head. "Darndest thing was, the next day he stole my snow shovel." Gertie shrugged and took another drag off her cigarette. "Like I said, you make allowances."

"What on earth was that woman talking about?" Mr. Pollard demanded as he watched Gertie walk down the driveway, leaving a trail of smoke like a jet across a summer sky.

Before Hannah had a chance to answer, there was a commotion from the front porch.

"That's it, Chuckie Belway," Sissy yelled. "I don't care how many love songs you sing me, I want artichokes!"

"Aw, sugar! Not that again," Chuck whined.

"Yes, that again," Sissy said as she got up off the swing and flounced off into the house, slamming the door behind her.

Chuck tried to follow. "Now you didn't lock me out again, did you?" He rattled the knob. "Come on, sweetness. Open the door."

Susie kicked off her Mary Janes and skipped down the steps barefoot. "Looks like Mom left Dad again," she said.

"Does that mean I can go now?" Andy yelled from the porch.

Mr. Pollard's baggy face slowly ripened to the color of an anemic strawberry. "This—*this* is the perfect family you've found for our ad campaign?" he sputtered.

Hannah opened her mouth to explain, to see if she could somehow try to finesse the situation one last time. But then she thought of Scruffy out on that thin ice. And then she turned and saw everyone, family, friends and neighbors scattered across the front lawn. A small crowd had gathered and she recognized faces from the grocery store, the drugstore, the department store. Even Uncle Tuffy was there. She sent him a little wave. He giggled and waved back.

"I know I was supposed to stay at Molly's, Hannah," he said, "but they didn't have my cartoon show on their television. Is it okay that I came back?"

"Of course it's okay," Hannah said gently. "You belong here." Then she turned back to Pollard.

"Yes," she said, confidently. "*This* is the Great American Family."

"Then, Miss Ross, you obviously need to rethink your choice. Because this," he said disdainfully as he swept his arm in an arc to include the entire tableau, "is certainly *not* perfectly normal."

Hannah got a lump in her throat as the poker club gathered around her like a polyester fortress. She'd never felt such support. She had to swallow hard before she could say, "Sorry. I stand by my choice one hundred percent. The Walkers are perfect just the way they are."

"Way to go, Hannah," Ina said. There were mutterings of concurrence from the group on the lawn.

"This is absurd," Pollard said. "We can't possibly use these people in our ad campaign, Miss Ross."

"I'm afraid you're going to have to, Mr. Pollard. Because they won the contest."

Pollard's anemic strawberry turned into an overripe tomato. "I warn you, young lady. You are in a lot of trouble. Get the legal department on the phone," he yelled to his assistant. "We're going to sue!"

DANNY WAS COMING OUT of Ludington's Drugs, tearing into a candy bar, when Tuffy came running around the corner.

"Danny! I was looking for you. Hannah's in trouble!"

"I know she's in trouble, Uncle Tuffy. But she's got half the town over there helping her."

"But I don't think they can help her with this, Danny. The cereal man, Mr. Pollard, says he's going to sue her."

Danny frowned. "Sue her? Why?"

"He wants her to change her mind about who won the contest and she won't do it, Danny. She said we belong on that cereal box."

"She did?"

"Yup. She said we were perfect just the way we are."

Danny grinned. "She said that?"

"Yes, Danny. Now, come on, let's go!"

Danny hesitated and Tuffy tugged on his arm. "What are you waiting for? Hannah needs us."

Danny laughed. He swore that sometimes Tuffy was the only one in the whole damn family that made any sense.

"Let's go," he said and they ran all the way back home and got there just in time to see a big guy with a red face say to Hannah, "You'll be hearing from our lawyers."

"Then you'll be hearing from ours, too," Danny said loud enough for everyone to hear.

"And who are you?" Pollard demanded.

Danny put his arm around Uncle Tuffy. "We're the guys who are supposed to be on that cereal box. If you sue Hannah to keep us off the box, we'll sue you right back to keep us on it."

Danny could see the wheels turning in the guy's litigious brain. Finally, Pollard went into a huddled conference with the suits he had with him. When they were through talking, he got out his cell phone and punched out a number.

Danny needed to talk to Hannah. And he wasn't going to put it off this time. She was standing in a cluster of women, his ma included. They'd all stuck by her. Danny wondered how he could have ever left her when she was in trouble. He took his arm from Tuffy's shoulders and walked up to her. The card club fell back to allow them some space.

"I'm sorry. I should have been here for you."

"No," she said. "I was wrong."

He shrugged. "Maybe we were both wrong."

"Yeah, we're both a couple of troublemakers," Hannah said.

Danny laughed and took her hand. "Quite a team," he said.

They were still gazing into each other's eyes when Pollard ended the call. "I'm prepared to offer you a deal, Miss Ross. If the Walker family agrees to forfeit the title of Granny's Grains' Great American Family, we won't sue."

Hannah looked at Danny. "I think it should be Uncle Tuffy's decision," she said.

"What do you say, Uncle Tuffy?" Danny asked.

"I don't mind not being on the box, if it keeps Hannah out of trouble. But, do you think we could still get the year's supply of cereal?"

There was gentle laughter from the lawn.

Pollard conferred with the suits again then grudgingly said, "Agreed."

"Then we're even," Danny said.

"And you're fired," Pollard said as he pointed at Hannah. "Come on," he called over his shoulder, "let's get out of this place."

Hannah relinquished the keys and Pollard himself took possession of the station wagon with the flying ear of corn on its side.

As they watched the Granny's Grains procession leave, Hannah said, "No job. No car. Looks like I'm stranded."

"I think we can offer asylum for such a firebrand of truth and honesty," Danny said.

Hannah laughed. "The Walker house is a little crazy but I wouldn't go so far as to call it an asylum. Let's just say that it's imperfectly perfect."

Danny looked at her for a long moment. "Do you know how much I want to kiss you right now?" he asked.

"Then why don't you?"

"Them," Danny said with a slight tilt of his head toward

the crowd on the lawn. "They're still waiting for the legend to come true."

Hannah smiled softly. "Should we tell them that it already has?"

Danny shook his head. "Let's show them instead," he said. And then he kissed her—right there in broad daylight, with half the town watching.

Timber Bay. Hannah's town.

* * * * *

Return for wintertime in
Timber Bay with Lukas's story—
coming early in 2005!
Don't miss it

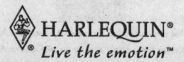

HARLEQUIN® *Blaze* ™

HARLEQUIN® *Temptation* ®

Single in South Beach

Nightlife on the Strip just got a little hotter!

Join author Joanne Rock as she takes you back to
Miami Beach and its hottest singles' playground.
Club Paradise has staked its claim in the decadent
South Beach nightlife and the women in charge are
determined to keep the sexy resort on top. So what will
they do with the hot men who show up at the club?

GIRL GONE WILD
Harlequin Blaze #135
May 2004

DATE WITH A DIVA
Harlequin Blaze #139
June 2004

HER FINAL FLING
Harlequin Temptation #983
July 2004

Don't miss the continuation of this red-hot series from Joanne Rock!

Look for these books at your favorite retail outlet.

www.eHarlequin.com   HBSSB2

Harlequin Romance®

THE WEDDING PLANNERS

Where weddings are all in a day's work!

Have you ever wondered about the women behind the scenes, the ones who make those special days happen, the ones who help to create a memory built on love that lasts forever—who, no matter how expert they are at helping others, can't quite sort out their love lives for themselves?

Meet Tara, Skye and Riana—three sisters whose jobs consist of arranging the most perfect and romantic weddings imaginable—and read how they find themselves walking down the aisle with their very own Mr. Right…!

Don't miss the THE WEDDING PLANNERS trilogy by Australian author Darcy Maguire:

A Professional Engagement HR#3801

On sale June 2004 in Harlequin Romance®!

Plus:

The Best Man's Baby, HR#3805, on sale July 2004
A Convenient Groom, HR#3809, on sale August 2004

Available at your favorite retail outlet.

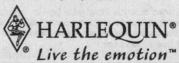

HARLEQUIN®
Live the emotion™

Visit us at www.eHarlequin.com

HRTWP

If you enjoyed what you just read,
then we've got an offer you can't resist!

Take 2 bestselling
love stories FREE!
Plus get a FREE surprise gift!